W9-BDJ-153

THE BARCELONA BROTHERS

THE BARCELONA BROTHERS

A NOVEL

TRANSLATED BY JOHN CULLEN

OTHER PRESS | New York

Originally published in Spanish as *Tarde, mal y nunca* by RBA Libros, Barcelona, Spain, in 2011.

Production Editor: Yvonne E. Cárdenas

Book design: Chris Welch

10 9 8 7 6 5 4 3 2 1

Printed in the United States of America on acid-free paper. For information write to Other Press LLC, 2 Park Avenue, 24th Floor, New York, NY 10016. Or visit our Web site: www.otherpress.com

Library of Congress Cataloging-in-Publication Data

Zanón, Carlos.
[Tarde, mal y nunca. English]
The Barcelona brothers / by Carlos Zanón ; translated by John Cullen.
p. cm.
ISBN 978-1-59051-518-1 (trade pbk.) — ISBN 978-1-59051-519-8 (e-book)
1. Immigrants—Spain—Barcelona—Fiction. 2. Murder—Fiction.
3. Barcelona (Spain)—Fiction. I. Cullen, John, 1942– II. Title.
PQ6676.A56T3713 2012
863'.64—dc23
2012000402

Publisher's Note:

This is a work of fiction. Names, characters, places, and incidents either are the product of the author's imagination or are used fictitiously, and any resemblance to actual persons, living or dead, events, or locales is entirely coincidental.

"I want my happiness!" at last he murmured, hoarsely and indistinctly, hardly shaping out the words. "Many, many years have I waited for it! It is late! It is late! I want my happiness!"

—NATHANIEL HAWTHORNE,
The House of the Seven Gables

1

SOMEONE ON THE TELEVISION IS SAYING THAT THERE were people back in the old days who earned their livelihood by reading the future in rivers, ponds, and mirrors. Salva, the bar owner, hears all that without listening to it. He jabs the remote control at the plasma screen as though wielding a magic wand whose powers are inexplicably fading.

Behind him, seated at the bar and clutching a glass of cognac, is Tanveer Hussein. He arrived with Epi a while ago, after a very strenuous night; nevertheless, he seems to have forgotten it, and he's in a good mood. He gazes ironically upon Salva's attempts to operate the pirated remote and asks him if he needs help. Supposedly, there was a day when he, Tanveer, installed satellite dishes. Salva doesn't reply. He lifts his eyeglasses from his nose to his forehead and holds the clicker close to his eyes, because it's early in the morning and he's already begun to doubt everything. He sees yellow buttons, red buttons, green buttons. All the same, all ridiculous.

When Epi and the *Moro*—the North African—came into the bar, Epi's brother, Alex, was sitting at one of the tables in the back. As Epi crossed the room in long strides, he glanced at his favorite Space Invaders machine. Like a jealous lover gazing down on his beloved, asleep and alone, he was relieved to see that the machine was off. Then he went into the bathroom. He was carrying a sports bag printed with the words MOSCOW 1980.

Female Bulgarian shot-putters, Alex thinks, automatically, as soon as he reads the legend on the bag. Epi didn't even gesture in his brother's direction when he came in. Maybe he didn't see him. *Hairy Czech armpits, sad blue Slavic eyes,* Alex muses, recalling the televised broadcasts of the Olympic Games boycotted by the *yanquis*. Sleep's pushing its way into his skull and affecting his vision. He looks at his watch: not even seven o'clock. It's strange to be here and not in his bed at this hour; he's never set foot in Salva's bar so early. But he didn't sleep much last night, and besides, he ran out of tobacco and coffee. And so, heroically, he got up, dressed, and went down to the bar, which he knew would just be opening. Now he's sitting in front of a tall glass whose contents are in a state of combustion. It will be a good while before he'll be able to take a sip, but to tell the truth, he's in no hurry today.

Tanveer and Epi. Epi and Tanveer. Alex has heard that his little brother and the Moroccan were friends again, but Epi hasn't said a word on the subject. Nothing good can come of it, as everybody knows. Everybody except Epi, apparently. Alex takes two successive drags on his cigarette and tries to pick up the thread of the TV program, because it seems to be the sort of thing he remembers his father liking a lot.

On the screen, an expert from some distant university is asserting that if no one looks at you, you're worthless. What an insight. You have a bag on your head. It doesn't matter what you do or what you're good for. Without eyes focused on you, you've got no story. No before and no after. You can't return anywhere because nobody remembers you were there.

"These windbags are always depressing," Alex mutters to himself. As if someone has heard him, the image on the television screen suddenly disappears. Salva makes what sounds like a triumphant noise. But now rifles appear, and camouflage outfits, ammunition vests, men in firing positions. Then birds in flight, a quail, followed by others, a bevy of stupid quail. Shots among the clouds, and what looks like a little bundle falls from the sky, provoking some mean, opportunist dogs.

Alex prefers blowhards to hunters, but nobody's asking him. Nor does he protest. Instead, he moves his hand closer to his glass. Failed experiment—still too hot.

Epi's in the restroom, standing in the dark. His eyes are fixed on the light switch, where there's a small pinpoint of red light. He's so tense he even notices the sawdust under his feet. The odor of bleach is starting to make him feel sick. Where do people get the strength for this? Cleaning the bathroom floor every morning, keeping their lives in order, doing things right?

A Pakistani enters the scene. He comes in smiling and gestures toward the back of the room. Salva, behind the bar, advises him that he can't use the john unless he buys something to drink. But the guy doesn't understand or doesn't want to understand, so he widens his smile by six more teeth and starts looking for the right door. Salva curses the Christian God and the armies of the Crusaders for not finishing what they started, but he goes back to his main concern: looking for replays of yesterday's soccer goals.

"Leave that on, man, leave it on. I liked that stuff with the birds. Look, look, now they're going after the pig," Tanveer drawls.

"Boar, dummy. *Boar.*"

The Paki pushes the restroom door, and Epi, who didn't latch it, blocks it with his arm. The other apologizes, takes a step backward, and prepares to wait as long as it takes. He turns toward Alex, still smiling. But Epi's brother doesn't react. He'd like to enlighten the stranger: *That's the way we Europeans are,* he'd like to explain. *Jerks first thing in the morning. Maybe it's something left over from the French Revolution, kid.*

Epi closes the door and bolts it this time. He still doesn't turn on the light. His sweat is soaking his T-shirt. He has to calm down. He starts to chant a prayer, the way he was taught to do as a child: say your prayers for a few minutes until you fall asleep. He starts the prayer once, twice, three times, but each time he reaches a point—bad sign—where he's forgotten the rest.

All the same, he knows he can't stay in here any longer; he knows there's no alternative. For the umpteenth time, he touches the handle of the hammer he's taken out of the gym bag, and a great deal of foolishness, a great many absurd, inappropriate ideas, enter his mind. He thinks about how mad at him Mari's going to be—Mari is Salva's wife—when she has to clean up everything again. Blood, brains, broken glass, footsteps in the sawdust, on the spotless, polished surface of the bar. And of course, he thinks about Tiffany in order to screw up his courage, which seems to be failing him right when he needs it most. After a few seconds he opens the door. He's surprised to find himself face to face with the Pakistani. Epi doesn't know him from the barrio. He's just another recently arrived pariah, looking at him out of deep black eyes and mumbling a few words that fall somewhere between Spanish and Urdu. Epi's hardly out of the bathroom before the other guy's already inside, relieving his cramps.

Tanveer's still hypnotized by the hunting scenes on the television. Death, the game of hunters versus prey. The talk has turned to animals, how they sense danger in silence, in the deep stillness of the forest. The off-camera voice whispers that when it comes to wild boars, you have to know how to wait. The image breaks up, flashes of other channels appear, and there's the blowhard program again, the same expert, covered with dandruff and enthralled by his own discourse, now talking about who the hell knows what.

Panic, Disorder, Crazed Confusion. The Gorgons. There were three of them, and they always kept one eye open, the cunning things. *Three, like the three of us: Salva, Epi, and me. Like the Three Musketeers, or the Three Little Pigs, and Tanveer, naturally, as the Big Bad Wolf.* As Alex thinks this, he watches Epi position himself behind his Moroccan friend. Surprised,

Alex looks on as his brother gently sets his sports bag on the floor, out of the way. Then Epi straightens up, keeping his arms at his sides. In his right hand, he's holding a big hammer; its head brushes his knee. The thing looks incongruous to Alex. A hammer doesn't fit in this scene. This is a bar. This is ordinary life. It seems more like a computer screen, like a video game: Epi has found the talisman in the bathroom, and he wants to use it right away. One thousand life points; user moves up one level.

"You're gonna have to pay for the clicker," Tanveer says. "You've never been any good at conning people, Salvita."

Suddenly, everything starts happening fast. Salva turns around to tell Tanveer that he's had it up to here with his comments. But the words won't come out, because he sees Epi standing two paces behind Tanveer and clutching a large hammer with both hands, as if he's waiting for Salva's best pitch.

The bar owner's sudden silence is a scream of warning to Tanveer that something's happening behind him. He starts to turn around, and because he does, the hammer doesn't hit him flush. Epi's plan was to strike a clean blow to the head, one only, so that Tanveer would never know who or what killed him. But it wasn't to be, and now he can't stop.

He puts all his strength into the swing, completing it with his eyes half-closed. It looks to him as though he's striking the reflection of something worn, burnished, metallic. In fact, he lands a glancing blow on Tanveer's clavicle, cracking it and sending all six-foot-two of him immediately to the floor. As he falls, the Moroccan crashes against the legs of his attacker, causing

Epi to stumble and fall, too. Epi knows he has to spring to his feet, he has to get on top of Tanveer quickly and break his skull.

Salva bellows and tries to scramble out from behind the bar as fast as he can. At this point, Epi would like to forget the whole thing. Stop what he's doing, tell Tanveer it was all a joke, rewind the tape to a point months, years, lives ago. Cast a spell and awaken his dead mother, break his fingers pushing through walls and roofs, and become a child again, an innocent child with an easy life ahead of him. But it's not possible.

Tanveer, tall and strong, clutches his arm in pain and tries to get up. He slips on the recently washed floor and tumbles against the slot machine. Now the hammer lands on his back. Screaming insults and curses, he grabs hold of Epi's T-shirt, pulls on it hard, and falls back again.

Neither Salva nor Alex can intervene, because the hammer blows keep raining down wildly, one after another. Tanveer crawls away on all fours and collides with a metal ladder left by the painters. He gets behind the ladder, using it to shield himself from Epi's blows. Epi keeps swinging the hammer until, in the middle of a swing, he loses his grip. The hammer flies out of his hand, slams into his favorite game machine, and shatters it. For a few seconds everything seems suspended. Maybe Epi's thinking that all is lost now. Tanveer, by contrast, sees his chance. Though badly hurt, he grabs the ladder with both hands and finds the strength to bring it down hard on his adversary's back.

"Fucking fag, I'm going to kill you! You crazy son of a bitch!

I know why you're doing this, candy ass! Can I help it if you're a lousy fuck? Son of a bitch!"

The blow from the ladder rocks Epi and drives him against the wall. As luck would have it, he finds the hammer at his feet. So he seizes it forcefully, dodges Tanveer's weak follow-up attack, rears back, and staves in the *Moro*'s forehead with one blow. Hussein staggers and hugs his assailant to keep from collapsing. Epi looks at him with no idea of how to free himself from this dying embrace. Finally, Tanveer slips down and sprawls in the bleach and sawdust. On the floor under his head, a pool of blood forms and spreads, gleaming colorfully with the reflected light of the video games. The various machines, seeing what has just happened to one of their number, seem to be holding their breath.

Finish him, finish him, says a voice inside Epi's head.

But he can't do it. He's gone that far, but now he'll go no farther. He stands there with slumped shoulders, staring at Tanveer's body. Epi has awakened from his dream, and he can't recover the strength that exploded in him a few moments ago. Exhausted and broken, he looks at his brother—he sees him now—who stands paralyzed, watching him. Neither of them manages to utter a word.

At this moment the restroom door opens and the half-drunk Pakistani appears. Puzzled, he sees a man lying in a pool of blood and two other guys staring at him fixedly, as if waiting for him to explain all this. When he scurries out of the bar, no one stops him. And Epi, with several seconds' head start on him, has vanished as if he were never there.

"Is he dead?" Salva asks insistently.

"Of course he is, shit, you didn't see his head split open?"

Obviously, there's no hurry about calling anyone.

"I'm going up to tell Mari to stay out of here so she won't faint."

"Call her on the phone."

"It's better if I go up."

"And I'm supposed to stay here alone with *him*?"

"Yeah, keep him company. I won't be five minutes. And when I come back down, I'll call the cops."

Salva leaves the bar and pulls the rolling shutter halfway down. Inside, Alex, to avoid watching the death throes, returns his gaze to the television set. For no apparent reason, it's changed channels all on its own, and now it's showing a Madonna music video on MTV. She's stepping along a horizon of flowering paths. Better than Christ walking on the water. It's nice to distract yourself with something beautiful when you've got a guy whose skull is oozing blood and brains a yard from your feet. Alex thinks it would be wonderful to take refuge under Madonna's skirts. To live in New York. To be immensely rich. Not to live in this shitty city full of bicycles and assholes.

The black wings of a premonition suddenly darken his head and freeze his nerve centers. His brother has killed Tanveer. Salva and he, Alex, have both realized that they can pin the murder on the poor Paki, whom Allah, Yahweh, or some goddess with fifty thousand arms and the head of an elephant brought to this place in an evil hour. But how innocent is Alex going to look if someone wants a cup of coffee right away, undeterred by a half-lowered rolling shutter? What's he doing standing over a corpse? Why is he still in the wrong place at the wrong time? Besides, there's that sports bag, the souvenir of the Bolshevik Olympics. Something tells him that this is the moment to go home and leave Tanveer in Madonna's pleasant company. Alex pulls down the sleeve of his sweater and uses it to pick up the hammer, which he sticks in the bag. He steps out onto the street. Feels cooler. With all that commotion, it's a miracle there isn't a group of people hanging around outside and speculating. Alex pulls his jacket tight around him, wipes his nose with his fingertips, tries to forget everything and go on to the next screen. He raises his arms and imagines he has some magic dust he can use to make the city disappear. He sees himself swinging between buildings like a large spider, his shadow falling on roof terraces and tall windows.

Inside the bar, Tanveer's eyes are open, but he can't see anything. He's at death's door, breathing his last. A song plays inside his head. He listens to the music while he smells his own blood, while he feels it filling his mouth. He didn't know that keeping your eyes open doesn't necessarily mean you're able to see. He doesn't know who Madonna is, either, nor does it matter much. But she seems to find his ignorance insulting, not funny. So Tanveer thinks his own urine is hers; she's the woman who pees on him in his dreams. Apparently, Madonna still has bad manners left over from her days on the street, when she lived on popcorn and remunerative sex.

2

TANVEER AND TIFFANY BRISETTE WERE SHUT UP IN THAT room. It was a narrow room, filled to bursting with objects evidently impossible to get rid of. And below the mountain of stuffed toys, of dirty, recently ironed, or perhaps forgotten clothes, of ashtrays and CDs, there was a single bed, a night table, a chair, a mirror.

In that room they could hear sounds from the rest of the apartment. Sounds moving closer or keeping their distance or fading away without a hint as to where they'd come from or why they'd gone. Aside from visiting the bathroom now and again, Tiffany's mother and sister never bothered them. Instead they spent the time looking at television and acting as though Tanveer and Tiffany didn't exist. For his part, Percy, Tiffany's little son, knew that he mustn't go near the room when his mother had company. Tanveer was convinced the child liked to watch. Not that he cared, but Tiffany refused to let the boy spy on them. So to avoid any detriment to their screwing, the *Moro* usually brought something the kid could distract himself with while they shut themselves up in the room. And if Percy wanted to watch, let him learn how to do it without his mother finding out. As he himself had done. As everybody did.

The soft click of the door when it locked was the signal for Tanveer to go up to the girl and stand behind her. He'd keep very still, and she'd remain with her back to him, without ever turning around. Automatically, they switched off the lights. She could hear him breathing and inhaled his scent, a mixture of sweat, tobacco, alcohol, and mint, or whatever the happy smell invading her nostrils was. Then a few seconds would pass. Tiffany could feel his fingers on her neck. In the beginning they'd barely graze her, as though not wishing to be mistaken for any sort of caress. Then the pressure would grow steadily more intense. Tiffany, well acquainted with the rules, would stand there unmoving, asking no questions, only waiting, as if suspended in a bubble formed by Tanveer's breath. After a few seconds, and without decreasing the pressure on her neck, he'd place the palm of his other hand in front of the girl's mouth, as though trying to feel some imaginary steam rising from her lips. Then the fingers gripping her neck would become an open palm pushing on the back of her head, while the other hand was now a fist a few inches from her mouth. Tanveer would now be in front of Tiffany, and at this point, he'd say, "Kiss it," and she'd pretend she hadn't heard him. He'd insist and push her face toward his fist, which remained immobile, practically under her nose. Eventually, she'd obey; she'd kiss his fist, his knuckles. On a few occasions, and without any obvious reason, he'd unclench his fist and give her a slap. A flat, simple blow to the face. The hand that caresses can also hit. That seemed to be the lesson. Although Tiffany could sense when the slap was coming, she wouldn't dodge it. After she kissed his fist, he'd open his hand and offer his palm for more kissing. And then, only then, would she speak. The Heartbreak Queen, she who paraded around the barrio like a commander, would start babbling and making funny faces and spouting nonsense; she was a woman pretending—badly—to be a child.

The *Moro*'s eyes would get blurry and moist, like the eyes of a drunkard. They could express nothing but the flood of desire that was surging through him. He liked to feel her through her clothes, to thrust his hands under her top, slowly spread his fingers, and cup her breasts. To fasten his fingers like clamps on her nipples, nipples that had suckled a child. He'd ask her to tell him how he could get himself inside her, all of him, big and ungainly as he was, so that he, and not Percy, would be her child. Tiffany would regress a few years, stroke his hair, take him in her arms, and suckle him, finding no words that weren't fantasies and dreams, lullabies and echoes of words and songs spoken and sung by so many before her.

Then they'd face each other in silence. He'd stretch out his arms, put them on the girl's shoulders, and slowly press her down until she was on her knees and waiting for him to put it in her mouth. Both of them liked everything to seem as though they were doing it for the first and last time. Tanveer Hussein's member pounded the inside of her throat; the more violent thrusts made her gag, but she said nothing. She'd get her payback later. When he'd raise her up, his hands clasping her ass, and make her explode with pleasure. When they'd hit the pavement at night with a group of people who were more or less friends and destroy themselves with gin and cocaine and laughter. When they'd go up and down other streets, streets outside the barrio. When he'd buy her clothes, dinner, and drinks, whatever she wanted, as the price for her sex and her freedom.

Sometimes Tanveer would cross the line, going beyond the agreed limits in the demonstration of his power and her submission. On occasion, something she misinterpreted or something he deemed a lack of respect was enough to set him off. At such times Tiffany would have liked to annihilate him, to tear him apart with her own hands like a clay figure. That sort of thing always ended in the wee hours of the morning, with her clinging to her poor mother's arm at the police station. The *Moro* would be arrested, and he'd leave the court with a restraining order against him. But neither he nor she could obey it, and the whole thing would become just one more papier-mâché prop on the stage behind the two protagonists. Nevertheless, it left Tiffany with a certain power over her man, a power whose savor was acrid in her mouth and aroused her senses, as if she could turn it into something physical. One call from her, and Tanveer would go to jail for violating a court order. Another kind of call, and they'd shut themselves up for the entire evening in Tiffany's room or in the safe house the Moroccan shared with people nobody knew at all. Tanveer was aware of both aspects of the game, and although it enraged him to lose the initiative, he felt something like the peace, the sense of order, the security that come from knowing that jails, stool pigeons, and guards still exist.

Before and after her meetings with Hussein, Tiffany hated herself. As she lay on the bed, alone, inhaling the scent of sweat and violence that emanated from the cotton bedspread, she'd think about what she'd done and felt and find it difficult to recognize herself, in the same way as when they were out in the street and she'd see him being so loud and boisterous, she'd look at him and remember asking him to describe fragments of a childhood neither of them could have had. At those moments, when their eyes met in the street, there was nothing more for them to say to each other. He knew that she knew, and vice versa. It was as if each of them had kidnapped the other's secret and neither of them had the slightest intention of paying the ransom.

And yet Tanveer, too, hated himself. For getting attached to Tiffany. For desiring her, and at the same time for getting her so easily. For not having been the first, and for knowing he wouldn't be the last. Hussein's mother was a Spanish woman from Tangiers. His father, a *Moro* and a Muslim—as his mother never failed to point out—had died several times, and it was therefore probable that he was in prison or that one day he had escaped from that woman forever. Tanveer was never able to get a clear answer about what had happened, but in his heart he knew the truth: Spanish women aren't generous, they make deals for everything, everything's a negotiation, and so no way his father would have stayed. He likewise knew that one day his father would come back for him, and that when that day came, he'd break the old man's jaw before deciding whether or not to return with him to Morocco.

Tanveer believed there was nothing that couldn't be stolen and no one who couldn't be fooled. The only exception, if he had to make one, was the ethereal figure of his paternal grandmother, who along with his mother had raised him after his father abandoned them. They lived in an adobe brick house, or at least that was the way he remembered it. In that house, and in those years of his childhood, Tanveer Hussein had left everything, absolutely everything: the Future, Propriety, Truth, Law. The streets, the money, the easy women, the poor saps who almost begged you to rip them off, the television shows, replete with tits, colors, and cars, that humiliated his family, or, much worse, the ones that sugarcoated reality with feeble, paternalistic speeches—all that was nothing but city lights, as attractive as only the devil can be. And in the end, they ruined the good boy from the country who only wanted to have a good time for a while over the holidays. They doomed the skeptical kid who didn't know how to get home after the first few drinks and so had to keep on going. Tiffany was a part of the pleasure trap that had orchestrated his life. Tiffany was the vice you don't give up today because you think you'll be able to give it up tomorrow. A weakness he would have been ashamed to confess to his grandmother, sitting at dusk in her whitewashed adobe brick house.

Tanveer was tall and dark. From the first moment he arrived in the barrio, he never tried to be inconspicuous, not that he could have succeeded had he tried. He'd swagger around with his shirt off, exhibiting tattoos, medals, bracelets, and abdominal muscles. He'd run here and there in his Nike sports shoes, doing a lot of drugs and drinking unspeakable quantities of alcohol. He bummed Winston cigarettes, he was good with a knife, and in street fights he'd land some really impressive whacks, the kind that ring out, bounce off the sidewalk, echo, and then climb buildings floor by floor. And every now and again, he worked with some guy who was in construction. He dealt drugs, of course, he'd had some prior arrests as a juvenile that counted against him as an adult, and he got to know the inside of a cell for a few months. If he felt like dressing up to impress a woman, he'd put on a tracksuit that cost as much as the rent on the apartment his mother paid for, bless her soul, by working in a plus-size clothing store; if he was bored, he'd go looking for trouble, robbing the exchange students in the barrio, terrifying people at random, or picking up whores with Epi around the city morgue. As he did the night before the morning when his companion in debauchery would, to his surprise, dash out his brains.

When Tanveer arrived, things in that part of the city had already begun to change. It was one of those moments when you perceive that everyday life has shifted, has been shaken up, and will be put back together again but in a different shape. The environment was changing, tenaciously, inexorably, and as the image of the barrio was altered, the older residents started feeling uncomfortable. Because little by little they found themselves being shut out of bars, squares, and streets, while—as they saw it—the others, those who had to suffer humiliation and to be grateful to find a job and a future, were getting government assistance, obtaining permits to hold bazaars on Thursdays, and taking up a lot of television time.

It was true that new renters had been succeeding one another in those buildings for years, entering and leaving, occupying the residences of those who once were alive and today were dead, of those who'd lived together there and whose names are now all that remain of the families that fled. Now there were strange kinds of music, unfamiliar words, and the newcomer's disagreeable determination to conquer the new world for himself. And what happened was that one fine day the original inhabitants of the barrio who still lived there reviewed the situation and realized that they'd been abandoned to their fate. They saw that many others, the farsighted ones, those with children gone from the barrio, had escaped to the mountains and left behind whatever was useless, slow, or dim. And that all that was left in the neighborhood were the impaired, the poor, junkies, drunks, and old folks.

3

ALEX ENTERS THE LOBBY OF HIS APARTMENT BUILDing. He runs past the mailboxes in the hallway, looks left and right, and decides against taking the elevator. Throwing an arm over the metal handrail, he launches himself up the stairs, two or three at a time. He doesn't want to meet anyone. It's very early in the morning, but too many things have happened already. He's not interested in running into neighbors, whether friendly or unsociable or enemies of long standing. To say nothing of shades or spirits. Thus far, they haven't made an appearance, but he hasn't taken his medication yet today, and he's sure they've been invited to the party. He's supposed to take a pill every morning, right after breakfast; otherwise, stomach acid will ruin his day. At the turning of every landing, the gym bag strikes his leg. He's already tossed the hammer into a Dumpster he passed on the way home. Nobody saw him. When it comes to taking precautions, being schizophrenic has its advantages.

He's breathing hard when he lunges into the apartment. He calls out to Epi, hoping against hope that he's taken refuge at home. As this wouldn't be a bad option, it seems pretty unlikely to Alex that his brother has chosen it; by now, Epi has surely come up with something ten times worse. At the end of the hall, the light in their mother's room is on. The light that never goes out. It never went out while the old lady was still alive, and for some idiotic, fraudulent reason, neither Alex nor Epi wants to turn it off now, three months after her death. They're probably afraid she'll start yelling at them the way she used to when they assumed she was asleep and switched it off.

His mother's gone, but Alex still sees her, hears her, senses her everywhere. It's surely her hand guiding his when he forges her "certificate of existence" so they can keep receiving her family assistance check from the government. She's what protects them from the social worker, who never stops calling. Obviously, the healthiest course would be for them to go into their mother's room and drive all the ghosts out of there. Break ruthlessly into closets and drawers. Burn the furniture and the holy pictures and the family photographs. But such an undertaking would be so titanic that instead, day by day, the room has been turning into a museum, and so it shall remain.

Another possibility is that Epi has gone into hiding at Tiffany's place. It would be a good idea to give her a call. Alex can still remember the first meeting between his mother and Tiffany. When the girl said her name, the old lady grimaced, made her repeat it two or three more times, and then asked, "What kind of a name is that?"

"Just a name."

"Which saint is it?"

"Saint Don't Bug Me, señora."

"You don't have very good manners. Didn't they teach you to be polite in your house? Where are you from?"

"From here," Tiffany lied.

"Well then, how about your parents?"

"From Peru."

"Ah, right. And how did you come to be born here?"

"Tell your mother to drop it, will you?"

Later, they learned to get along quite well, but in her last days, the old lady didn't recognize Tiffany, either. The hepatic poisoning she suffered from severely limited her ability to understand almost anything. She persisted only in watching television and talking to the husband who'd left her, to her first sweetheart, to her last lover, to her dead grandmother, to Jesus Christ, also dead, and to Elvis Presley, who was, indeed, forever alive.

Suddenly, the telephone at Alex's side starts ringing. It takes him a few seconds to grasp the fact that the sound is coming neither from his pocket nor from inside his skull, but rather from the cordless phone right there, within reach of his hand. He hesitates to answer the call. He doesn't recognize the number that appears on the display, but he knows the caller's not using a cell phone. What to do? It might be Epi, calling from a pay phone.

"Alex? Is that you?"

"Yes."

It's Salva, maybe on the phone in the bar.

"Man, you left me with a real mess on my hands."

"I'm sorry," Alex replies, summoning enough strength to keep on replying, and forcing himself to think. "I was scared shitless. I don't know what—but look, if someone comes in and finds me with a dead body, then I'm sure to get busted. Nothing's going to happen to you, you own the bar. It makes perfect sense that you'd be there, but not me—"

"I told them you were with me," Salva interrupts him.

This revelation definitively activates the alarm in Alex's head. He rapidly considers the possibility that Salva's call is being monitored, that Salva has given him up to the cops, him and Epi both. Alex has to be careful. He says, "Why shouldn't you tell them that?"

Salva doesn't reply. He hesitates. It may be that he's sensed Alex's mistrust, or that the *Mossos d'Esquadra*, the Catalonian police, really are in the room with him.

Alex, beginning to lose patience, waits for the bar owner to show his cards, once and for all, and then asks, "Where are you calling from, Salva?"

"From home."

"Is there anything else you want? I have stuff to do."

Alex walks into his brother's room. *I wish he was back, I wish he was lying in his bed right now,* Alex thinks, as though trying to replace the nightmare of what's happened with his own desires. But no, no such luck. The sheets are in disorder, dirty clothes are strewn across the floor, the computer's screen saver is shedding green, blue, and red tears, and one of Epi's thousand sneakers, lost and disoriented, is propped against the door. Alex says to Salva, "Don't worry."

"What's to worry about?"

"You told them I ran out after the Paki, right? He went into the subway. I couldn't catch him. He ran too fast. You know how those guys can run."

"In any case, the cops want to talk to you."

"What about?"

"Alex, for Christ's sake, I don't feel like playing games. You witnessed a murder, what do you expect? You think you can send them a postcard? Drop by the Embajadores police station. I didn't have your cell number, so it's lucky that Mari has your home phone number—I don't even want to think about why. Anyway, go and talk to them, because if you don't they're going to come looking for you at home, and nobody likes that."

"I'll go down there. I wasted my time running after that Paki. The bastard took off like a man possessed. I lost him in the subway."

"Alex, will you please calm down? You just told me that."

"I know I just told you that."

"Okay."

"So what about Tanveer?"

"You won't believe it, but when the ambulance came, he was opening his mouth a little."

"Think he'll live?"

"No."

"May Allah take him to His bosom."

"Don't be a jackass, Alex."

"I'm serious."

"But Tanveer was half Spanish."

"What does that have to do with it, Salva? A man believes what he believes."

"Right."

"Wait till my brother finds out."

"Maybe he already knows," the bar owner replies mysteriously.

"How could he know?"

"All right, Alex. I have no idea . . ."

"I gotta go, Salva."

"Okay."

"One more thing."

"What?"

"Thanks."

So Epi well and truly wasted Tanveer, Alex thinks. Up until this moment, it's been as if it wasn't real, or at least not as real as it actually was. Alex's legs start trembling again. He looks up and finds himself staring at his reflection in the mirror. He can still recognize himself. He's not a dead man's ghost—not yet. But he *is* old and tired. His hair's disheveled, unruly, like a patch of woodland a fire has weakened but not destroyed. Years ago, Alex had an angular, bony face, but now he's got bags for cheeks. His skin is waxy, with violet shadows; the more obstinate ones look like tattoos under his eyes, which are small and set wide apart.

No, he wouldn't like it if the *mossos* came to his apartment. Still, before he sees them, he's got to talk to Epi. He calls his brother's mobile phone for about the thousandth time, but it's either turned off or out of range. He looks for Tiffany's number, but he lost it when he changed phones and didn't do anything to recover it. If Epi's got to forget her, every little bit helps.

He goes into Epi's room again, giving the vigilant sneaker a swift kick. The shoe skitters away and hides under the bed like a fearful dog. Alex is looking for he doesn't know what. Maybe the girl's telephone number. Maybe a clue that will tell him where his brother is. He checks the objects on the table. It occurs to him that Epi's cell phone might be somewhere around here, but fortunately there's no trace of it among the miscellaneous litter. However, he does find some paper napkins with notes addressed to Tiffany and written in Epi's horrendous, childish hand. Alex starts to read them, but he can't go on. They make him sick. For caution's sake, he decides to take them with him. Better if no one ever finds them. He thinks about another occasion, when he saw a girl, a different girl, lying on that same bed. Alex had overslept and was going to be late for his shift in the parking garage where he still works today. He staggered out of his room and found the bathroom door closed. Epi was inside, and Alex could feel the presence of someone else in the apartment, in Epi's bedroom. He opened the door of his brother's room a little wider and intuited rather than saw her, lying under the jumble of sheets and blankets, entangled in disorder, surrounded by the reek of sweat, tobacco, and sex. She was the source of the soft snoring he heard, the configuration of soft flesh filled with heat, guts, and straight razors that his brother had introduced him to a few days before.

Not that Tiffany was something out of this world. She was rather short, with a moon-shaped face and big eyes. Her tattooed blue eyelids were the only feature that distinguished her from any other girl. You could tell that as she grew older, she'd get fat and lose her curves, because having the baby had already broadened her hips. But she had something that lit you up if you were next to her, something that made you shine. There was no need for explanations; the mere fact that she'd chosen you proved you were someone special. By the same token, to be left by Tiffany was to return to eternal, impenetrable, unyielding darkness. *A skillful player would know how to leave her ten minutes before she left him*, Alex tells himself. Alex knows he would have been better at the game than Epi, but Tiffany was never his. Once upon a time, she was his brother's. Now, in fact—Alex sees the matter more clearly than ever, if possible—it's as though Epi won the prize and lost everything, all with the same ticket.

Alex lies down on his brother's bed. He closes his eyes and tries to calm himself. There's no time to waste. He must get up and take his medication before everything starts to get complicated inside his head. He knows perfectly well that after he swallows the pill, it will be easier for him to decide what to do. But he stays there, lying on the bed with his eyes closed. It's ridiculous, he thinks, to be forty years old and still in custody, a prisoner in almost everyone's eyes. To pay attention to the doctor, who tells him not to drink or take drugs and to stick to his medication schedule. To obey his mother's former commands: Take care of your brother. Pay the rent. Greet those who greet you, and also those who don't. And then there are all those voices he hears and recognizes, both inside and outside his head, always giving him orders, warning him, frightening him.

He leaves Epi's room and turns toward his. All he has to do is to cross the hall, but the bad news keeps coming. Near the door, he thinks he catches a glimpse of a long robe, disappearing as its wearer takes cover. It's too late; he's already seen it. He shuts his eyes, enters his bedroom, gropes unseeing for the box of pills, rips off the packaging, and takes one, swallowing it with difficulty. At his first opportunity, he'll wash the pill all the way down with a nice glass of water. In the darkness of his own room, he can control his movements almost without opening his eyes, but the minute he steps out into the hall, he'll wind up breaking something. So he'll have to open them. And he must keep his panic in check. He knows that. He'll see absurd images, the door of the bedroom stained with blood, Lazarus returned from the dead and sauntering down the hall like John Travolta. He'll see such things and more. "It's nothing but illusions inside my head," he tells himself, and he remembers that he's right, that he has to concentrate on reality, as his doctor has counseled him to do. But if he sees what he sees and hears what he hears, what more is required for something to be real? All sheer madness. His mother always called him by his little brother's name, never by his own. And things like the one stationed out there, wearing a robe, are nothing but the shit his mother crammed into his head. So many saints and martyrs, so much dust, so many wounds, such a desert. He can feel the pill stuck in his throat. He swallows saliva repeatedly. He could go to the bathroom or the kitchen, but he can't move, he doesn't dare. He ought to run. Do it quickly and trick all the shapes that'll come out at him along the way. He runs into the kitchen and locks the door behind him. Taking a glass from the sink, he turns on the faucet. He empties the glass in one gulp. The water's tepid. It's disgusting. Of course—the water heater's on. Maybe he's the one who forgot to turn it off. Maybe it was the others. But the kitchen's always a place of refuge. Sacred ground. The bright fluorescent lights chase away the undead. He disconnects the heater and lets the water run. A good swig of cool water will soothe him. After he drinks, he opens the kitchen door and starts running.

There's no one who can see him, no one who can reprove him, as his mother used to do, for running in the hall with his eyes closed. At the same time, he pats his pockets to make sure he's got his keys, his wallet, and his cell phone, and then he accelerates toward the door. He thinks there's someone behind him, someone who wants to touch him. It's Christ, beseeching him. Maybe He wants him to believe in Him, wants his help with the loaves or the fishes, or maybe He wants him to stop downloading music for free, because he and everyone else who does that are killing the artists. No matter. Go back to Nazareth, nutball, Alex thinks. But he's immediately frightened by his blasphemy. "God can read your heart," his mother used to tell him. When he closes the door behind him and heads down the stairs, he hears the screams of the ghosts, which stay inside, growing like trees behind our backs, crossing off, one by one, the minutes left until we return and they can go back to scaring us.

4

EPI HALTS AT THE CURB AND LOOKS AT THE STOPLIGHT. It's green. He can cross, but he's already ignored so many red signals that he's on the point of forgetting the rules for drivers and pedestrians. For a few seconds, he hasn't the slightest notion where he is. Inside his gym shoes, his feet are burning. He crosses over to the opposite corner, attempting to catch his breath, walking with one hand clutching his side, as he did when he was a boy and he was trying to quiet his heartbeat. Several cars pass. A bus. He walks to the next corner. Maybe he can get a better idea of where he is from there. He's left the barrio, but he knows he has to go back. He looks at his cell phone, then turns it on. His brother's calls appear on the screen, but the little chirp that means his battery is near death sounds almost at once, and he decides to turn the phone off. He's sure the battery will have better occasions for chirping later that very day. When he reaches the corner, he stands still for a good while. With his mind blank. He's not carrying the bag with the hammer. Maybe he left it in the bar or threw it away somewhere. He doesn't remember. It's not that he expects to get out of the fix he's in, but it seems he could at least not make the law's job too easy.

He's cold. He touches his lip, which feels strange, as if it were swelling. Then he looks at his fingertips, checking for blood from his mouth. His temples are pounding. Everything's so confused. Even now, after he's made his decision and acted upon it. Things are still until they start moving fast, and then they don't know how to stop. He looks at the corners of the buildings, at the terraces and the cars, but his eyes have degenerated from so much staring at computer screens and squinting at video games. He's so far gone that the act of shutting and opening his eyes feels to him rather like closing and restarting the same game.

Actual violence, it turns out, is not only sordid and unaesthetic, it also possesses a tremendous capacity to generate desperation. Your blows don't land where you want them to. You're not as strong as you think. It hurts to receive, but it also hurts to give. And the terrible thing is the certainty that it's all or nothing. There are no second chances. You have to keep it up. There's nothing behind you. The sad truth is that adrenaline tastes like fear.

Epi prefers not to think very much about what happened. His obsession is focused on Tiffany. His wish is to see her face, to hear himself speaking, to talk to her and realize that she's listening attentively to what he has to tell her. The building he's in front of has a low windowsill he could sit on. Maybe stopping for a while would help him to think clearly and figure out what he should do next. A taxi's about to pass him. Nobody's going to look for you inside a taxi. Epi raises his hand, but the cab doesn't stop. Then he notices what he looks like. His sweater is stained with blood and his face—surely—with fear. He takes off the sweater, turns it inside out, and puts it back on. Without realizing it, he's been trembling for who knows how long. His whole body's beginning to hurt. Especially his back. The son of a bitch got him good with that ladder. He won't be able to move tomorrow. One of his feet is starting to bother him, too. It's possible that he broke a toe. A few minutes pass, and then another taxi comes along, this one with its green light turned on. Epi raises his hand; the cab slows down and pulls up to the curb.

The driver's a woman. She scrutinizes him at length in her rearview mirror. The cab's front and back seats are separated by a security panel with a little basket for passing money back and forth. Epi has never been in jail. He imagines that the visiting area must be something like this. The lawyer committed to justice, the devastated girlfriend, her hand trying to touch his hand through the glass as she says, *I'll wait for you, I'll be there when you get out, but tell me, you know you can trust me, where did you hide the money?*

"Where shall I take you?"

"I don't know."

"Well, if you don't know . . ."

"I mean I don't remember the address."

"Anyway, I'm turning on the meter."

"I'm going to my girlfriend's. She doesn't live far from here. I'm late. I'll tell you where to turn as we go along."

The taxi heads for Tiffany's place. Epi should probably give her a call first. But it's still very early, and Miss Tiffany Brisette has a hard time waking up. Something's not working right, Epi thinks, when the fugitive has to wait outside the girl's door until she's ready to soothe his bad temper with the morning's first cup of coffee. Such things don't happen to superheroes. Whenever they want, they just go in through the windows. They go down stairs inside burning buildings and step out into smoking alleys. Women are always waiting for them to appear, and they, of course, are guys who make women wait.

The morning stretches and yawns, gradually waking up. Another sunny day, another good day for recovering from a cold. Indifferent to living things, the orange light is welcoming the buildings, illuminating them in such a way that they appear to Epi like new discoveries, things that weren't there last night, and now it seems to him that the light is raising them from the ground and trying to set them on their feet. Or worse yet, that they haven't left yet, despite all the warnings. Like dinosaur fossils, the concrete towers stay in place, and the light tries to straighten them up so they can start walking, but it isn't possible; they remain anchored where they are, waiting for time to bury them once and for all.

"Can I make a call on your cell phone?"

"I'm sorry. It's only for work."

"That means it's only for making calls to your dispatcher?"

"No. It just means it can't be used for certain things."

"What things?"

"It can't be used by customers, for example."

"This is an emergency."

"What kind of emergency?"

"In bars, customers can use the restrooms."

"What kind of emergency?"

"Never mind." Given the driver's attitude, Epi changes his tone and says to her, "But at least try to drive in a straight line. That is, if your husband taught you how."

"Careful what you say. This is my car, and I decide who gets to ride in it."

"It was only a joke."

"Real fucking funny."

Things like this exasperate him. He can't comprehend them. He doesn't understand why people choose to be jerks, just because. But at least the discussion has been useful for something. The cab driver has begun to concentrate hard on making all the lights. Now it looks as though she wants to get to their destination more than he does. They're very close. A few more intersections. As they drive on, they pass a *mossos* squad car, going in the opposite direction with its lights flashing but no siren. Epi figures they're going to Salva's bar. Then it's as if he can hear Alex scolding him, telling him that only a moron would kill Tanveer and then immediately go to see Tiffany Brisette. And he'd be right. As usual. Incredible as it seems, Epi hadn't thought about the police. He knows he had to do what he did, and he supposes that's enough. He chose the way of doing it without weighing many other options. He picked up whatever lay to hand. As to afterward, what would happen afterward, he simply hadn't thought about it, except to envision Tiffany receiving the news. He'd pictured himself in prison, but not how or where he'd be held. He'd also imagined himself on television, handcuffed, getting into a car while one of those pigs clapped a hand on his neck and thrust his head down. Why do they always do that? Because they saw it on TV one day and they're copying it? As far as he knows, nobody likes to whack his head against the roof of a car.

Now that he's on the point of seeing Tiffany, he realizes he ought to have prepared some sort of speech. Explanation's not his forte, and, slow as he is, he's never allowed to finish a thought. He needs to be given time, space, air. People—especially her—always keep interrupting him. But today's different. What he has to say has only one voice and a few words: his. As though a flash has lit up his consciousness, he becomes aware that he needs to go somewhere else and think some more. He says, "Change of plans."

Epi gives the driver the new address. She makes a popping sound with her lips and keeps her thoughts to herself. She puts on her turn signal and changes direction at the next intersection. Epi turns on his phone and calls Tiffany. Three rings, four, and then he ends the call. Let her wake up first. He sees the driver looking at him in the rearview mirror. He repeats the operation and hangs up again. "Fake call," he says. "I'm making a fake call."

Epi smiles. Teasing the taxi driver amuses him. He can picture her later, being asked in an interview whether she noticed anything strange about that particular passenger, the one who wore a sweater turned inside out and asked if he could use her cell phone. She'll declare with pride that she stood up to him and refused to let him make a call. As he's imagining this, Tiffany at last answers the phone.

CHARACTER IS DESTINY. Those words are written on a metal plaque over the main entrance to the Michi Panero Secondary School. Alex takes his hand out of his jacket pocket and, without breaking stride, thrusts a finger between the bars of the wrought-iron fence. Clack, clack, clack, clack. Like when he was a boy, and a student in that very school. He doesn't even look at the plaque, which time is steadily deteriorating. But he remembers how it gleamed when he was a schoolboy. Every morning he read that declaration. His father was a teacher at the Michi Panero School. He would always endorse the school's motto, word for word, even though he was never willing to reveal to Alex the ultimate secret it surely contained. "You'll understand it when you grow up," Alex's father would tell him. But then Alex grew up, and he still didn't understand it.

Nor was his father about to explain it to him. It was very hard to have him for a teacher, to be in his class and watch him walk up and down the rows, the butt of the jokes and stories invented by his classmates. Alex usually turned a blind eye and a deaf ear to those obscene, hellish spectacles, but sometimes he went so far as to join in them. His father's appearance contributed to the general derision: eyeglasses thick as bottle bottoms, old-fashioned vests, dark jackets covered with cat hair. Professor Dalmau occasionally lost the thread of his own explanations, it was practically obligatory to copy during his exams, and anything could happen in his classrooms. Beyond all that, what Alex found most ridiculous about his father was his absurd, anachronistic passion, which he never lost. The gleam in his eyes when he spoke of wrathful Achilles, of the death of Patroclus, who learned too late that Troy was defended by mighty warriors, and that the mightiest of them all was Hector. In the end, Alex's father turned out to be a mysterious man, too, for no one would have imagined that he could fall in love with another woman. That one fine day, he'd go out the door and never return. That all in all, he didn't give a shit about Ithaca.

Alex knows he's got to talk to the *mossos*, sooner rather than later. But no one likes going to a police station or an outpatient clinic. You can never be completely sure that the door closing behind you will open for you again. In any case, he has to talk to Epi first, so that the statements they give the police will gibe. However, his brother's still not answering his phone.

He turns into the street on his right. In Salva's bar, no doubt, they're gathering evidence and all that sort of thing. Alex walks past the barrio basketball court, next to the high school. It's only a few minutes before classes will begin, and some boys are making their final moves. Their schoolbags lie in piles under the baskets, and their sneakers squeal on the cement court. A little farther on, feigning indifference, a group of adolescent girls watch the game. They're chewing gum nonstop, the tiny strings of the thongs they all wear are showing, and they're having a try at choreographing a confused rhythm that goes *sha la la ra la la.*

It's nine o'clock, and the doors of the Michi Panero School are opening. Alex walks through one of the mobs of students stampeding toward the main entrance. If only he'd be lucky enough to meet Tiffany taking her little boy to nursery school! That would save him half the trip.

Epi's brother wonders what's passing through Epi's mind right about now while he, Alex, slips though the multitude of kids without taking the trouble to notice whom he's pushing or where he's putting his feet. Up until now, he hasn't asked himself why his brother has chosen to fuck up his life the way he has. On the other hand, he probably hasn't wondered about that because the answer seems so obvious. Therefore, it's more than possible that Epi's with Tiffany, or that at least he's contacted her.

Alex turns left at the next corner, enters a pedestrian zone, dodges a van, and reaches the girl's street. He hopes she's still living with her mother, but the truth is that he's hardly seen her in the past few months, not since Tanveer got out of jail. Everybody assumed she'd go back to him, and as Epi grew increasingly embittered and bad-tempered, he only confirmed that assumption.

Tiffany Brisette and her son live with Doña Fortu, her mother, and Jamelia, her older sister. The girls' parents are separated, in part thanks to some maneuvers by Tiffany that have never been clarified. The whole episode served to reaffirm Tiffany Brisette's ascendancy in the home, especially over her mother. The end result, however, also entailed the defeat of her sister, a sad, slow-witted girl who arrived that way on the plane from Peru; always dressed in grandmotherly clothes, always clinging to her mother's everlasting arm, she was addicted to Oreo cookies and the songs of Luis Miguel.

Doña Fortu's obsession with extravagant names seemed to have infected Tiffany like a sickness, for she had named her son—she was a single mother—Percy José. As if a name were something more than a name. As if it were a kind of magic spell with which you summon the future to play and you win the hand. The years to come may bring all that's good, luxurious, and exotic to someone named Tiffany Brisette, but what can they bring to girls named Pilar or Amparo? Maybe that wasn't it; maybe Doña Fortu's penchant for fancy names was just a roundabout way of taking a special sort of revenge. Having probably read books doesn't give you the right to name your daughter Fortunata Jacinta, as Doña Fortu's mother had done.* Nonetheless, it's more than possible that Doña Fortu harbored hopes for her arrival in Benito Pérez Galdós's homeland, hopes that her mere name would immediately cause the Spanish to consider her an extremely cultured distant cousin.

* Translator's note: *Fortunata y Jacinta*, an outstanding example of Spanish literary realism, is a popular novel written by Benito Pérez Galdós in 1887.

But obviously, that wasn't what happened. She looked like an Indian, in Peru she'd been poorer than the rats, and nobody in the barrio was going to waste time with realistic novels. And so, as soon as she set foot there, Doña Fortu secured a position as something like a character out of a child's comic book, an object of pure mockery, a figure very far from the one in her illusions.

Her home was a disaster in spite of, or because of, her attempts to make it the opposite. She spent money she didn't have, she waited for what never arrived, and she had no trace of an education. All this drove Tiffany to desperation. During the periods when circumstances obliged her to stay under her mother's roof, dealing with the girl was impossible. She turned into an unpredictable, irritating creature. Without notice, she'd disappear for weeks or months, leaving her son with Grandmother Fortu and Aunt Jamelia, only to reappear like a biblical plague, tormented by remorse and bad luck.

At one end of the street there's a financial institution, at the other a bar, and more or less in the middle, number 36. Alex is almost certain that the apartment's on the fourth floor, letter A or letter B. He rings both, but neither responds. He tries again and again: useless. He finds this odd; it's very early, and someone must be there. He heads for the bar and looks inside. Not many people. And no Tiffany Brisette. Suddenly, something makes him turn his head. He sees people leaving Tiffany's building. It's Jamelia, taking the boy to nursery school. In fact, they're walking in Alex's direction, holding hands, stepping out briskly because they're already late.

5

IT'S HARD FOR ALEX TO TELL WHETHER JAMELIA'S SEEN him or not. She has, however, come to a stop in the middle of the sidewalk. They're separated by a distance of about thirty feet, far enough to exasperate Alex. He'd like to shout the news to her, to tell her he's got a murder to pin on somebody and a jerk-off for a brother who's liable to fuck up all their lives and a bunch of *Mossos d'Esquadra* waiting for him at the police station. All at once, woman and child start walking again, and when they draw even with him, Alex cuts them off. Jamelia's options are to push Alex out of the way or to step down off the curb and walk in the roadway with the child, who's doing his best to free himself from his aunt's hand.

"Hello, Percy, how's school?"

"Epi, Epi, Epi . . ."

"Yeah, yeah, I hear you. But it's a bad connection. I'm not Epi, I'm his brother Alex. Do you remember me? You used to come to my place a lot, don't you remember? Say, listen: Where's your mama?"

"Epi, Epi, Epi."

It occurs to Alex that the little details are the ones that let you know you're getting old. For example, the way you can't maintain a squatting position for more than half a minute, or the way you have less and less patience with children.

"Jamelia, I need to talk to Tiffany. Do you know where she is?"

Alex hopes that sooner or later she'll say something that might qualify as a response, but for the moment she doesn't answer him. All things considered, his question is neither dangerous nor hard to understand. The girl looks frightened. Or mortified. But then again, that's her natural state; she always seems to be on the verge of apoplexy if someone speaks to her in the street. He repeats the question, but Jamelia remains silent, looking at the ground, as though counting the seconds remaining until her interrogator finds his task impossible and gives up.

"Please, I'm looking for Epi. It's important."

"Epi, Epi, Epi . . ."

"Right, exactly, Epi. Tiffany surely knows where he is. Is she still at home right now, sleeping off last night? Fuck, Jamelia, at least tell me whether or not you've seen Epi."

"Epi, Epi, Epi . . ."

"Percy, honey, you're going to have to shut up now, please." The child seems to understand and obeys. "Has he come around this morning? Come on, Jamelia, this could be a matter of life and death."

He says it without thinking. But suddenly he's seized by doubt: Is what he just said true? Was the scene in the bar with Tanveer just the first act of the Great Fuckup? But no, that wouldn't make any sense. Tiffany's participation in Tanveer's murder must have been limited to inspiring it, with or without her consent. It doesn't make sense to think anything else about Epi. Alex says, "Jamelia, I need . . ."

Maybe it's the change in her respiration, maybe it's the slight movement of her head, but Alex believes he can make out the promise of a glance, and even of a reply, behind the tangled curtain of her hair. And so he decides to wait and speak not a word, to wait and let her be squeezed by the silence and her thwarted haste. He employs the time in examining her as a man examines a woman; he lets himself be carried away by the fantasy of becoming her lover and dragging her out of her self-absorption. How much love she must have pent up inside, waiting for someone to let it escape! To penetrate her, to hear her moan in her little girl's bedroom. But without Alex's knowing exactly why, the erotic image he's contemplating suddenly turns miserable.

"I, I, I don't know—"

Alex defends himself against his own meanness, thinking that if Jamelia is to become a woman a man can desire, she'll have to stop bleaching her hair, get rid of her fuzzy sideburns, and give up looking at people with those demented eyes, which are now looking at him as she begins to speak.

"I—"

The worse thing about loquacious interior voices, loud music inside cars, and sexual fantasies is that they distract you. That may be the reason why Alex realizes too late that he's being lifted off the ground by the crotch and shaken.

"What's up, man? What are you doing so far from your burrow?"

"Son of a bitch, you scared the shit out of me!"

"Have you heard about Tanveer?"

Allawi's an Algerian, a handsome guy with slightly Asian features. He's also the only person alive on earth today who still drinks Diet Coke with Lemon. He's the official barber of the barrio, and he sports a vertical tattoo that runs from his right ear to the base of his neck and reads, in English, *I LOVE VANESSA*. But if there's anything Allawi doesn't like, it's people inquiring about the said Vanessa. He's calm and congenial, as if the lotions he inherited from the previous barber, Señor Juan, a man known for calmness and congeniality, had promoted these qualities. From inside the café on the corner, Allawi spotted Alex and decided to step out and talk to him. Today he's wearing his hair short and dyed platinum blond, but there's a good chance that tomorrow he'll have a different color and a different style.

"What about Tanveer?"

"He was killed in Mari's this morning."

Alex glances over his shoulder at Jamelia's terrified face. He wants to get rid of the Algerian as soon as possible so he won't lose his chance; the girl seemed to want to talk. As if

Alex doesn't have enough problems, Percy José starts singing his little song again: "Epi, Epi, Epi . . ."

"They shot him a couple of times."

"Holy shit . . ."

"It was the cops. Those fuckers are going to kill us all, because we're not lily-white like you."

"Are you serious?"

"Apparently they tried to frisk him, and Tanveer wasn't up for that. You know how crazy he could be sometimes and . . . hey! Kid!"

Percy has run away, heading back toward the apartment building where he lives. When Jamelia takes off after the child, Alex prevents her, figuring that the boy will stop when he gets to the main door. But that's expecting a lot of him. Percy reaches the building, keeps on running, turns right at the corner, disappears. Alex lets Jamelia go after him. She runs awkwardly in her low-slung shoes, which are no match for Percy's sneakers.

"They took him off to the hospital. The police don't do things halfway, as you know. Apparently the problem is us Africans. We're fucking up everything. Because of us, there are more cops around here than ever before. You'd think we blew up the *Sagrada Familia*."

"It wouldn't surprise me."

"You're a racist Catalan pig."

Alex has failed to take into account the barrio's extraordinary capacity for inventing fables. But he tells himself he'd do well not to confide in anyone. He remembers the Coyote. The enormous boulder that seems to be rolling away can reverse direction and squash not only Epi but also himself. It's not for nothing that he's the murderer's brother, or that he was there when Tanveer's head got itself split open.

"Will you come in and have a drink with me?"

Alex is on the point of refusing the offer, but he knows Allawi's powers of persuasion are practically invincible. Besides, it occurs to him that it would be a good idea to start damming the neighborhood's free-flowing fantasies. He saw that Paki waste Tanveer, so why not proclaim it to the four winds? Why not begin with the most popular barbershop in the barrio?

"Come on, a quick coffee, I've got things to do."

At this point the cell phone in the inside pocket of Alex's overworked jacket begins to ring. It's Epi. Alex stays outside while Allawi goes back into the bar. There's a man in there who calls himself "Professor Malick, Master Keta," whatever that may mean. He's a black man, sitting at the end of the bar, near the corridor leading to the kitchen and the restrooms. A kid he says is his nephew hands out flyers offering the Professor's services to the customers. Alex, who enters the place in a vile temper, also receives one of these announcements. He doesn't even read it. He knows the green-and-yellow photocopies all too well. The charlatan's marketing department has inundated the barrio with the miraculous catalog of his powers: solutions for all the problems in your life. He can convoke the swiftest spirits in existence and resolve any romantic difficulty radically and immediately. The Professor receives from eight in the morning until ten at night. In point of fact, Professor

Malick, Master Keta, hardly ever rests. Results within a maximum of three days, one hundred percent guaranteed. Problems related to marriage, work, and business; illnesses of unknown origin; love problems; how to get your mate back, how to attract people you're fond of, how to break spells; problems of sexual impotency; legal problems; how to be generally and euphorically lucky in life. Professor Malick resolves all, thanks to his innate, supernatural power. In addition, he speaks to Jesus and Mohammed. To the dead and the absent. It goes without saying that his work is serious and guaranteed.

Alex locates the barber and sits across from him at an isolated table, which he notices is damp.

"Not a very long conversation."

"We got cut off. Out of range, I guess."

"Who was it?"

"What's it to you? It was my brother."

"He called you on that Nokia I got him? He doesn't have any idea how it works yet, that's for sure."

"For sure."

Alex puts the phone on the table, hoping that Epi will call him again, right away. The black faith healer has begun to speak. The waiter listens to him spellbound, but with a mocking smile on his face. To avoid wasting time, Alex decides to go to the bar and order his own drink.

". . . and the person you call Jesus wasn't the Christ, he was a man, one who was inhabited by God for the time that He was within him. A spiritual power capable of changing shape and moving at the speed of a ray of light. So therefore, men didn't crucify Christ, they crucified Jesus, and maybe not even Jesus, but someone else. The writings say—"

"A coffee and cognac."

"Coming up."

"—that Jesus Christ transformed into Simon of Cyrene after Simon offered to help him carry the cross. They say that once the cross was carried to the top of the hill, Jesus went over to another hill near Golgotha and laughed as he watched the Romans and Jews, his dupes, crucifying Simon inside Jesus' body . . ."

"I guess Simon was the one who didn't think it was all that funny," says the deliveryman, who's waiting for the pink copy of the invoice to be signed so he can continue his route.

His remark catches on like a flame throughout the bar, and the resulting merriment is so general that even Professor Malick recognizes the prudence of changing the mask of his face into a smile filled with white, gleaming teeth. He accepts that his discourse has been overwhelmed, at least for the next few minutes.

"It's true that the good Simon did the wrong person a favor . . ."

"Hey, butane man!" shouts another of the regular customers, a noted jokester. He addresses a group of Pakistani gas-bottle deliverymen, who are having breakfast under their turbans. "Isn't this Simon a model for you folks? You exchange hugs with the first guy you meet on the stairs, and then he goes on up with the gas canister!"

The audience appears to be irrecoverably lost. Professor Malick could try to get it back and maybe even return it to the state of respectful silence it was in just a few moments ago. But telling that tale was obviously a mistake. Whether a story works or not always depends on the ears of those listening to it. Maybe it would be better to work one-on-one for a while, or to wait until there's a big turnover in the clientele.

Alex sees him approaching. He looks in his direction and happens to catch a glimpse of a silhouette slipping behind some cases of wine and going through a door that must lead to the storeroom, or maybe to the toilets. Whenever Alex enters a room, any room, his head goes into the darkest corners of the space and places there shadows and persons that he alone can see. On this occasion, perhaps it's Simon of Cyrene. The thing is, no one likes being laughed at after having been cruelly put to death on a cross.

The Professor is carrying a cup of hot coffee. "What's the matter, son?" he says to Alex, placing the cup in front of him. "You didn't laugh."

"I'm not much in the mood for laughing."

"This is missing a shot of cognac. I ordered a coffee with cognac."

"Are you sure?" the man behind the bar asks.

"Yes."

"Coming up right away."

The Professor remains at Alex's side, staring at him fixedly. His insistence disturbs Alex. No chance he's going to pay any attention to him. He knows these guys who aim to fill the gap left by the loss of faith. He thinks they make priests and nuns look good. Priests and nuns at least have enough decency not to guarantee one hundred percent success within three days.

"You won't laugh until tomorrow. There will be no laughs for you today. But the person you're waiting to hear from will call."

"They always call in the end, don't they?"

"Not always."

"Yes they do." Thanks to the *barista*'s diligence, a coffee with cognac is now steaming on the bar in front of Alex. He asks, "How much do I owe you?"

"Nothing," Professor Malick replies. "Save all the money you can. You're going to need it. She's crazy. Everyone is. You're the one sane person in a ship of fools. Come back whenever you want. I'll pay today. The next time, tomorrow, you'll pay."

"Thanks . . ." Suddenly embarrassed, Alex pronounces the word in a stupid daze.

Professor Malick lets out a guffaw, which serves among other things as a warning to the competition. He's in a jocular mood today. So much so that he didn't and doesn't care about what happened a few minutes ago. When Alex gets back to his table, Allawi's just about finished perusing the last page of the newspaper.

"No calls."

"That lunatic over there bought me a drink."

"Malick? He's a good guy. Smart, too. And he's got a good business strategy. I should set up something like that in my own place. Do you like soccer?"

"Not much."

"But the team you root for is Barça, right?"

"Espanyol."

"Fuck! How is that possible?"

"It has to do with my father."

"You like my sweater?" Allawi asks Alex, modeling it for him. It's white with brown, blue, and yellow stripes running over the shoulders and arms. "Cheap and good-looking. You want one?"

"Is it stolen?"

"Springfield. On sale."

"Tell me about Tanveer."

"Just what I told you. People are fed up. Some because they've had it up to here, and others, well, sure, because they're bored, and as far as they're concerned, any kind of ruckus is a party. They all want to organize—what do you call them?—mobilizations, or some such. You people from here, you love that sort of thing, don't you?" Allawi doesn't expect an answer. "The truth is, I still don't know whether I liked Tanveer or not. He was practically my fellow countryman, but his soul wasn't right."

"At the moment, the state of his soul doesn't make much difference."

"No, it doesn't."

"What about Tiffany?"

"Tiffany? I suppose it's a matter of indifference to her, too."

"Why do you say that?"

"Just to say something."

"Allawi, I hate to spoil your . . . mobilization, but it wasn't the cops who broke Tanveer's head open. I was there."

"No shit? Who did it, then?"

"Well, look, I was in Salva and Mari's bar—"

"Mari? I thought it happened at dawn . . ."

"Let me explain it to you, all right? It was very early in the morning. They had just opened. Mari had been there, cleaning up, but she'd already finished and gone back up to the apartment. I like your sweater."

"Alex, come on, leave me alone about the sweater."

Allawi pays close attention to Alex's explanations, but seems to give them little credit. Maybe that's because he doesn't take Alex seriously. He's known the two brothers for some time, and even though they're good people, he thinks both of them are a bit cracked, one more than the other. Someone whom Allawi has seen go completely blank, someone who he knows is prone to obliviousness, someone for whom names and instants are empty holes, someone inclined to dizzy spells, spiraling down vertiginously into himself—signs, perhaps, from the past that he missed because of drugs, which according to the word in the barrio he used to take like aspirins—such a man, Allawi thinks, makes no very reliable witness. Or how about the times when his paranoid visions overwhelm him and he gets it irremovably in his head that he's being followed or bugged or God knows what?

"A Paki?"

"Didn't say much. One of the quiet ones with the dark looks, you know what I mean? So he comes into the bar, this

Paki, and goes into the bathroom. He was in a hurry to get there. He stays inside, I don't know, something like five or ten minutes. Then the son of a bitch comes out fast with a hammer in his hand, zips over to Tanveer, and busts his head open. He hit him three times, one, two, three. Salva and I tried to stop him, but he was an animal. Not a very big guy, either. That hammer must have weighed a ton."

"What a way to go: hammered to death."

"Tanveer falls to the floor. The Paki looks at us, at Salva and me, warns us with signs that we haven't seen shit, and runs out."

"That's it?"

"Yes. End of story."

"Well, now I'll explain to you what I know. Hey, kid! You want something?"

"No, thanks."

"All right, never mind."

"What do you mean, now you'll explain to me what you know? I'm not repeating hearsay. I'm telling you what happened. I was there."

Professor Malick walks past. He smiles at Allawi, who responds with a comradely, affectionate "What's up, Malick?" It's not a question. Nor does it appear to be an invitation, but the African stops beside their table. The next coffee and cognac arrives, as though sprung from the folds of Master Keta's cape. Alex tries to meet his gaze and smile back at him, but at that moment the cell phone on the table goes into action. It begins to ring; its display screen shows Epi's name, flashing on and off; and it vibrates so hard that it rattles the little saucers and spoons and cups on the table. Alex raises the telephone to his ear and stands up to leave, but he stops at once; the connection, barely established, has been abruptly cut off. The problem's not the range. The problem's his idiot brother. He presses the callback button but stays inside the café because without knowing very clearly why, he doesn't want to leave Allawi and the witch doctor alone together. It's as though he's afraid they might exchange confidences, as though Professor Malick and his swift, efficacious spirits were going to determine how many days of life Alex has left or reveal another of the thousand secrets one sometimes keeps without knowing it. "The mobile phone number you have dialed cannot be accessed," a robotic voice tells him. He skips the voice mail. This whole thing is a screwup of epic proportions. He goes back to his seat.

". . . they say that for listening to lewd secrets or blasphemous conversations, the most appropriate instrument is a peach pit. It has the ability to retain the echoes of words, but only if they're conspiratorial, words spoken in erotic conversations or murder plots . . ."

"And the CIA wouldn't be able to stop the attacks. Shit, plant peach orchards all over Houston. You like peaches, Alex?"

"No."

"Well, I must leave you. Clients are arriving," says Professor Malick, rising from the table and pointing to another farther back, where a blond prostitute is taking a seat. "By the way, barber, your business idea for helping my brothers seems very interesting. We'll have to work together."

"What the fuck is he talking about?" asks Alex after Malick has gone.

"How should I know? He's a medium. He reads your mind. I play along with him. You working today?"

"No. Tomorrow."

"Listen, I meant to ask you this. The personalized van with the fancy windows and carpeted interior and all that other stuff—that's your brother's, right?"

"Yes. What about it?"

"Yesterday evening, pretty late, your brother came looking for vitamins. He's been buying dope almost continuously these past few months. Also, I don't know about last night, but lately he and Tanveer or some other jewel have been getting into that van and going for long rides. What they do or leave undone, I don't know. But I've heard the cops are looking for a van like your brother's."

Behind the bar, the bartender makes signs to a guy who's just come in. He points to the barber, who's left a notice on the door of his shop, indicating where he can be found should anyone be looking for him, whether with good or better intentions.

"I'm coming, I'm coming . . . So look, I thought that one thing went with the other. Epi's van and Tanveer. I thought maybe the cops followed them and took them by surprise last night, and then Tanveer did his Braveheart act, and—"

"Allawi, I saw it. It was with a hammer or a heavy stick. In the face, man. And I wish there *had* been a cop in the bar."

"I don't know. Of course, I wasn't there. If you want the scoop on the van, ask the *mossos*. They'll know."

Allawi gets up, puts his hand on Alex's shoulder, and gives him a pinch that's meant to express complicity but actually causes pain. For a few seconds, Alex's brain considers the possibility that the problems caused by the *Moro*'s murder aren't going to be as easy to resolve as he thought. At the same time, out of the corner of his eye, he sees something like a shadow slip under one of the tables and settle down to observe him. Alex pretends not to notice it. Ghosts don't exist. Shadows don't walk or hide themselves under tables in cafés. Surely, at some point in the course of the day, his brother will be able to overcome the inopportune difficulty with his cell phone and things will begin to sort themselves out. That will surely happen. And tomorrow he'll laugh the way the warlock predicted he would, he'll laugh and laugh and never stop.

6

MAYBE TIFFANY HAS HEARD ABOUT THE BLACK HOLES that gobble up everything around them. You throw a stone, and it neither falls nor comes back to you. Like women waiting for calls from men who are never going to call. Calls they know from the beginning are not going to be made. Who'd have thought she'd become so much like those women? Clinging to Tanveer, putting up with that retard Epi. Who'd have thought she'd throw stones that would never fall back to earth? And really, in general, Tiffany Brisette tries not to get too absorbed in thinking about herself. Today, however, she's got the feeling she has to. She has to look around and interpret the things, the words, and the signs she finds here and there. And she must remember. Like running backward, that's how she must do it. But it's hard for her to keep her attention on her thoughts, to keep a steady balance as she goes backward.

Sometimes images assail her like flashes, and she doesn't know if they're real or fantasies. But if she thinks they can do her harm, she shoos them off with a wave of her hand, as one does with pigeons in a public square. On one occasion, Epi's mother explained to her that in former times there never used to be pigeons, neither in Barcelona nor anywhere else in Europe. That pigeons were brought from the East to cure a rich woman's melancholy. And that they never went back home. To this day, something keeps them in our squares and on our roofs. As if they were prisoners of something indistinct and unknown. A little like Tiffany herself.

She has always been the one who got to choose. The one who made others wait. Giving free rein to her whims, making things happen, causing earthquakes, and—if she felt like it—healing wounds and repairing losses. But she wasn't unfair, or at least she doesn't see herself that way. She never got a guy hot just to leave him hanging, the way other girls would. Nor did she ever deceive anyone or act in bad faith. Of course, sometimes she liked to have fun, all girls did, but she didn't go much beyond that.

She's sitting on the floor in the half-empty apartment Epi asked her to meet him in. The window shutters are down, but the slats have so many holes they look bullet-riddled, and the first direct light of the morning enters through them. The dust is getting into her throat. She remembers the time when bees built a hive in the housing above some other shutters. Where did that happen? Was it just after they arrived in Spain? Yes, on the second floor, where they lived in practically complete security. Papa didn't let anybody go into the room. He sealed it by stuffing cloths under the door so that the bees, once they were driven mad, couldn't escape. The action wasn't particularly heroic. The nest was treated with poison, after which there was nothing to do but let a few days pass and then check the honeycomb to see that it was empty. But to Tiffany, the long wait on the other side of the door, then her father coming through it with that strange construction in his hands, and the floor of the room thickly littered with insect carcasses—all that seemed to provide yet another demonstration of the value and authority her progenitor exuded at certain fixed hours of the day. That was her father's good side, which on no account compensated for the other one.

Now she regrets having added so much fuel to Epi's flame. She reflects on his unexpected call, his apparently urgent need to see her, his almost literally yanking her out of her apartment and summoning her here, to the safe house Tanveer Hussein and his pals use. Epi tricked her, assured her that she absolutely must not remain at her place, because they'd be coming for her, too. But who? And why? Tiffany didn't understand a thing. But she was mixed up in so many shenanigans that she decided to err on the side of caution rather than incredulity.

"What's that supposed to mean? What happened?"

"Nothing, honey, nothing. I'll explain when I see you."

Tiffany hated it when Epi called her "honey." It wasn't just a casual, unimportant filler word—far from it. Epi deployed it to reconstruct a familiarity that no longer existed between them, to go back, little by little, to that part of their lives. It was a bit like a little story she remembered from her stay in the convent school. The camel, which is sin, stands outside your tent and begs you to let it enter because a terrible storm is raging. First it thrusts in one foot, then another, then its head, and eventually, almost without your noticing, the damn camel's inside and you can't get it out of your life. Tiffany reproaches herself for having allowed him to use that "honey" without hanging up on him. But she wanted to find out what the devil had really happened, what on earth would cause him to telephone her at eight in the morning. Not exactly an hour for heroic exploits.

"I don't want to play games, Epi. Stop fucking around."

"But why not do what I'm asking you to do, just this once?"

He was very nervous. It had been a long time since she'd last known him in such a state. Tiffany had a bad feeling. She didn't want impatience to get the best of her. She lifted the medal with the image of the Virgin to her lips, kissed it, and put it in her mouth, completing the unconscious gesture she had recourse to when she was trying to calm down a little. She stood there in the middle of the room, barefoot, wearing the XL Mala Rodríguez T-shirt that reached down almost to her knees and served as a nightshirt. She'd jumped out of bed to get the phone, and Epi wasn't making himself very clear. She was having trouble hearing him. When she did, his voice had a metallic echo. Tiffany decided to jump in the shower and get dressed quickly. She'd probably get breakfast in the bar, so she wouldn't have to give her mother any explanations. Thus distracted, she hadn't noticed that the older lady, awakened by the telephone, was behind her, wrapped in her pink dressing gown and clutching it as though holding in her life.

"Nothing's going on, Mama. Go back to bed."

"Who is it?"

"Nobody, goddamn it, nobody! And don't yell! The child's still asleep!"

"Tiffany, please." It was Epi's supplicating, half-human, half-robotic voice, coming from the receiver.

"For Christ's sake. You've woken up the whole family. Now I'm trying to get my noble mother to return to her bed, and besides, I can barely hear you."

"How about now? Can you hear me better now?"

"Yes."

"Either my account's getting low or my battery is, I don't know. I have to keep turning the phone off and then turning it back on. I'll see you in the Granada Street apartment in fifteen minutes. It's important, I promise."

"But don't leave me like this! Tell me what's going on!"

"I'm all right."

Tiffany left the room where the telephone was and went back to her bedroom. She got dressed and, standing in front of a mirror, thought for the umpteenth time that maybe it hadn't been such a great idea to have her eyelids tattooed. She also found time to spray her hair. Before she went out, slamming the door, she wondered whether she should tell her sister where she was going. In the end, she decided not to. Now, in the other apartment, she regrets her omission in a remote, imprecise way, with a feeling close to apathy. The same feeling that stops her from reaching in her purse, pulling out her cell phone, and calling home this very moment.

Tired of sitting on the floor, she rises to her feet and shakes the dust from the seat of her pants. It must be years since anybody swept up in here. She goes to the bedroom, where there's a mattress and a wardrobe with a few articles of clothing. She knows entering the room is going to bring back bad memories, but she won't and can't resist the temptation to go in. Everything looks the way it did the last time she was there. All that's different is the blue T-shirt on the floor, or maybe the cruddy glasses by the mattress. There are some little glassine envelopes with tiny traces of cocaine. Tiffany runs a finger inside the envelopes and then rubs the finger on her gums. The drug tastes dusty, of course.

She rummages around in her purse until she comes up with her cigarettes. She lights one. There's no ashtray, so she uses one of the little envelopes. She sits down on the mattress. She knows she's still not alone; she knows she'll have no secrets, no privacy, as long as those invisible eyes keep looking at her. Eyes that never sleep. Eyes that look in no other direction, not yet, not for the moment. Tanveer's eyes.

Tiffany drags on her cigarette, sets it on the chest of drawers, and thinks about opening them. The surface of the chest is rough. Once the piece of furniture was in place, they promised each other they'd sand and stain and varnish it, but Tanveer never had time for anything. Nor was this place ever his home. Other people were always staying there—you could meet all kinds. The bottom drawer is empty. The drawer above it contains a pair of clean panties that Tiffany had forgotten about. In the top drawer she discovers the little paperback novel she never finished reading, no matter how much Alex insisted. It wasn't only that reading didn't interest her; it also put her in a bad mood. She always felt that someone was making fun of her, of her inability to keep her attention focused on the plot, of her tendency to get lost among the lines of black ants that seemed to move around, for no good reason, right in front of her eyes. Under the book she finds some lilac-colored packets of condoms.

She shuts the drawer, takes another drag on her cigarette, and lets herself drop onto the mattress. Exhaling the smoke, she stretches out, face down. She lies still and closes her eyes. She feels sleepy, thinks she's going to doze off. But first she wants to smell Tanveer. To relive the last time she was there with him. No, not the last time. All the times before that, yes, but the last one, no. She wants to smell other women, too. Other scents, other sweat, not Hussein's.

The last time they were together in this apartment, the Moroccan was in a strange mood. She'd never seen him like that before. They were trying out a brand-new, shiny kind of separation, according to the terms of which Tanveer didn't come near Tiffany until she decided when and where they would see each other. This game delighted both of them, but on that night, Tanveer wasn't himself. He made her wait a long time. She was unable to get in touch with him the entire afternoon. If it hadn't been his birthday, if she hadn't bought him a Raider T-shirt, she would certainly have given up waiting for him. When he finally arrived, he told her some asinine story he didn't even try to make believable. Then, when she didn't believe him, he tensed up and tried acting tough, but Tiffany was in a good mood and decided to give him the benefit of the doubt. She wanted to enjoy herself; she wasn't up for having a bad night. However, Tanveer kept thinking about other things, maybe about another woman. He took her out to dinner, yes, but he hardly drank anything. At the end of the dinner, when she blurted out that he was acting strange, he apologized and said he was wasted. The previous night had nearly killed him.

"Don't exaggerate so much, Tanveer. We've all had wild nights."

"Last night was different, babe. We went too far."

"It could be you're getting old."

"It's not that. Or let's say it is—it makes no difference. Your thing is you always have to be right."

"Were you out with Epi?"

"Yes."

"Just the two of you?"

"Of course."

"Where did you go?"

"Around here."

"Did you score?"

"That, too."

After dinner, Tanveer didn't want to go to any of the usual places. He insisted on dodging friends and chance meetings. They left the barrio, and in a Colombian joint whose rolling shutter was halfway down, Tiffany drank herself crazy. The cheap alcohol made her head spin and caused her to puke her guts out, first in the ladies' room and later in the street. The alcohol and her fear, and her certainty that Tanveer was escaping her, and the sensation that he found no pleasure with her or had any idea what she was thinking at any given moment.

Why not erase that last night with Tanveer from her memory and concentrate on the other times? When he'd turn into her father and her son, when he'd scold her for being so good and for being such a whore, when he'd adore her for taking pity on him and healing him. She'd explore the thick, curly hair on his chest, as if she wanted to make sure there was a heart underneath. To hear it beating and tear at it with her teeth. And then to feel herself the female again and ask him for forgiveness, for mercy, for the harshest punishment imaginable. Or to leave him outside the room while she stretched out naked on this very mattress, under the covers. And he'd come in like a thief, without knowing how he'd be received, and open her legs and put it in her. And afterward she'd hit him, thrust her fingers in his ass until it hurt, scratch him, and hate him as much as she desired him.

Or why not recall, for example, that time at the gas station? That Thursday when she was so angry at him, and she went with some girlfriends to a disco where she knew Tanveer would come looking for her. She spent a little time before he arrived chatting up some poor chump whose name was Luis or Ángel, she can't remember now. When Hussein appeared and saw them sitting so close together in the corner, he rushed over to them, looking as though he was going to kill the guy.

He grabbed him and shook him and pressed a fist against his face so hard it seemed it might go through his skull. Tiffany was frightened by the scene, by the violence she saw seething in Tanveer. But she had to admit it was a little like what she'd been hoping would happen. It felt godlike, determining future events, capriciously provoking moments of blinding intensity. The guys from security showed them the door, and they obeyed. It was better to leave than to have the management call the police. Then they all piled into Epi's van. They drove around looking for Luis or Ángel or whatever the fool's name was. It took more than an hour, but at last they saw him and his friends standing near a metallic Skoda in a gas station, fueling up. After telling Epi to park several yards away from the first pumps and keep the engine running, Hussein got out and headed straight for the soft drinks machine into which Luis or Ángel was inserting coins. After half a minute, Tiffany also stepped out of the van, but without any specific goal. She was afraid, and she didn't know whether she'd rather calm things down or enjoy her fear. Epi and two of Tiffany's friends, tired girls with their war paint quite faded, were remarking that the whole thing was madness. One of them got out with the intention of walking to the avenue and catching a cab. The other girl hesitated, but in the end she told Epi good-bye and ran off after her friend. They stood on a corner of the avenue, waiting for a taxi with a green light to come along and take them home.

Tiffany's erstwhile suitor became aware too late of Tanveer's presence. The *Moro* punched him in the face, causing him to stagger and fall backward; he landed hard on his back and had the bad luck to strike his head against the curb. As he lay on the ground unconscious, the kid began to shake. Later they would learn that Tanveer hadn't killed him, but the sight of that body shaken by spasms, with a protruding tongue, a pool of blood spreading around the head like a Gothic nimbus of sanctity, and eyes starting from their sockets, made them anticipate the worst. Little by little, Tiffany got closer to the scene. She was surprised and fascinated. She couldn't turn her eyes away. What she was looking at repulsed her, frightened her, and attracted her, all at the same time. Then Tanveer snatched away the fuel hose one of Luis or Ángel's companions had been using to fill his tank. The terrified suitor lay on the ground, sometimes shaking, sometimes unmoving, as Tanveer doused him with gasoline. Then the *Moro* turned to the Skoda and pumped gas all over it; two other guys who had taken refuge inside the car sprang from it in terror. Tanveer flung the hose to the ground, next to Luis or Ángel's body, and walked away from the filing station at a decent clip, but without running or even looking back.

"You killed him."

"*Ná*, I only punched him out."

The van pulled away and ran through the lights at the first three intersections they came to. The first light was green, the second amber, and the third red. It was like one of those PlayStation games where you keep eating up obstacles. As they hurtled along, nobody spoke. It was always awkward when Epi, the ex-boyfriend, drove them to the Granada Street apartment, but this time it seemed more awkward than ever. After his passengers got out, Epi, who loved routine, usually pulled away violently so that Tiffany would know that once again she'd broken his heart. It was a little like the old *Avengers* comic books, where the Falcon yields Jane to a nonhuman. But Tiffany's considered conclusion was that it wasn't her fault if Epi had no pride and continued to act as their facilitator. If he didn't want to go out with them, all he had to do was to say no and pass up the chance.

They didn't take the time to go up to the apartment; they did it in the lobby. Tiffany closed her eyes. All those images flooded over her—the gasoline, the smell of fear and perspiration, the alcohol, the spasm of violence, the young man jerking in convulsions on the gray asphalt, the streetlights hurtling toward the van at top speed—and paralyzed her senses. Once inside the apartment, they did it again. Tanveer's hand was swelling up. His fingers, constrained by the rings he wore, looked as though they were going to explode. A face is full of bones. Sometimes one forgets that. In the bathroom, he turned on the faucet and took off the rings, one by one, holding his aching hand under the cool running water.

"Whore."

"I knew you'd come."

But the last time they saw each other is obstinate, it imposes itself on her memories. It wants to come forward, it wants to be present. Tiffany can't always prevent bitter images of that last night, the night when they celebrated Tanveer's birthday, from filling her head. Yes, that night was different. Passion hardly deigned to make an appearance; it was her rage and jealousy, not her romantic passion, that bit Tanveer's face and shoulder. When they entered the apartment, he hit her, but only to get her off of him. He didn't want to fuck and decided to leave again shortly after they arrived. Jealous and confused, Tiffany demanded that he stay, but he paid no attention to her. It was then that stories about abandoned women sounded inside her head, women in limbo waiting for a call that never comes, women driven mad by rejection. Stories about players who don't know enough to withdraw from the game in time and so lose everything.

That night, Tiffany made a vow: never again. Sooner or later, as he'd done before, more than once, he'd come creeping back and beg her to go to bed with him. And she'd refuse. She would, indeed she would. Before too long, the alcohol knocked her out. When she woke up some minutes later—it was still night—she felt dirty and discarded. In a few hours she'd be taking Percy to nursery school. She thought she couldn't bear the day, and it was only beginning. She went down to the street. In a bar, she drank a cup of coffee, which did her good—and strengthened her resolution not to see Tanveer again. Out of the corner of her eye, however, she glanced at her cell phone to see if there was a call from him. There wasn't. Maybe it was too soon for him to request a second chance. But that morning was nearly a month ago, and she hasn't heard from the no-good son of a bitch since. He drives her crazy.

She's fed up. Fed up with men and fed up with waiting. That's why she rises from the bed, resolved on leaving the apartment at once. She doesn't want to meet Epi there anyway, nor does she care whether he explains what's going on or not. She's Tiffany Brisette. The girl with the tattooed blue eyelids. The one who never cries. The one who doesn't wait for anybody.

7

EPI THOUGHT HE COULD MAKE USE OF THE TIME TIFfany would need to get to the apartment on Granada Street by talking to his brother. But the call was cut off, so he decided to go home and wait for him there or call him on their apartment's landline. Now, however, he doesn't want the taxi driver to drop him off in front of the building. A certain paranoia has come over him, and he asks the cabbie to let him out a few blocks away. Though limping, he walks rapidly, almost militarily. He's aching and exhausted. If he lies on the bed, he could sleep for years. He meets no one in the lobby or on the stairs. When he goes into the apartment, he locks the door behind him. Unfortunately, Alex isn't home.

He looks for the cordless telephone, which as usual is not in its cradle. He presses the search button and locates the receiver. On his way to get it, he raises the blinds in his room and the dining room in two swift jerks, using so much force he fears he's broken something. At those hours, the sunlight crosses the apartment from one side to the other, creating walls glistening with golden dust. *The sun regenerates sick bodies and minds.* He remembers a period when his brother used to say that. It must have been one of the adages Alex had been made to learn by heart in one of his detox centers. Epi can tell that Alex has been rummaging around in his stuff. On the computer, some eMule files have been completed. He takes the opportunity to clear the list. Then he dials Alex's number on the landline phone. Busy.

In the bathroom he takes off his bloody T-shirt. He turns around in front of the mirror and looks over his shoulder at the impact marks on his back, blue-and-purple welts, some scratches. All the blood is apparently Tanveer's. It's true that his face is yellowish, or maybe it just seems that way to him. The long, straight hair, the little ears, the elongated countenance. The small eyes look frightened, like a child's eyes in an adult's face. He empties his pockets. He ought to look for his cell phone's charging cable, but he'll do that later. He calls Alex on the landline again. The number's still busy.

He sits on the edge of the bathtub and takes off his shoes and socks. The little toe on his left foot looks bad. It's so small he can't tell if it's broken or not. He reaches out an arm, inserts the stopper in the drain, turns on the cold water tap, and sticks his foot under it. He won't dedicate much time to this activity—he knows how little Tiffany likes to wait—but his toe feels better already. Cupping both hands under the bathtub faucet, he washes his face. Then he puts his socks back on and leaves the bathroom with the intention of looking for another T-shirt, a clean one, if possible. And in any case, he thinks he'll take the bloodstained shirt along with him. He doesn't yet know how he'll get rid of it, but he's convinced that leaving it in the house or wearing it would be an extremely bad idea. As he's pondering this problem, the telephone rings.

"Epi!"

"Don't yell."

"Are you home?"

"You called here, man."

"Right, right, of course."

"Alex, you have to help me."

"Don't pull any more stupid stunts. Everything's under control."

"I had to do it, man. I had to kill him."

"Epi, don't say anything, all right? Do you understand? You do, don't you? I'm coming home, and we'll talk. Don't move from there."

"Better hurry. I've got to go."

"Where are you going?"

"I can't stay here."

"Sure you can. Let me explain when I get there. Nothing's happened yet."

"Yes it has. It's been happening for days now, lots of days."

"What the hell are you talking about? Look, we'll see each other in a minute."

"Just one thing."

"What?"

"Do you know where my cell phone charger is?"

Alex doesn't know. They hang up. Epi lets the conversation end without answering his brother's question, because he doesn't want to tell him where he's in such a hurry to get to. Now, sitting on the chair beside the little table the telephone has always rested on, Epi wonders how long it's been since the last time he sat there. He looks at the wallpaper in that part of his home. There was a time—so long ago now—when it was the fashion to wallpaper everything, absolutely everything. As a boy, Alex stared at that wallpaper so much he could see things in it, things nobody else could see—just like he does now. Antelopes escaping from ferocious lions, clouds in the shape of gigantic winged creatures, elephants with huge ears, Egyptians with perfect profiles, heroes struck down by treacherous arrows. Epi makes a vain effort to find some of those things in the wallpaper. No doubt, the figures are all angry with him for his stupidity and disdain, for always passing in front of them without paying them the least attention, but the fact is, he never could see what Alex saw. Epi always admired his brother for being able to do such things. It took time for him to become convinced that many of Alex's accomplishments, which Epi had considered brilliant when he was young, were nothing but a series of malfunctioning circuits in his brother's head.

Back in his room, Epi opens the closet and takes out the first T-shirt he comes across. He puts it on and then pulls on a second T-shirt over it, in case he gets cold. He looks for a different jacket; he wants to avoid being connected not just with what happened in Salva's bar this morning but also with what happened last night with the whores. Until this moment, he hasn't thought about that. And he prefers to keep on not thinking about it. Maybe he can use it in his defense. Everything's piling up in his head like shapes in a nightmare, swelling until they can no longer fit inside the narrow confines of his brain. He puts the bloody T-shirt in the pocket of the jacket and promises himself to get rid of the shirt as soon as he's outside. A sewer would be a good place for it.

Tiffany must be waiting in the apartment already. He ought to get a move on. He's very thirsty, so he goes to the kitchen and drinks two glasses of water. The sink is piled with pans, plates, cups, and cutlery. He takes the opportunity to put the stopper in and fill the sink with boiling hot water, as if it were still possible to preserve a certain sense of routine on a day like today.

He dials Alex's number again on the landline, but at that very moment his cell phone display announces that Tiffany's calling him. Epi has to choose. He searches his desk for the charging cable again but doesn't find it. By the end of the search, Tiffany has hung up. Cursing, he leaves the apartment. When he steps out onto the street, he's lucky enough to find a cab right away. In five minutes he can be with Tiffany. The traffic lights help. He has a pain in the center of his chest. Maybe from a blow, or maybe it's his heart. He should have followed his first impulse and gone straight to Tiffany's place. The cops don't move all that fast.

"Drop me off right here."

He strides quickly to the building on Granada Street and enters the lobby, determined to go up as fast as he can to the apartment where he's sure Tiffany is, doing what she least likes to do: waiting. At that moment he gets a phone call. Alex again. He can barely hear his voice.

Alex is in front of his apartment building. He's been inside and seen that Epi was there but isn't anymore. And now Alex is standing as if planted on the sidewalk with no idea of what to do. He's like an ungainly antenna, waiting to pick up some transmission, some signal that will tell him where to go, where to start looking. It's so frustrating. He touches his face with his hands. He takes a few steps to one side and then to the other, trying not to lose control. Whatever he decides, it would be a good idea to take his medication again, though it's been hardly any time since the last dose. But he knows his stomach will burn and phlegm will fill his throat. He sits down on the curb in the space between two parked cars. His cell phone's in his hand, because he's waiting for Epi to call him back, and Alex wants to be sure it's him calling before he answers. Suddenly, a pair of legs is standing in front of him, blue, spread legs that end in two impeccably polished police boots. The legs call him by name. Apparently, a neighbor woman has pointed him out as Alejandro Dalmau, and Alex doesn't have the nerve to deny a thing like that.

8

NIGHT IS NOT A LOYAL ALLY. AND ON MOST OCCASIONS, waking up's a relief. Epi hadn't trusted the dark for a long time. Even so, that night, barely a few hours earlier, he'd raised his arm as though trying to touch the darkness. He'd stretched out his hand until his fingertips met the windshield. The effort appeared to calm him down. Or maybe disappointment was what shone in his face, disappointment at not having been able to dip his fingers into that enormous liquid plasma screen, which was what the night sometimes seemed to be when he was behind the steering wheel of his van.

Everything that happens at night seems incomprehensible later in the sun. By night, things are done that wouldn't be done by day. And on the following day, you don't believe you did most of the things you did the night before. Maybe everything can be summed up in those two worlds his father used to speak about. Two opposed worlds: one dark, the other luminous. Crimes and sexual acts perpetrated at night shouldn't be judged, punished, or kept up in the light of day. When the sun shines, white lines on asphalt can't be seen.

In addition to being disloyal, night wears you out. At night, it's a mistake ever to come to a stop. You go to pieces. Ghosts chase you. When you're young, you don't realize it, but little by little you begin to learn. Not that he's so old. Twenty-something years aren't much, but they're not nothing. If he could take all his nights, with their parties and drunkenness, their many disappointments and few fucks, if he could take them all and line them up the length and breadth of this avenue, he could almost fill it.

The problem occurs when you find what you want and then lose it. Without warning. You find it on an ordinary night, almost by chance. You recognize it, it's yours, and despite trying to hold on to it with all your strength—as in his case—you lose it. Then you grow old abruptly, then you've seen and known and you can't go back to not seeing, not knowing. And of course, you have to keep setting out every evening in hopes of finding again what made you happy the first time, as if miracles were frequent occurrences, but you suspect that nothing will be as good as what you had. No matter how much you seek and seem to find, you think it will always taste, in the end, like failure, like too late, like a mistake.

His brother says if at first you don't succeed, try, try again. But he also says the best thing Epi could do would be to forget her. Alex says so many things, too many things. In fact, everybody talks too much. There's a reason why talking is free. It's something that has impressed him ever since he was a boy. On television, when a question is posed, the person being asked always knows how to answer rapidly and at length, to establish links, to give his reply a convincing appearance of the purest truth. However hard he might try, Epi could never find so many words in his mouth. He doesn't trust them. There are people who hide behind words. People who use them like cords, like electrical tape they wrap around your body and over your lips until you're immobilized and speechless. People like Tiffany. People like Alex.

Words had never helped Epi. It didn't matter how much of an effort he made to explain his feelings to Tiffany; he'd never been able to express them. There was no way. His sentiments died on his lips. It was love, yes, but also something more. Tiffany produced in him the sensation that everything was right only when she was at his side, that there was no need for him to go on looking, that what everyone else thought, said, and did was of no importance. Only she and he knew what happened when they were alone. When he kept her inside, when he was sure she wouldn't go out that night, when he knocked on her door, when he went to their date, when she smiled at the sight of him, when he said to himself yes, now she was his, now he knew waiting for her and striving to get her had been worth it.

In the beginning, it was the two of them, him and Tiffany, each holding a frosty bottle of beer, in a dark, seedy bar in this city. The music loud, the walls weeping from humidity. Surrounded by strangers, high on something, anything, smoking, drinking, kissing, knowing they'd make love later, knowing the goal was in sight, close but not yet attained. How could he explain an avalanche of emotions like that in words?

Epi noticed his nose was wet. Snot was running from it. He let one of his hands, which were covering his face, slide down and wipe his nose. Then he realized it was bleeding. He shouldn't have snorted so much coke, but now it made no difference. Tanveer was taking longer than he should. If only he wouldn't come back at all. If only someone would kill Tanveer for him.

In the projects, sometimes the simplest—and at other times the most terribly complicated—thing you can do is to find the drug dealer. There's no logical reason for it, that's just the way it happens. What would he do if Tanveer appeared all bloody, clutching his guts, dragging himself toward the van? Would he run away, or would he act the comrade, take him to the hospital, and save his life? He can't help thinking that some people are superfluous, while others seem to fit in perfectly; it all depends on the moment and the circumstances. Because he'd go to his death with that guy if it weren't for Tiffany. He would be his blood brother. He may even love him more than he loves Alex, because his brother always winds up showing contempt for him and making him feel like an idiot.

He knows that, in a certain way, he fears and needs Tanveer, just as he fears and needs Tiffany. He needs them because when they speak to him or seek his company, they take him out of his anonymity; they make him feel important, singled out, visible to the rest of the world.

Tiffany, Tanveer, Epi. Yes, there's one person too many in that world, which could otherwise be idyllic. In fact, a very simple equation applies: Without Tiffany, Tanveer and Epi would be inseparable buddies. Without Tanveer, Tiffany would be with Epi. She was already with him. Because for Epi, at that point, all mathematics were coming to an end.

"Let me out of here, man. Come on. I . . ."

Epi had completely forgotten the whore. She was in the back of the van, also waiting for Tanveer to return. Maybe he'd dozed off, or maybe he'd just been concentrating too hard on his thoughts. He looked at her. A rather ugly woman, probably past thirty, maybe younger. It was difficult to be accurate on that point, owing to her makeup, the hour of the morning, and the state Epi found himself in. She had cheaply dyed red hair, coarse features, and incredible tits. He tried not to look at those tits, or at her face, either, because of an absurd feeling of shyness, and also because he didn't want her to be able to recognize him afterward. So he replied without turning toward her: "Look, don't be a pain in the ass. We're going to pay you. My friend went to score some shit, he'll be right back. If you behave, we'll let you do a few lines."

"No, no, I don't do any of that stuff."

"Good, better for everybody. Just settle down back there and don't be a pest."

"Where are we? Will you take me back to where you picked me up, afterward?"

It was more a way of sizing up the situation than a real question, Epi thought. Like cabdrivers who talk your ear off.

They're gauging you. They know where you're coming from. Then the woman tried to get into the front passenger's seat. Epi blocked her way, thrusting out his arm as far as he could until he made her back off.

"At least give me a light, chatterbox."

"Okay, but don't fuck up my carpet. Here's an ashtray. Come on, settle down."

The woman gazed at the glass ashtray in her hand and dropped her ashes calmly and precisely into the center of the transparent circumference. However, she didn't retreat to the back of the van. She stayed where she was, on her knees, leaning with her elbows on the two front seats, with her head a hand's breadth from his and her ass pointed at the van's rear door. It reminded Epi of when they took the watchdog along; he did the same thing. The same except for smoking and screwing, obviously.

"I'll suck you off if you want."

"I don't want."

"I'll charge you separate, not much. That way we'll be doing something."

"We're already doing something: we're waiting."

There was a silence, and then the woman started in again.

"Your friend sure is taking his time."

Epi opted for making no reply. If he shut up, maybe she'd realize he wanted to be alone and silent. Refocused. Smoke was filling up the inside of the van. He shook the lavender air freshener that was set over the dashboard vent. The device gave off little waves of an almost pleasant scent, and the woman got the message.

"What time is it? Ooh, good God! Look, why don't you pay me, and I'll beat it and catch a cab . . ."

"Listen. What's your name?"

"My name? Carmen."

His patience was running out. By then, he didn't care if she could see his face perfectly or not. With all this time spent at close quarters, he figured she could probably sculpt him in wax. "Look, Carmen," he said. "We're right at the entrance to a very fucked-up barrio. If you get out, you won't make it to the first streetlight. My friend can't be much longer."

"The thing is, since we've been here all this time without doing anything—"

"Come on, keep quiet. He won't be long."

Her face disappeared as though hidden in the black roots of her red hair, and the curtain with the gray and red squares that separated the van's front seats from its cargo area fell closed. At that moment, Epi had the sensation of being in one of those films where a bank robbery is just starting to go very badly and nobody knows for sure what's fucking things up or how to stop it. It was all so ridiculous. He was out there on the edge with a guy he intended to kill that same night, or tomorrow, or as soon as he could gather the strength he'd need to eliminate the superfluous member of the cast. What sense did that make?

Something was going wrong. For sure. Tanveer should have been back a long time ago. On the other hand, Epi's premonitions were mistaken twice as often as they were accurate. He tried to calm himself. If something *has* happened to Tanveer, so much the better, right? What he'd give at this moment to be in front of his PlayStation or in Salva's bar, killing Martians. Or at the slot machine. Like that glorious afternoon when, like Moby Dick, the third lemon appeared. One in a thousand. But Epi knew he wouldn't be pressing the fast-forward key this time. If Tanveer didn't come back right away, Epi would let the whore go, lock the van, and start looking for him in the two or three places where they'd go to score drugs when they ran out of whatever they'd got from the barber. He'd go looking for him. It was hard to explain. A question of masculine, feudal loyalty. As if it was easier to kill someone than to leave him in the lurch.

When Tiffany arrived in the barrio, Epi was the first person who saw her. She wasn't like the other girls, the ones he'd seen grow up, the ones he'd liked and stopped liking. The way it happened, it was like something in an old story. She'd appeared out of nowhere, abandoned on the street for whoever wanted to gather her up. And he did want to, indeed he did. But she refused to be easy. She flirted with him, confused him, flattered him. And all the other men's eyes were on her, too. It was crazy. Once, in the doorway of her building, she let him kiss her. At first she didn't open her mouth. But then she did. That night, Epi could hardly sleep. The following morning he picked her up at her place and they went for a drive, stopping here and there. Nobody understood how that Indian girl could go out with him. His own family couldn't believe it.

All he heard were warnings and dark hints about problems to come. But they saw each other every day; every day they went to some raucous party and got wasted or walked around the shopping center, dreaming about buying everything while she devoured colored popcorn and they decided whether to see a horror film or an action film.

Naturally, they also had quarrels and attacks of jealousy, rumors abounded, and Tiffany constantly seemed to be somewhere other than where she was supposed to be. But she always knew how to twist things around in her favor. He believed her, because as long as they were together, he felt complete. Everything was going fine, or at least that's the way he remembered their affair after he lost her. As his mother was ill and Alex condemned to his work schedule at the parking garage, Epi would often bring Tiffany up to the family apartment, and they practically lived the fiction of being a married couple. They would make love at all hours—he remembered how she'd push his head down when he started going too fast, how she'd lie there purring when the spasms were over—sit on the sofa and watch movies, or plan mountain excursions that never happened because they'd oversleep, or because they understood they weren't missing anything up there on the heights. It was all idyllic, until Tanveer came along to ruin everything.

"Listen, man, I . . ."

You had to say this for the woman, she certainly had the gift of opportunity. The anger that exploded inside Epi surprised even him. He found himself rolling around with the whore on the carpeted floor of the van until they collided with one of the walls, in which the most deafening amplifiers in the city were installed. He sat on top of her, pinning her wrists, and her blouse rode up, revealing a teat badly injected with silicon and half supported by a red brassiere that was more functional than pretty. Epi looked at the whore's terrified face and stopped. He asked her if she was going to keep still, and she answered with a nod. He had no plan for her, and so it was only out of curiosity that he pulled down one of the cups of her bra, uncovered one fat, black, sagging nipple, like a light switch, and took it in his mouth. He didn't go so far as to bite it. He merely sucked it and made it hard, fully intending to go back to the driver's seat.

Then there was a strange silence while Epi tugged furiously at his hair. He heard the click of the van's rear door and pretended not to hear her run off. Almost immediately, Tanveer was back, climbing into the passenger's seat with a shout of relief.

"Man, that Gypsy! Holy shit!"

"Everything went all right?"

"Like a fucking dream! He wouldn't let me go. They're having quite a party. Listen . . . where's the slut?"

"She left."

"What do you mean, she left? You let her go?"

"Yes."

"Then let's go get another one."

Judging by how happy he was, Epi figured Tanveer had brought some of the party with him.

9

AFTER POLISHING OFF THE UMPTEENTH CIGARETTE, Tiffany gets up from the floor. She picks up her purse, takes out her cell phone, and hesitates over whether to make one final call to Epi. But no, she's not going to do that. Not now, not ever. Let him drop dead, the retard. A retard like his brother, like his mother. No wonder the father let the city swallow him up forever as soon as he glimpsed a brighter horizon. Disappeared without a trace, without a warning, without a forwarding address. Tiffany's cell phone interrupts her musings. It's her sister, explaining that Percy's school has called. They want somebody to go there and pick up Percy, who's running a few degrees of fever. He acted strange that morning, Jamelia says; he even ran away from her down the street. Jamelia can go and pick him up—that's not the problem. The problem arises when she tells Tiffany she can't keep the child for the rest of the morning: she's got a job interview at one of the supermarkets they've been opening in the barrio, the first job interview of her life. People say the pay is good there, and she'll even have a few days off. Jamelia sounds very excited at the prospect. Tiffany's reactions are contradictory. On one hand, she's glad her sister can start to lead a normal life. But on the other hand, Tiffany feels a twinge of jealousy. It's as if Jamelia, for the first time ever, were closer than she is to building something good and solid.

But Tiffany's never hard on herself for very long. She immediately thinks that if she wanted such a job, it would be hers for the taking. At the moment, however, garbage work like that, a job in a supermarket, is not for Tiffany Brisette. Jamelia keeps on apologizing, which always exasperates her sister. It looks like today's the day when she has to exercise patience with everybody, because all the assholes in the world are latching on to her.

"Girl, what the hell are you trying to tell me? That you don't give a shit about your nephew? I know that, I'm used to it." The dose of unfairness and cruelty she injects into her voice begins to have an effect on her, like a sweet, strong antidote. "I'll take care of him myself. I had things to do, but that's all right, it doesn't matter. What I've got going on is never important. Mama's not there?"

"No, she's out shopping."

"The thing is, you have to bring Percy here."

"Where? The interview's in forty minutes."

"You've got time. It'll be close, but you'll make it," Tiffany assures her, knowing full well her sister will have to run all the way if she's to have any chance of arriving at the appointed hour. An excellent joke on her, then. "I'm in the apartment on Granada Street. The one illegals use. Yes, stupid, 20 Granada, third floor, second door."

"But I'll have to take the bus, because—"

"If you leave right now, you won't need the bus. Touch the doorbell, I'll buzz the door open, and Percy can come upstairs by himself," Tiffany says, making a concession to her older sister. "You don't have to bring him all the way up. Come on, get a move on. I'll wait for you, but remember, I have things to do, too."

Tiffany insults her sister as she hangs up, not caring whether she hears her or not. Now she has to wait. Shit. As she does every morning, she thinks about making up some excuse and calling Tanveer, but no, she's not going to do that today, either. Tiffany's eighty percent pride and the rest self-esteem, as Doña Fortu likes to say. She's not about to humble herself for the sake of that son of a bitch. Furthermore, tonight she'll stop being good, she'll go out and party. She'll go out to a few places she knows. Either he'll show up, or there'll always be some informant who'll tell him how Miss Tiffany Brisette was doing. How pretty and stoned she was, how much fun she was having. Who she was with in the wee hours of the morning. She'll go to bars and clubs, and he'll have to leave as soon as she appears. The restraining order that says he has to stay a thousand meters away from her can be a bar of cold iron or warm rubber, depending solely on the quality of her mercy. And she has a feeling that tonight she's going to use that iron bar to break his knees.

The street door slams shut and footsteps begin to mount the stairs. She figures it's Epi and decides to add a little drama to their meeting. First, some sulking for having been made to wait and kept in the dark about the reason; then we'll see. She hastens to light another cigarette and goes over to the other end of the room, casting a glance at the window that someone, but not her and not the rain, ought to clean sometime. It's a pretty day, she thinks, a good day to take a walk around the barrio or head for the beach. Anything would be better than hanging around in a dreary, empty apartment. She's surprised that Epi's taking so long to walk up a few flights of stairs. Deciding to abandon her pose—femme fatale, waiting in the farthest corner of the room—she goes to the door and partly opens it. From there she's able to verify that yes, it's him. He's halfway up the last flight of stairs, leaning on the wall, with one leg raised and resting on the banister. He's talking on his cell phone to someone whose identity he apparently wants to hide from her.

What's this all about?

When she's not with Tanveer, fooling around with Epi—a purely gymnastic exercise for her vanity, sometimes—never ceases to be like toying with a bomb that could explode at any moment. For that very reason, the only way to defuse it is—as in the films Epi likes so much—to remove the red cable when the red cable needs removing and to remove the blue one when the blue one does. You can do that, or you can get fed up with the whole thing and yank out both cables at once and let the world go under. Tiffany believes she controls the game because she's the only one who knows for certain that there's a game. That's always an advantage, isn't it?

Men are obtuse creatures who occasionally appear to be extremely wary and even devious. But they only appear so. She discovered that very early on. When she was a girl, when she practically had to exchange her dolls for a real baby. Wasn't that one more proof that the world is shit and has always been shit? She can't even remember what he looked like, the guy who got her pregnant one night during the neighborhood celebrations in her old barrio. Her mother acted the victim; her father wanted to kill the seducer and tried to force her to have an immediate abortion. But that effort backfired; the maternal instinct rose up in her out of who knows where, perhaps because she wanted to upset everybody, and the upshot was that she moved to another barrio with Percy in her arms.

From that moment on, her father, who'd already exercised more rights over her than he possessed, began to wonder: if she'd already had sexual relations with another man, then why not with him? By way of self-protection, she's forgotten almost everything. And she's made up the rest. She remembers quite clearly, however, seeing him once when his back was to her. Maybe he was looking for something in the dresser. That naked backside of his, fitter to arouse compassion than desire: white buttocks, flabby flesh, a doughy mass you could write on or ripple, like a flag of surrender.

Now he too knows that you don't play games with Tiffany. She gets money out of him. Almost as much as she wants. Including the use of the apartment for Doña Fortu. Did she or didn't she know, Doña Fortu, what had been taking place in her home? It was difficult to say. Besides, once you arrive at the truth, what can you do with it? It's no good for erasing or hiding what happened, and nothing stable can be built on it, either. But that information, the possession of that secret, gave her power over her mother's reproaches and subjugated her will. In fact, she separated from her husband without wishing to do so. She did it because Tiffany wanted them to separate. As clear as that. Doña Fortu denied her suspicions; childish foolishness, according to her. And so, as often as she could, she and her husband met in secret and went dancing. To salsa music, of course, and real close together. He'd hold her hand when they walked down the street, take her to afternoon tea, and give her flowers that Tiffany would find later in the most ridiculous and remote corners of the apartment. A genuine soap opera. Just like when they were girlfriend and boyfriend, back in Peru. When Tiffany found out about their deceptions, she felt betrayed and swore again she would denounce him. But in the end, she didn't, because she needed Doña Fortu to manage the household. And also, a child needs a place to live. A certain order.

Epi can't manage to open the door. He keeps trying keys; he doesn't remember which of them is right. Obviously, Tiffany doesn't even think about helping him. And if she were to do so, it would be with a violent gesture that would proclaim, loudly and clearly, her intention not to receive him but to clear out herself. However, everything's become more complicated now. Her sister will arrive with Percy at any moment, and

Tiffany has to wait for them. She's irritated at having been rousted out of bed in the early morning and commanded here and there ever since, all for the sake of other people. That's why she's finally decided to get out of there and resolve the matter of her son after she's in the street.

Epi's face lights up when he sees Tiffany. As for her, she's so furious at him that if she were to do what her body yearns to do, she'd throw herself on him, give him a couple of good smacks, tell him to go fuck himself, and threaten to have him tossed in the slammer if he ever so much as gives a sign of life again. But she compels herself to wait a few moments. Curiosity gets the better of her. Besides, Epi's disheveled and pallid, and his elongated face, with the isosceles triangle formed by his brows and his long, slightly upturned nose, looks dazzled, as though by some marvelous discovery or some deep tragedy; it seems equally possible that he's suddenly become a millionaire or that the subway was blown up this morning and he's the only survivor. His eyes are glittering, they want to tell her everything, but his tongue is silent. He smoothes his hair and rushes over to kiss Tiffany, but she steps aside.

"I'm sorry I'm late. I wasn't able to come earlier."

"But you *were* able to make me wait a little longer while you had a phone conversation on the stairs."

As soon as she says the words, the girl regrets them. For nothing in the world would she want Epi to believe she could harbor the least shred of jealousy on his account.

"I was talking to my brother. His phone doesn't have much range."

Realizing that Tiffany isn't going to kiss him, he crosses the room and stands at the window. Like a character in a film about a cornered man, he looks up and down the street. He hopes to spot a long black car with a passenger in the back seat, a short guy wearing a hat and enveloped in a cloud of blue smoke. But nobody's in sight. Nor is there a trace of the country's patriotic police. He lowers the blinds. That's quite convenient, he thinks. It gives him time, enough time to stop looking scared and to explain to Tiffany why he killed Tanveer. Time to assess her reactions. Time to be so convincing that she bursts into tears and takes refuge in his arms, knowing that their nightmare is over and that now they can be happy again.

"Was anyone here?"

"When?"

"When you got here."

"No."

Epi looks around the apartment and like Tiffany before him notes the clues indicating it hasn't had many tenants recently. It does, however, appear dirtier and untidier than he remembers. In what would be the living room in a conventional apartment are two black bags filled with cables and wooden boards, unusable PlayStation controls. There's also the sofa with its transparent plastic covering, a piece of furniture Epi remembers from forever. He walks over to it, intending to take a seat.

"It's been some time since he's been here."

She doesn't reply. Mentally, she's counting up to fifty or a hundred or two hundred before she clears out without a word. Inside her purse, her hand strokes the bundle of keys and selects the apartment key, the longest one on the ring. Epi lets himself drop onto the sofa. It offers little resistance to his weight, and he sinks all the way into it. Amused and absurd, Epi finds himself twisting around on the floor, surprised that life can be so unpredictable. How readily you can pass from the most difficult thing to the simplest, from killing a man to stifling a guffaw, the latter unsuccessfully. He hopes the situation has struck Tiffany as funny, too. As he rolls on the floor, picking up all the dust on his arms and clothes, he hears a muffled sound but fails to identify it as the main door slamming shut. Nor does he immediately grasp the fact that Tiffany has locked the apartment door from the outside to protect her flight. The girl goes down the steps two at a time. She's not afraid. It's more like running away after a prank. When she reaches the street, she gazes in all directions, just in case she could be lucky enough to locate that imbecile Jamelia. But she isn't, and so she starts running, planning to intercept her sister while at the same time trying to call her to find out where she is and whether she's walking or taking the bus.

By the time Epi succeeds in opening the door and reaches the street, it's impossible to know which way the girl has gone. Fed up with the way things never turn out right, he represses an urge to burst into tears. He decides it's best, all in all, to go back up to the apartment, calm down, and think about how to get out of this whole mess, how to get five minutes with Tiffany so that he can explain to her why he did what he did and who Tanveer was, the Tanveer that only he knew.

10

PEP MANAGES TO FIND A PARKING SPOT CLOSE TO THE police station. He's just in time for his shift. He rubs his cheeks and chin, pleased by the smoothness of his skin and by the memory of the pleasant shower he took a few minutes ago. Also, the music on the way was just right, and last night's dinner was great. And that's all the good news. The bad news is that he's been notified of a murder in the barrio. In Salva and Mari's bar. This strikes him as strange, because the woman has always tried hard to keep dealers and unpresentable types out of her place. He doesn't yet know who the victim is or why he was done in. The bad news continues: the shift partner he has to work with today is Rubén, a handsome blockhead worthy of being seen and admired but not of being listened to. Pep utters a sigh of resignation, grabs his jacket, and with difficulty gets out of his car. He thrusts out his long legs, which seem to construct themselves as they exit the vehicle. When he stands on the sidewalk, a pleasant gust of wind blows his blond bangs over his eyes. He tosses his hair back and smoothes it. After he locks the car and turns around, his attention is drawn to the opposite sidewalk. There's a guy walking down the street in a peculiar way. He looks like a character in a silent film. Stepping along at a good pace, taking long strides. As if he's escaping from someone or something. We'll all wind up like that, Pep thinks. He drapes the jacket over his arm. Now he has to hurry; he goes on duty in a minute.

The guy Pep's looking at with some surprise is Alex. The older of the Dalmau brothers is hearing voices behind him, but he's not about to turn around to confirm anything. He keeps walking quickly. No need to run. There are few things more suspicious than breaking into a run while leaving a police station. What do those voices want? Who are they? The police, maybe, with one more question for him. Or maybe he's forgotten his identity card, his medical certificate, or his prescriptions in the station; it's even possible there's another document that needs to be signed. He scolds himself for being so nervous, for having such sweaty hands, for the way his shirt is stuck to his armpits. He tells himself he has nothing to hide. Nothing bad can happen to him. If all else fails, it's Epi who'll have to pay for the crazy thing he did, not him. Then again, with the police, you can never be absolutely certain you're clean. And besides, they're apparently concerned with more than the killing of Tanveer Hussein. As their questions proceeded, it became increasingly clear that they were also interested in matters that Alex knew absolutely nothing about: a van, consumption of and perhaps trafficking in drugs, attacks on prostitutes . . . And the chief effect of all that was to make him, if possible, more nervous. Obviously, as it turned out, he'd taken too much for granted—for example, that Epi had killed Tanveer out of jealousy or spite. Now Alex thinks there might have been other reasons.

He tries to synchronize his strides with his breathing, as the psychologist has recommended. But the corner around which he intends to disappear seems to be moving farther away, as in those nightmares where the curb keeps receding while the automobile bears down on you, bent on breaking your spine. His medication. He has to stop in some bar and wash down another pill. When he does that, he doesn't hear voices like the ones he's hearing now, behind him and around him. Alex needs to think clearly and well. And not just about what may happen to his brother, but also about how to make sure the foul soup Epi's got himself in doesn't splash on him, too. He has to talk to Salva. And he also has to talk to Epi. He has to find out what the van Epi uses for work, the one the cops had so many questions about, has to do with all this. But above all, he has to stop hearing these voices and stop seeing shadows like the ones now looming on his right.

Alex is barely twenty or thirty paces from the corner he's designated as his salvation. Out of the corner of his eye, he sees a shadow that's adapted itself to his gait. He acts as though it's not there and closes his eyes, but he feels nauseous, begins to fear he may fall, and decides to stand still and confront it.

And so the elder of the Dalmau brothers stops and addresses a shadow, keeping his eyes fixed on the ground.

"What do you want? Get out of here!"

But nobody replies. Alex hesitates. Maybe it's disappeared. Or it could have been just a passerby, walking in the same direction as him, and all a new invention of his imagination. He opens his eyes and, unfortunately, he's not alone. It's not Jesus. It's not the devil. It's not the police, and it's no angel, either. It's not Salva or Epi. Or his mother, or Tanveer. No.

"Who are you?"

"An inhabitant of the lepers' cave in *Ben-Hur*, and I've come to touch you."

It can't be true. He's wearing a wristwatch, Alex tells himself. His rags are the remains of a ruined executive's business suit. It's true that he has a beard and long hair. That he's barefoot, and that his fingers are black and covered with sores. It's true that his clothes are bloody from his having been dragged through the sand, like Messala. But he's not real. Inside his own four walls, Alex can go so far as to accept that his visions are real, but outside in the street, he can't let himself do that. *No, please, no, you don't exist, you're the product of my paranoid schizophrenia, and of Papa's bright goddamned idea to see that stupid goddamned movie on that Holy Week afternoon a thousand years ago.*

"That's not true. You're just part of the confusion in my mind."

"Then touch me and see for yourself how my flesh falls off in shreds."

Alex looks over toward the police station at the other end of the street to check whether anyone might be watching him. He sees nobody, except for a woman who crosses the street, draws near, and looks at him with an expression between fright and surprise, when the normal thing to do would have been to stare at the bloody, scruffy, dirty leper. The confirmation that his ragged companion is part of a film being shown exclusively inside his head encourages Alex. That's his unique and sole reality.

"What are you doing?"

"I'm removing my ear and exchanging it for my nose. A bit of change is a good thing."

And the leper does as he says.

"I'm not afraid of you. You don't exist."

"Well then, touch me and tell me where the cave is."

"Leprosy's not contagious like that, idiot."

"Aren't you the smart one? Then tell me what Saint Martín de Porres died of."

Alex reaches out, not expecting to touch anything, thinking that everything will disappear, as it does when one awakens from a dream. But that doesn't happen. He touches a body that doesn't disappear. It's like touching wood. It feels clammy and cold, like a bad fever. Terrified, Alex snatches away his hand and begins to run. He has no intention of stopping until after he reaches the barrio. And then he'll need to find an antidote to leprosy before his flesh starts coming off in tatters, or at least to take his medication again and keep taking it until his stomach turns sour and all his nerves fall asleep.

At this very moment, Epi has come to the realization that he's alone, terribly alone. His brother, Tanveer Hussein, and Tiffany Brisette are all he has. Thoughts and arguments get muddled in his head. It used to happen to him when he was a boy. His mother would tell him to look inside for the thread, the first word, and when he found it, he'd be able to draw out the rest. Easy, right? But everything's always dark in there, there are many paths, and apparently every one of them is wrong. He would say what he was supposed to shut up about and shut up when it was his duty to speak, and whatever he said was always and in every case the opposite of what others expected to hear from him. Faced with so many daily fiascoes, he decided to do whatever he was ordered to do. If he obeyed, he reasoned, he'd commit fewer errors. But of course, he'd also receive less satisfaction.

He could go over to Salva's, he thinks. Or call him up. Except that he doesn't remember the number. Still, he needs to know what's happening. To see it all from outside. But leaving the apartment strikes him as the craziest idea conceivable. The typical mistake that fucks up everything. No, he won't do that. He prefers to stay inside these four walls. A text message, he thinks, regretting that it hasn't occurred to him sooner; he can send a text to Alex's cell, tell him where he is, and ask him to come. There's still time. He turns on his phone, disregards its chirping death throes, implores it to hold on a little while longer. If he can just key in an address, the text will fly through the air and arrive at its destination. He sends the message, but he has no way of knowing whether Alex has received it, because his phone fades out before the reception is confirmed. He tells himself he'll try again later. If only his brother would show up here, and soon.

At first Epi thought Tiffany would turn around and come back; storming out was just the culmination of one of her tantrums, he imagined. But she hasn't returned, nor does it look like she's going to. He should have followed her when she ran away. Once in the street, he should have chosen a direction at random and run after her and caught up with her. Maybe she'd been angry with him only because he'd made her angry. Or maybe she was jealous because she thought he'd been talking on the phone with some other girl when he was on the stairs. If only that was it. If it was, it would be easy to convince her that she was mistaken. Because he, Epi, loves her so much he's even committed murder in order to be with her for the rest of his life. That sounds pretty good to him, so he tries to memorize it, to say it by heart. They'll leave the barrio right away. He'll get a good job. She'll be able to study modeling or languages, which is what she used to say she wanted to do in the very beginning, when they were practically engaged. They'd have children. Lots of them. He should have played the game harder in those days; way back then, he should have bound her tightly to him.

But who could have imagined that everything would change? Only Alex, naturally: "That guy's stealing your girlfriend."

He was referring to Tanveer, obviously. His brother's superior airs have always annoyed Epi. Typical Alex, like the way he always figures out how movies will end when they're halfway through and tells you just so he can brag. When he made that remark about Tanveer, Epi chose not to pay attention to him. He remembers the scene perfectly: he was lying in his bed, killing time while waiting for a phone call from Tiffany that should have come more than an hour earlier. But his brother didn't know that. He was just leaning in the doorway, with no apparent purpose other than to get on Epi's nerves.

"Don't talk nonsense."

"You know it's not nonsense."

"Anyway, so much the better, right? From the very first day, you've been giving me a pain in the ass with all your shit about how that girl's going to fuck up my life. So if she walks, terrific! There's no problem."

"But you're already jealous."

"That's not true."

They both knew he was lying. Epi remembered that he'd been falling in love forever, and that it had always been unrequited. He never could understand it. It wasn't just that teacher whose silhouette against the window made you forget what a dope she looked like with her big eyeglasses, or that friend of his mother's, the one who wound up bored and alcoholic in a fancy house in the Zona Alta. After those two impossible fantasies came the girls of his own age, classmates, shadowy figures in bars and discos, and the same thing kept on happening. There was something in Epi that made women not want to go very far with him. He wasn't so ugly that they didn't want to be in his company. He wasn't dirty, he wasn't rude, and he always treated people politely, keeping his distance more from caution than from insecurity. But no one went so far as to love him. At most, girls might sit and talk to him at one end of the metal tables at Sunday afternoon gatherings while the other boys' entire attention was captured by the racing cars speeding around on the TV screen. At most, a girl or two might consider him a friend, someone she could trust. But none of them thought about him with desire, none of them thought about loving him, and no female had enough interest in toying with him even to try to break his heart. As she leaned toward him so that he could light her cigarette, a girl whose breath smelled like disinfectant once said to him, "You have hands like an undertaker." Epi hated clever people like her, maybe because they showed up the confusion he lived in. After he got home, he imagined a thousand replies and insults and even a couple of smacks he could have given that painted, drunken idiot, with her tight black clothes and her suicidal mug, when she dared to provoke him. But in real time, he gave her a light, smiled, and failed to utter a single word. If he had an undertaker's hands, he thought, his embrace would be like a coffin. But it was too late; the comeback occurred to him six hours after it would have been appropriate.

"Be prepared. The *Moro*'s going to take her away from you. Guaranteed."

"Go fuck yourself."

Epi wasn't such a fool as not to recognize that his brother could be right. And it wasn't possible to lay all the blame on Tanveer. It was more than obvious that Tiffany was flirting with him. In the past several months, whether they were alone together or in a group, Epi could tell that her attitude had changed. Tiffany no longer liked staying home or hanging around with old pals. Now she wanted to go out almost every night. They no longer went to the same joints, and if Hussein wasn't in the new ones, he soon showed up. She spoke ill of him in private, she seemed to hate him, and when he appeared, she ignored him or sometimes was even rude to him. But if someone changes the way she is when someone else appears, it's because she cares about him. Or likes him. Or is already sleeping with him. Considering how late she'd been for some of their last dates and how she kept forgetting the time she was supposed to call or the fact that they were supposed to do something together, Epi asked her about Tanveer. Miss Brisette denied everything, and as usual, Epi's role switched from injured party to offender without his being very clear about how he'd crossed the frontier between one position and the other. He soon learned not to show that he was jealous or cross. Because after every row, or even after a simple conversation, Tiffany would tell him she was sick of his jealousy and possessiveness and disappear for two, three, or four days, during which she neither answered his telephone calls nor returned to her apartment. People talked about having seen her here or there. With Tanveer, often enough. The gossip made Epi feel broken inside, but he forced himself to wait and welcome her back and forgive her without so much as a reproach, assuming all the blame, giving the best of himself, bowing to her every whim, avoiding any mistake that could give her a fresh excuse to disappear again. And then, one day,

Tiffany went away and didn't come back. Somebody told him she was with the *Moro*. He called her up, and on this occasion she answered his call. Epi asked her if what he'd heard was true, and Tiffany spun out her spider's web.

"You've been seeing each other behind my back for a long time, right?"

"Don't be so paranoid. It's not anything yet. You and I—it wasn't working out for us. I want to be alone. Tanveer's only a friend. And that's all. I don't want to keep talking about this, okay?"

He trotted behind her like a puppy. He was so obvious and pathetic that it was painful to look at him. But Epi didn't care. He was proud of his love, proud of his wounded heart. Because loving her was the best thing that had ever happened to him.

11

ROCÍO BAEZA'S PROBABLY A FOOL. SHE DOESN'T GENERally hear that suspicion inside her head, nor would she acknowledge it to anyone. But she knows she's foolish, or if not, then she's extremely unlucky, or maybe both at once. It's not a good night. The competition is numerous and merciless. All these damned immigrants, all this foreign flesh, black or mulatto or pale as milk. Whores and transvestites with silicon breasts, bubble-butts from Colombia, underage Senegalese girls, junkies with gleaming eyes and transparent adhesive strips on their arms. Rocío Baeza has some bad nights and some very bad nights. This night is one of the worst.

One day a colleague told her that having to be a whore is bad enough, but if nobody wants to hire you, that's the worst. The other women are getting in and out of cars. An unbearable scent of pride and triumph emanates from them; they exhibit a certain overacted fatigue; they know where the center of the world is and how much to charge for it. Meanwhile, Rocío and another woman watch the scene out of the corners of their eyes and pretend not to notice all the activity. They stand around the flaming oil drums and prattle, as if they weren't there for the reason they're there, as if they've come to chat a bit, to reminisce about the old days, to gossip about Isabel Pantoja, the singer, and other famous women.

Rocío Baeza feels like the last of a vanishing breed, fading away little by little, but that's because her pride is as deceitful as her memory of a time when she was young, beautiful, and desirable. When the national product ruled the market and the sex worker's life was different, pleasanter, simpler, better organized, easier to understand. Even the clients were something else. They came looking for what men have always looked for, but they did it differently. Now you gaze into those eyes with their dilated pupils, into those mouths as deep as hell, and fear makes you turn your eyes away. Fear of knowing. Fear that fear has no bottom. Fear of pain, of humiliation, of dying with your head bashed in, like a plastic doll left over from a Nativity scene.

Anyone who chooses Rocío Baeza does so because he's as poor as a church mouse and because nobody—with the possible exception of old Josefa or some drug addict with skin like cigarette paper—will do it cheaper. Or because he's a guy in his fifties and afraid of black women who tower over him or unwilling to risk the horror of finding a dick firmly set between what he thought were a girl's thighs. The best cases are the clients who pick her because she has big, in fact enormous, tits.

And Rocío Baeza's probably even more of a fool than she seems, because she's cheating on Antonio, her husband, by working as a whore. He doesn't know. If he knew, he'd kill her—even though she occasionally thinks he's looking the other way when he doesn't ask how she got the money to pay for this or that. She prostitutes herself because she can't make it to the end of the month. It's sad, it's moronic, Rocío tells herself, it's God knows what. And their household can't make it until the end of the month because Antonio's salary doesn't cover anything. Because they have four children. And she's a fool because she's thirty-seven years old and she's pregnant again, three months now. He likes children a lot, and she's always careless about contraception.

Maybe she could have avoided falling so low. Now she's giving six-euro blow jobs with a child in her belly, her children at home, and her husband on the road in a truck burdened by bank loans and Cofidis debts. Her companion around the fiery barrels receives a call on her mobile phone. She's got a sick kid, and the grandmother calls her every hour with a report. Rocío seizes the opportunity to move away a little, get closer to the road, and try her luck. She's got only twenty euros in her purse, and it's almost four in the morning. There are no other girls around, so no one will be watching when cars stop next to her, refuse her, and drive on. Rocío Baeza's head is still filled with the royal family's problems—that princess is so rude—and with the sweet-talking thief who's got poor Isabel in so much legal trouble. A car's approaching, and she smiles. She turns up the collar of the denim jacket she's pinched from her oldest daughter and crosses her legs to show more of her flesh, blotchy from the cold and bruised by Antonio's fingers. The vehicle comes closer; the driver slows down before pulling onto the shoulder of the road, but when the two young guys inside get a good look at her, they laugh in her face and speed away.

The whore looks one way and then the other to see whether anyone has observed what just happened. She can make out Berta and Irina, but they're far off. Tears of helplessness and shame well up, and she lets them fall from her eyes. Protected by the darkness, she turns her head toward the new cluster of cars bearing down on her. The beams of their headlights pass through and behind her legs, forming columns of light that illuminate the gravel of the roadway. After the cars pass, the blackest and dampest darkness imaginable closes around her. Rocío Baeza prays to her beloved Virgin. The same one her mother used to pray to. And her mother, too. The Virgin who stands behind the iron screen and the pile of lighted candles in the chapel of the beautiful white village she used to visit in the summer every year, when she'd stay in her uncle Nato's house. The Virgin who worked the miracle that cured Inés's awful sickness, the protectress of the girl who waited for the return of the soldier who wouldn't keep his promise when he got back. Rocío prays to the same Virgin, and her words come out as though she's speaking them for the first time, although she becomes muddled and mixes up the prayers and has to start over from the beginning. Now a pair of powerful headlights is shining on her back. Rocío hears the car stop a few meters behind her, and the driver dims the lights. She hears music playing at an extremely high volume; someone has opened a door and stepped out. She thinks she recognizes the song. It's the one Uncle Nato used to hum along with when Bambino sang it on the radio. Rocío has a good feeling, and she turns around expectantly. A guy with his arms akimbo is standing next to a van and waiting for her. The other's still inside, behind the steering wheel.

"Hello, sweetheart. Want to go for a ride with us?"

He looks tall and strong, possibly a *Moro*. The one inside looks Spanish. He's punier, dragging compulsively on a cigarette with his face turned away. Rocío doesn't like threesomes, or *Moros*, either. But she also doesn't like going home with only twenty euros in her purse. She won't even be able to take a cab and get back in time to fix breakfast and get the kids ready and go out for groceries.

"I don't do two at a time. If one of you gets out, all right."

"We're not going to hurt you."

"That's what they all say."

"Okay. I don't argue with women. First one of us, and then the other."

"Fifty euros. Each."

"Not a chance. Eighty for both of us."

Tanveer's wearing an open shirt. He looks handsome. Rocío figures he's well under thirty. His eyes are embers. If they're still kids, why do they want whores? Can't they get women, normal women, without paying for them?

"I want to see the cash first. We get all kinds out here."

"Take a look, you suspicious girl." Tanveer pulls a couple of fifty-euro notes out of his pants pocket and shows them to her. "You're going to have to earn them."

"All right. So one of you gets out of the van, and when we're finished, the second one gets in."

"I know, I heard you the first time. Don't be a pain in the ass."

"Park the car a little farther ahead, over there."

Rocío points to some hedges ten or twelve meters away. The driver follows her instructions, the gravel crunching under his tires. The van has smoked glass windows; its wheel rims shine like knife blades. These boys look pretty clean. The *Moro* points to the driver, who steps out after he parks the van. He'll be first. Epi, making an effort to look shy, tries to keep her from seeing his face. With a turn of the ignition key, he kills the sound inside the vehicle. Tanveer bows to Rocío, and before opening the back door of the van for her, he says, "You'll be amazed. It's going to be like you're a queen. The queen wasp."

And he's right. The interior of the van looks almost like one of those Arab tents you see in adventure films. The floor, the walls, and the roof are carpeted with what appears to be tiger skin. Imitation, she supposes. There's also a little table with a few whiskey bottles and some tall glasses. The dim light inside the van keeps changing color. Red, yellow, blue. Like in the night clubs where she used to make out with her boyfriends when she was little more than a kid. She feels like she's dreaming, like she's entered one of those television programs where they take an ordinary person and turn her into someone special for a few hours. The *Moro* doesn't help her get in. She grabs hold of the door and struggles hard for a while because her skirt's so tight. Once she's inside, she turns and sees Tanveer bound into the van with one jump, shut the door, and move close to her. Rocío's not sure he's a *Moro*. A Gypsy, maybe. Not a good sign, either, not as far as she's concerned.

"You want something to drink? How about doing a line?"

"No, no drugs. But I wouldn't mind a whiskey with anything, please."

"Fix it yourself. You think I'm your waiter?"

Rocío Baeza doesn't understand this sudden mood change. She looks around. The door's closed, but it wouldn't be hard to open it and hit the ground running and ask one of her coworkers for help. On the other hand, she thinks, why be so touchy? It won't be the first time she's been treated like crap. First come the nice words, but then, when you set to work, you're just a hole, a disgusting hole.

No, she's not going to run away. She stands to make a pretty good haul. It'll take a little while, and then it'll be over. She can't go back home with empty hands, cold and sad with nothing to show for it. Besides, her colleagues will know she's turned her share of tricks this morning. Rocío Baeza isn't through yet. And so, while the man is hunched over one of the four big speakers that stand in the corners of the van's interior, snorting a few lines of coke, she goes over to the little table—it's carpeted, too—where the liquor bottles are. A bag of ice, the kind they sell in gas stations, is under the table. The bag's open, and she has no trouble extracting a couple of cubes and putting them in one of the tall glasses. Surreptitiously, she wipes the rim of the glass with the sleeve of the denim jacket—she'll have to put it back in her daughter's closet before the girl goes to school—and pours herself some whiskey. She reaches inside her pocket and touches the cigarette pack where she keeps a supply of condoms. *Moros* like to do it bareback, but she can't let that happen. For the sake of the baby inside her. For Antonio.

Rocío lifts the glass to her lips and lets the amber liquid fall into her mouth. A shiver runs through her whole body. With whiskey, she never knows. Sometimes it makes her feel good, sometimes it's deadly. She decides to sit down on one side of the van and take out a condom so that it will be in plain view and she won't have to explain anything. Suddenly, spasmodically, Tanveer straightens up and turns around. His movements are rapid but somewhat clumsy. He's really loaded. Rocío perceives that, and she feels a little scared. Let it be over fast, let the dawn come. The *Moro*'s bloodshot eyes stare at her. He stands before her, undoes his fly, and puts the palm of one hand on her head to force her to her knees. Rocío feels like she's in a press that's trying to crush her. She resists. She's afraid of dropping the glass, because she doesn't think this bastard would find that very funny, considering how immaculate the goddamned van is. And unless she can pull up her skirt a little, the damn thing won't let her kneel down. Without knowing exactly how, she manages to put the glass on top of the nearest speaker and falls on her knees. The hand clasping her head doesn't stop pressing on her. Her skirt's torn somewhere.

"Let's go, bitch, put it in your mouth! Come on!"

She obeys. Now the hand's pressing the back of her neck. She gags at each thrust. As she sucks, she starts praying. And thinking about her children. About her husband. About her promise not to be a fool and never to do this again. She also thinks that you forget everything eventually, even the bad times. You drink a cup of hot coffee and milk in the market. And when you leave the café, all you take with you is the money you've made. A few euros to buy what the kids don't have, to play a card in the bingo hall, to keep paying the rent. Finally, the *Moro* ejaculates. He shouts with pleasure, lifts his arms, and furiously pounds the ceiling, as if he were a great ape.

"Come on, yeah, come on, let's go, let's go! *Bambino*!!!"

Rocío Baeza wipes her mouth with a paper handkerchief. She's swallowed as little of this guy's spunk as possible.

She's still on her knees when she feels the van begin to move. Bambino's music thunders from the four loudspeakers.

I had the pride of a hundred runaway colts
And laughed when I gave it to a woman.
And now I'm a stuffed toy for life.

Suddenly, a blow from a fist knocks her down. The vehicle gathers speed. Nobody hears her cries when Tanveer punches her in the face, throws her on the floor, rips her blouse, and yanks her breasts out of her bra.

Rocío knows her life's on the line, and so she bites, screams, and hits out, weeps, prays, and begs. She tells him about the baby she's carrying, about her Gypsy friends who'll slit his throat, and about many other things until she tastes the blood in her mouth and impotence and weariness make her stop. For more than two hours, Tanveer keeps on penetrating her and striking her here and there. His attempt to sodomize her fails when the woman's hemorrhoids prevent him, which infuriates the *Moro* even further. Both his erection and his rage seem endless. Nothing assuages him, nothing satisfies him.

When nobody loves you,
When they all forget you,
And implacable fate
Brings you close to the end.

The van stops at traffic lights. Rocío screams, and the monster's so sure of himself he doesn't even stop her. Both of them know that no one will be able to distinguish her howls from the thunderous music flattening them against the floor. Every now and then he insults her. He tells her she's old and ugly, that she has blue veins around her nipples. That he's got a gorgeous girlfriend with tattooed eyelids, and he satisfies her each and every day. That the baby the whore's carrying in her belly will be born dead after this night. That she'd better be careful about running off at the mouth . . .

At a certain point the van stops. Tanveer tells her she can go. He takes her bloody, beaten face in his hands and kisses her gently on the lips. Then he grabs her purse and steals her money and her cell phone. Rocío implores him to leave her enough to get a cab and go home. The man seizes her by the arm, drags her across the carpeted floor of the van—causing abrasions on her back—opens the rear door, and pushes her out.

I'll be on the road where you left me,
With open arms and immortal love.

With difficulty, Rocío Baeza rises to her feet. She hasn't the vaguest idea where she is. She walks around awkwardly for a good while, looking but not recognizing any of the buildings that surround the open ground where they've left her. Only the neon sign on top of one of the hotels gives her a little help in getting her bearings. She understands that she's hours away from her house, that the dawn is breaking, that her daughter's jacket is ripped to tatters and stained with blood. She looks at the van as it pulls away and fears that they'll return and run over her. But they don't do that. The driver has stopped a little farther on. When the light turns green, he takes off. She needs some coffee. She needs a pistol she can kill with. She needs Antonio to return as soon as possible so she can sleep in his arms and tell him she fell down the stairs, but the baby's all right, she can still feel him inside her, alive and as big as hate.

12

AS A SUBSTITUTE FOR THINKING, EPI LOOKS OUT through the window, his eyes dazzled by the dirty light refracted in the glass pane. In a spasm of clearheadedness, however, he decides to limit his break to five minutes, and then he'll go back to thinking about going back to thinking about what to do. This important decision calms him down immediately, and he remembers warm summer nights when he looked out of windows very much like this one. At the neighbors' roof terraces, at the street, at some noisy passerby or other, still echoing the racket in the bar or open-air dance he was returning from. Sometimes the sweltering heat was so oppressive that Epi could fall asleep only if he stretched out on the floor tiles. His neighbors all had very large families, cousins and siblings by the dozens, all of them together night and day. The men would play cards, sing to themselves, or cause upsets. The women carried baskets of wet clothes upstairs to hang on the wires that crossed the flat roof from one end to the other. Slender women, with their hair caught up behind, dark complexions, and naked legs under floral-print skirts. The slap of their rubber flip-flops, which were barely held on their feet by a plastic thong between their big and second toes, would shatter Epi's voyeuristic universe. Apparently the women liked wearing those rubber sandals as much as their own daughters did, though the girls would toss them into the air ecstatically at the least provocation.

Still today, when his family no longer exists, Epi can recognize within himself the hatred he used to feel toward his parents. So Catalonian, so civilized, so urbane. The balanced family unit, with four members. Now just two of them are left, Epi and Alex, but a brother isn't anything, hardly more than an acquaintance you don't always feel like greeting. His mother: a professional in dissimulation. The only inhabitant of a cyclothymic world which seemed to be reborn every day with new rules and procedures, from the most overwhelming affection and protection to the handful of salt rubbed into the infected wound. His father: an angelic sluggard, lacking in all the masculine attributes one hopes to find in a father. He knew a great deal, indeed he did, but nothing a kid could brag about in the barrio. His histories of the Greeks and Romans, all those books standing in bookcases and glass cabinets all over their apartment, and the reverential respect given him by the next-door neighbors—what good was all that? What good was he, if he didn't know how to sort out anything at home, if he couldn't so much as kick a soccer ball, if the only time the neighbors across the hall invited him to play *tute* he didn't take off his shirt the whole afternoon, they relieved him of all his cash, and he was a laughingstock at the card table for the rest of the summer? When the old man disappeared—in a perfect escape, treacherous and even admirable—Epi (in contrast to Alex) found it a relief. He'd no longer have to avoid him, or to excuse and defend him in front of the neighbors.

"Mama, I'd like to have a family."

"You already have one."

"No, more family."

His mother would run her hand through his hair and kiss him on the head, inhaling his child's smell. She seemed to understand him. They'd remain together at the window, looking out at the terrace filled with people, lights, cries, and songs, which were coming from their neighbor Sonia's little Cosmos record player.

"You'll have one someday. You'll have lots and lots of children. And your wife will have brothers and sisters with children. It'll be a really big family, and you all will invite me to your terrace, and I'll join you there, of course, I'll join you there."

Now, stepping back from the window, he asks himself how everything could have gone so wrong. He looks around to make sure he hasn't forgotten anything or left any traces. He can leave and maybe head over to Salva's bar, the murderer returning to the scene of his crime; let all the world know the truth, and God's will be done. Nothing will change from now on; his faith isn't great enough for that.

He's on the point of leaving when the doorbell rings. As he's closer to the window, he looks out, but he can't see anyone. So he picks up the intercom. Maybe it's Tiffany. He says nothing and listens, then presses the buzzer to open the main door. Now he's sure the girl will soon be retracing her steps, because her son is coming up the stairs.

ALEX IS GETTING over his fright. He feels better already. So much so that he begins to think the leper's only a nightmare he once had. Now it's returned, he concludes, regurgitated into his brain. Like one of those flashbacks that punish you for doing acid. Goddamned drugs. If only his brain were still intact. And to think, when it came to playing chess, he used to be the pride of the barrio; now he wouldn't know how most of the pieces move. Pawns and kings. That's all he sees around him. And queens, of course. Queens like Tiffany.

He's in Salva's bar. He's taken his medication again, hours ahead of schedule. He's going through a lucid phase. Such phases sometimes last minutes and sometimes hours. The fact of having been to the police station has reduced the pressure sufficiently for him to start thinking he can straighten out this whole mess. He knows, all too well, that he doesn't have much time. That there are matters he's completely ignorant about. Like the van the cops mentioned, for example.

Goddamned drugs, yes indeed, but what he wouldn't give to be high right now. How he longs for a good fix. Just one, and he'd sort everything out in a minute. The memory of the drug lays him lower than the drug itself ever did. The bittersweet aftertaste of his nostalgia. The shadow of the glorious past, before and during his addiction. And the memory also brings back a sensation of struggle—from the moment of awakening—against something you need and hate at the same time. Every day the same effort, the same defeat. And then the knowledge that you're off on one side, watching the big wheel turn without you.

And before? Are there memories from before the first fix? In his case, not many. One of them comes from his teenage years, a memory of going downstairs carrying a paperback book in his pocket—the already-read pages bent backward, as one does with an arm in a fight—to enjoy the sun outside. He recalls choosing, in various corners of the barrio, one or another of the mountains of rubble the municipal workers left behind, whether out of forgetfulness or malice was never quite clear; he'd use the debris as a place to sit and read. If Alex believes in coincidences, if he believes that a map of energies with crisscrossing lines exists, surprising us only because we don't know how to read it, his beliefs are now about to receive some support. In Salva's bar the usual crowd is gathered, but the news of the morning's events has left them chattier and more excited than ever before. Actually, there's nobody near the part of the bar where Tanveer lay bleeding. The police examined whatever they wanted and said nothing about it to anybody, but no one wants to sit over there. *El senyor metge*—"the Honorable Doctor" in Catalan—is present, along with Abel and Professor Malick, the last-named on his daily tour of all the bars in the barrio, and sitting at a table in the back, twenty-something years older than the image of him Alex has had in his mind until a few seconds ago, is Helio. In an unfortunate encounter one day when they were both teenagers, Helio tore Alex's book into a thousand pieces just because he was reading it. From that day on, Alex stopped looking for a sunny place to read outside. In fact, he hardly read at all anymore. Now, many years later, Helio—Alex knows this by hearsay—is in the construction business. He recruits laborers, carpenters, and night watchmen from among the roughest guys he can find. It's not so much good workers that Helio's interested in; he wants to sign up violent or desperate rabble. He keeps them for a couple of months. In general, he calls them by nicknames or insults that Helio and Helio alone finds funny. Ecuadorians, Moroccans, recent residents of Modelo prison rise and follow him, willing to put up with the steady abuse and humiliation because they know, or they've heard from others who know, that the more humiliation you put up with, the greater your reward will be.

"You monkey son of a bitch, fucking Indian . . . look how ugly you all are!"

Salva's observing the scene, unaware that Alex is at the bar, barely a few paces away from him. Mari asks Alex what he'd like.

"Give me some coffee. It'll make up for all the tranquilizers I've got in me."

Salva's surprised to see him but keeps drying a glass that has actually been dry since the spectacle—Helio paying his workers their week's wages—began. Evidently, Salva's not pleased with what's been going on in his bar today. He says to Alex, "What are you doing here?"

"I need coffee. Since when is your bar Helio's office?"

"Don't talk to me about it. I must have stepped in shit right after I got up this morning. First there was what happened before, and now this."

"But I heard he puts on this circus at Jacinto's."

"Jacinto's has closed. We don't know why. But for God's sake, I hope they reopen soon." He turns a little to address Mari: "Just think, the joint was crawling with cops all morning long . . . It wouldn't be a bad idea for a few of them to drop in right now."

"*Com el Colombo que sempre tornava*," says *El senyor metge* in Catalan.

"Shit, Salva, Colombo! You remember?"

"Fuck Colombo, and fuck his mother, too."

"Salva, instead of cursing and swearing, how about going over to that table and telling him you don't want him here?" While she's speaking, Mari points to the sign that says the proprietor has the right to refuse admission to anyone.

"You want to be a widow so you can sell the bar."

"Not a bad idea, not at all."

The shouting in the corner continues. At regular intervals, one of Helio's workers leaves the café, counting his money or already carrying it in his pocket, his head bowed down, his eyes burning with hatred.

"Salva . . . can I talk to you?"

"What's up?"

"Nothing."

"We'll talk in the john."

Professor Malick sits on the barstool Alex has just vacated. At the same time, Alex and Salva enter the storage room where the toilet is, the same room where Alex's brother, a few hours that seem centuries ago, lingered for a long time in the dark. Making sure they have no company, the bar owner opens the stall door and in a purely routine movement pulls the flush chain. The room is fairly large and filled with refrigerators and towering stacks of plastic bottles, which surround the two men like statues in a pagan temple. Salva stands in the doorway, positioning himself at an angle so that he can spot the cops if they come through the front door, with or without Colombo.

"First of all, I want to tell you what an asshole I am. I covered for your lunatic brother."

"You did right . . . ," Alex manages to say.

"I'm not so sure. Look, I knew your father and your mother and . . . fuck, we were all friends! All the doors in the barrio were open back then—people were always offering kids snacks." Alex is quite familiar with the evocation of these golden memories, but now is not the right time to get smart. "And all of a sudden, nobody respects anybody anymore. That Tanveer was just another worthless son of a bitch, living on my taxes and whatever he could get dealing drugs, filling his pockets with public subsidies here in Spain, because the people in his country don't have the balls to get out in the street and protest against the sheikhs. He's dead, and it's a good thing he's dead."

Up close, Salva looks a good two heads shorter than he does behind the bar. Maybe that's because he's hunched over, as if protecting his lungs from all the smoke in the place.

"He was dead as a doornail when they took him away," Salva goes on. "But to tell you the truth, I've heard all kinds of rumors. What the hell was your brother thinking?"

"I don't know. I don't even know where he is."

"Well, the cops are looking for him. If he can get control of himself and talk to them, maybe nothing happens to him. The thing is, there aren't any witnesses." Here Salva lowers his head even more and speaks very softly, but his words sound like a warning: "So now, if he fucks up, they're going to screw me to the wall for covering for him."

"You could have told them you didn't see anything."

"That's what I did." As a sly gleam lights up Salva's eyes, a loud row begins between Helio and one of his subordinates, and Salva shows himself in the doorway for a few moments. Then he continues, "I already explained it to you: I was in the kitchen, I heard a commotion, I got out there as fast as I could, and I saw the *Moro* on the floor and the Pakistani leaving in a hurry. What did you tell them?"

"He's my brother. I saw the whole thing."

"But you must have told them *I* didn't see anything, right?"

"More or less."

"What does that mean, more or less? You're going to fuck up my life! I knew it! I knew! . . ." All at once, Salva tenses up and starts waving his arms around.

"No, no. Calm down. I told them the fight scared me so much I didn't see anyone. I said if you'd been there too, you would have intervened. And you didn't. I said I saw you afterward."

"Are you sure?"

"I told them the fight scared me so much I didn't see anyone."

He keeps repeating the same things he's just said. Salva wants to believe him. He looks into Alex's eyes, trying to discern whether or not he's sincere. Alex turns his head away, not to hide the truth from him, but because Alex can't hold anybody's gaze. The older man takes pity on him. Salva can practically span Alex's shoulders with one hand. He sees the incipient wrinkles, like cracks in parched clay, around Alex's eyes and considers his childish face, one of those faces that will look more and more like a bulldog's with the passage of time. For a moment, Salva retreats into the past. He remembers Alex when he was a little boy, sitting in the back seat of his mother's car as she drove him to visit his grandmother so that she—the mother of Alex and Epi—could have a few hours alone with Salva in a room somewhere. Who's left to remember that passion, which they managed to keep secret during the ten years it lasted? It's the source of Salva's loyalty, whose origins Alex will never know.

El senyor metge approaches the restroom. Upon seeing them, he tries to say something, to make some joke, something neither indecent nor very stupid. But his tongue, swollen with alcohol and routine, finds nothing special to say, and so he opts for excusing himself and entering the toilet stall. Alex and Salva remain silent and wait for the explosive flush. When the alleged ex-physician is back in the bar, Salva once again asks Alex if he's absolutely sure about what he said to the police. Alex swears by all that's most sacred.

"Tanveer was bad company," Salva says. "There was a lot of talk about him, and recently about your brother, too. And judging by the questions the *mossos* asked me, they've heard those stories."

"What do you mean? Stories about what?"

"What do I know? Various atrocities."

"Be a little more specific, Salva. I have to know what I'm stepping into."

"I didn't get many details myself. Drug-related stuff. Vice crimes. I don't know. You know I don't like to hear about that kind of thing, especially if it concerns someone I've known since he was a little kid."

"But Epi doesn't deal drugs. I'm sure of that. If he did, I'd know."

"I have no idea. Ask him when you see him. I've got to go. If I stay in here any longer, Mari will kill me. And I don't want to talk to you again for at least a year."

"Wouldn't that look suspicious?"

"Well . . ." The old man hesitates. "Then don't come back before tomorrow or the day after."

When Salva leaves, Alex steps into the toilet cubicle to urinate. Before leaving he looks at himself in the mirror. He's sweaty, weary, worried. And he has something more than a premonition. It's as if everything has only just begun, as if Tanveer's murder was only God's excuse for throwing the dice against the wall and betting against himself. Alex wets his face. That will do him good, he thinks. He can picture Epi in this restroom. He evokes his brother's obstinate insistence on ruining his life.

"I drank your coffee," Professor Malick says to Alex when he goes back to the bar.

Then Helio's at his side, asking Mari how much he owes her. He doesn't recognize Alex. Why should he? Alex means nothing to this thug, but just in case—is he still afraid?—Alex chooses not to look at him. He smells of cognac, sweat, and cruelty. And if he'd pay attention, he'd probably smell the fear on Alex. Helio pays for his food and drink with interest, disdainfully dropping the banknotes on the glass surface, below which Russian salads and Galician-style octopus and eggs languish like corpses in their niches. After the brute starts to leave, but before he's out the door, Mari blurts out, "When's Jacinto opening again, Helio?" but she gets no reply.

Alex asks Mari for another cup of coffee. With a flick of her wrist, she puts his cup under the machine and presses the proper button, which pops out and lights up with an efficient-sounding click. It must be hard for her, Alex thinks, to navigate these waters, to survive amid so many loudmouths, so much violence, so many fearful children hidden inside men's bodies. Why has she stayed here, too? When the smart people left the barrio, why couldn't she escape with them?

"In God's Holy Book," Professor Malick begins to explain, "there are towns called Cities of Refuge. Do you know what those Cities of Refuge were?"

Alex shakes his head at the yellow eyes embedded in the black-and-pink surface of his interlocutor's face.

"Say you killed somebody. Either on purpose or accidentally. For example, you were hoeing and the blade flew off and killed a person. Something like that. The dead man's family could demand retribution from you. That was the Law of Men. If you ran away from your town and reached safety inside the walls of a City of Refuge, you were protected. There you would have a right to a just judgment. Nobody could take justice into his own hands, because the law in force in those cities was the Law of God."

"Why are you telling me about this?" Alex asks, searching for his cell phone so he can keep trying to call his brother. He puts a hand in his pocket, comes across Epi's scrawled notes, and decides it wouldn't be a good idea to take them out in front of the Professor.

"Because you're going to pay for the coffee I drank. What are you looking for?"

"My cell phone."

"You've lost it."

"No shit."

No, he doesn't have his phone. What could have happened to it? Alex can't imagine where he must have left it. He probably dropped it on the street after leaving the police station, but he doesn't have the nerve to retrace his steps. Maybe Malick himself swiped it as a way of confirming his prowess.

"Don't look for what you don't have."

"Then come on, Mister Wizard, you tell me where it is. Salva, let me pay you—I need change."

Mari immediately extends her hand and places three coins, wet with water and detergent, on the bar in front of Alex. He picks them up and heads for the public telephone at one end of the bar. Alex figures those three coins will be enough. In fact, the call turns out to be as useless as the dozens of other calls he's made to Epi during the course of the day. But Alex doesn't despair. He'd like to regain the feeling of control over the situation that he had in the already distant past of a few minutes ago. If it weren't for the loss of his cell phone, everything would be back on track. His conversation with Salva has indicated to him that there's no reason why this affair should come to a bad end, but only if he can get in touch with his brother, talk to him seriously, and convince him of what he has to do. And he's sure it's true that there are a whole lot of other problems festering here and there, problems hinted at in the questions the police officers surprised him with, but Alex decides not to think about those for the moment. His responsibility toward his younger brother is limited to the murder of Tanveer. If the stupid little fool has gotten himself involved in other bad stuff, that's a problem Alex is not going to try to solve.

Now, after a prolonged but ultimately successful effort to remember his number, he calls his own phone. As it starts to ring, he can't wait any longer to pull out Epi's paper-napkin notes and spread them on the bar. They immediately become soaked with some other customer's spilled beer. He doesn't try to rescue them, knowing it would be better for them to disappear. He doesn't even understand why he still has them. Once again, he reads them over. Some of them look as though they were written in blood. A third-rate psychopath, his sibling. The profusion of spelling mistakes makes Alex's desperation and obsessive desire for knowledge about his brother seem less than genuine, as if the errors created an insuperable distance between the writer and the reader and formed a barrier to any kind of empathy or compassion whatsoever.

The good news is that his cell phone's turned on and ringing. The bad news is that no one seems interested in answering it. Maybe it hasn't been found yet. It's ringing as it lies on the sidewalk, or in the happy thief's pocket. For a few moments, his mind plays him a nasty trick and then pokes fun at him. Maybe the leper stole his cell phone, and now he's making hurried calls to Saint Martín de Porres before his ear or his mouth falls off. The joke's not funny, not even to Alex.

Before the answering message starts, Alex hangs up and redials. With his free hand, he rips the wet paper napkins into a pile of shreds and puts them in the ashtray. Another redial, and then another. He watches Mari as she cheekily serves a tall man in his fifties, wearing a big black belt and a knockoff designer shirt with side slits. Alex doesn't recognize him from the barrio. He's not Spanish. Or maybe he is, who knows?

"Yes, hello . . ."

"Hello, who's this?"

"You're the caller. Identify yourself."

"Listen . . ."

"You're calling the district police station."

"Ah, hello." With dizzying speed, Alex seems to understand and take fright at the same time. "I was there this morning, and I think I left my cell phone, and—"

"A black Sharp?"

"Yes, of course, the one I'm calling."

"You left it at the security desk. You can drop by and pick it up whenever you want."

As he hangs up, Alex clearly recalls leaving the phone in the basket. He apparently didn't pick it up after passing under the security arch. Terror at the thought of going back there, along with everything else, overcomes him. It's an illogical fear, he knows that, but knowing what it is doesn't make it any less real. Nevertheless, if he wants to avoid problems, he has to go back to the police station as soon as possible. The guy who was talking to Mari picks up his coffee with cognac and carries it to one of the tables, not far from another table where four old fellows are whacking dominos against the marble top.

"Do you know who that is?" Mari asks Alex.

"No."

"Tiffany's father. Almost, almost a member of your family," jokes Mari, smiling under her mustache.

"I thought he was doing time," Alex answers, looking at the man again, curious to discover signs in him of the bad vibrations that radiate from his daughter.

"In prison? That's one of the girl's inventions. He often stops by when he's in the neighborhood. All in all, it's like a movie about the Wild West in here today, don't you think?"

"How about the restraining order his wife got against him?"

"It's not restraining him all that much, kid. If you keep believing everything women tell you, you're going to have lots of trouble," Mari exclaims, plunging her hands into the hot water in the sink. A little water splashes on her nose, which she wipes on her shoulder, talking all the while. "As my sainted mother used to say, women are very wicked; it would never occur to any man to fake an orgasm."

"Can't argue."

"Wait a little while. You'll see him step out of here and cross the street, and then he and Doña Fortu will walk off, heading for a place where their witch of a daughter can't see them."

Alex can't stay any longer. But Mari likes to talk so much that there's hardly ever a pause in her conversation long enough for Alex to get away without interrupting her.

"That guy's a bumpkin, I grant you, but he's nice. I don't know—he's got something. They say he has Brazilian blood. Maybe it's that. Did you know he speaks German, too? He learned it by himself. He'd go to the Mercat de Sant Antoni on Sundays and buy Nazi books from World War II, and he learned to read them with a dictionary."

"You shouldn't believe everything men tell you, either."

"That story I believe. He's a smart guy. When he arrived in the neighborhood, he had a family but no work. So he got into installing air conditioners. You see the one in here? He installed it. It's still working. Then he found out there was a congregation of Jehovah's Witnesses in the barrio, and zap! Every Saturday and Sunday, there he was, him and his wife and the two girls, sparkling clean and dressed to the nines in the tackiest getups imaginable, singing praises to the Almighty. Within three months, all the faithful had bought air conditioners, serviced and installed by the gentleman himself. Then, who would have thought it, the family lost their faith."

"I have to go, Mari. I have to pick up my cell phone."

In the street, Alex checks to see if he has enough money to take a cab. That would be the fastest way to get to the police station, but he appears to be out of luck. No matter; the buses are usually running smoothly at this time of day.

13

A SHAKEN JAMELIA WALKS DOWN THE STREET, HER FACE still burning from the slap Tiffany gave her a few minutes ago. They were standing in the middle of the sidewalk when Tiffany struck her, and now Jamelia's seething with aggression. She mustn't let this chagrin wipe out the illusion she was savoring when she ran into her sister on the street. She has to recover her calm, even though she knows she's not going to be on time for her job interview.

It's all Tiffany's fault, hers and hers alone. With all her airs, like she's the queen and everybody else has to make way for her. And yes, maybe Jamelia should have listened to Tiffany and not caught the bus. That way they would have met up sooner. And Jamelia probably should have taken the cell phone when she left home. Also, maybe she should have escorted the kid upstairs to the apartment where his mother was supposed to be waiting for him, but Jamelia was already late for her interview, and besides, he was surely capable of going up there by himself, wasn't he? Hasn't his own mother left him alone in front of the TV for hours and hours at home? Jamelia figured Tiffany was upstairs, waiting for him. What was the sense of all these scruples about the boy now, when the little guy's already seen much more than any child should see? Somebody buzzed the door open, didn't they? So the kid must be with Tanveer or Epi or whoever her sister's current boyfriend is. Jamelia's not Percy's mother, *she* is, Tiffany is.

Her tears, her running nose, her perspiration from walking so fast, without time to think . . . She was going to arrive disheveled as well as late, and she'd prepared for this interview with such special care! She'd scented herself with talcum powder and perfume stolen from her sister; she'd showered first thing in the morning so she'd have time for her final preparations. Jamelia feels herself bathed in sweat, something nothing and no one can avoid or alleviate. She's sure she'll reek at the interview. She's afraid they'll laugh at her, at the poor silly fool. She's afraid of disappointing the neat, well-dressed, handsome gentleman who's so eager to meet her, who must be waiting for her and wondering why she's late. She didn't do anything wrong. She only obeyed when she shouldn't have. But Tiffany's bad and mean. Mean to her, mean to Mama. Mean to Percy. Mean to Epi. Mean to everybody. And someday God will punish her. Jamelia's convinced of that. Nobody can be so selfish without getting punished for it in the end.

For Jamelia, the interview's much more than a good job opportunity. It means she'll be able to show she can work and do things well, earn a little money to buy clothes and gifts, get an ice cream, whatever she wants. It means popcorn at the shopping center. And going to the movie theater to see romantic films. Besides, it's the chance to get out of the apartment and meet the man of her dreams. She's aware—as she looks at her wristwatch and discovers she's already almost ten minutes late—that she sometimes imagines life as a television soap opera, like the ones Tiffany loathes so much. Just after clearing the table, or while she's sewing, Jamelia likes to sit on the sofa next to her mother and watch an episode in a serial followed by some celebrity gossip shows followed by an episode in another serial. Five hours of not thinking about yourself. Such sessions connect mother and daughter with the irremovable truths they left on the other side of the ocean, truths that reconfirm both women's faith in life and love: goodness makes its way through tragedies and the traps evil people put in its path; love is irrepressible and overcomes all obstacles; it makes no difference if you're not rich or very beautiful or outgoing or Spanish, because to emerge triumphant it's enough to be good, feminine, hardworking, and faithful. When you meet the other half you lack before your life can be full, don't think twice about it, give yourself totally, inundate him like a rushing river.

Even so, she'd been on the point of turning around, skipping the interview, and going back to the apartment to pick up Percy. But then her sister appeared, raging and furious in the middle of the street, shouting so loud Jamelia was stunned. She tried to explain herself, but Tiffany wasn't listening. She never listens to anyone, least of all her dim-witted sister. Jamelia's mother has told her and anyone else who would listen that it was the nurse's fault. It was Papa's fault for spanking her. It was the doctor's fault. Doña Fortu's unhappiness, her disappointments—it was their fault. For all those reasons, she says (the excuses vary according to her mood and the level of frustration in the house), Jamelia seems a bit slower, more withdrawn and silent, less impulsive than other girls, but Jamelia knows appearances are deceiving. Hasn't this happened in every serial she's ever seen on television, ever since she was little? The good girl's bad, the ugly one's pretty, the poor one's rich. Only she knows how loving she'd be if she were alone with the right person, just as she alone knows how she changes when she shuts herself up in her room, puts on the radio, and starts to dance. She looks pretty, she thinks, dancing in front of the mirror, imitating Shakira or another of those young actresses who shake out their blond hair, gyrate their hips, and give boys an ultimatum: *Now or never.*

Jamelia stops in front of the supermarket offices, where her interview was supposed to start fifteen minutes ago. She knows that if she could think up a good excuse and present it with smoothness and conviction, she could still pull it off. One or two more steps and the doors will open by themselves. All she has to do is to go in and ask one of the cashiers where the personnel interviews are conducted. But she can't. Petrified, she feels the echo of her sister's mocking insult like another slap. And there's also her smell, the smell of a perspiring woman, which perfume and cologne haven't been able to mask in her rush to get here. Maybe if she wouldn't squirm around too much, if she wouldn't raise her arms, if the room were very well ventilated. Actually, she's just doing what everyone expects her to do: giving up, stepping away from the door that opens to the world of normal people.

But then she imagines herself going home and closing the apartment door behind her. She imagines her mother, bursting into the hallway while drying her hands on a kitchen towel, welcoming her with a smile from ear to ear, and asking her how it went. She'd be excited, her mother, she'd make her sit down and recount everything, right down to the tiniest detail. And Jamelia would begin to lie, speaking in generalities, but when she had to give details, the game would surely be up. You can't trick your mother just like that. And then the disappointment would be all the greater. And sooner or later, Tiffany would subject her to fresh mockery. God would punish Jamelia's lie by making sure she'd receive no more job offers and leaving her a spinster. It's fate that's brought her to this point. As in her soap operas, nothing happens just by chance. Everything's written in the Lord's kind hand. These thoughts make Jamelia change her mind. She tries not to notice how her whole body is trembling, tries not to stutter when she addresses a store worker, who has to concentrate to understand what this girl is asking. Fortunately, the worker's a South American, too, and maybe that's why she has sufficient patience to hear Jamelia out, raise what looks like an extremely long finger with a fuchsia nail, and point to one of the doors in the hall.

Jamelia walks toward it. It's been a long time since she's felt the way she does in these precise moments. Everything looks so nice. The waxed floors shine glossily, like a frozen lake. She knows the song that's playing through the loudspeakers, just as she knows almost every song broadcast on the radio. It's Chayanne. What a handsome guy he is! Even the people pushing their grocery carts along seem to be following an established choreography. Everything in its place. Located here and not there. Labeled. Pressed. Packaged in reds, greens, and yellows. It reminds her of going to the company store with Papa on paydays when she was a little girl. Standing at the wooden counter that could be raised and lowered like a drawbridge, her father—who was always so self-assured—would request the items his family needed: rice, lentils, milk, sugar. Then he'd put everything in a cardboard box and carry it home, and when they got there, he'd let her take all the packages out of the box and then put them back in again, or she could play the salesclerk, with invisible banknotes and garbanzo beans for coins.

Jamelia stands in front of the wooden door, which is painted blue, and knocks on it cautiously. Nobody responds. Finally, she turns the knob and enters. Fortunately, things are well behind schedule. Now she's just one of several women, gathered in what seems to be a waiting room. There are women younger than she is, but some older ones, too. Women from the Maghreb, Spanish women, South Americans. Fat and thin. And there's an empty seat for her. Jamelia inquires whether this is the waiting room for the interviews, and when they answer affirmatively, she asks who's the last person ahead of her. She takes a seat, very nervous but also very happy. Because of a lot of things. Because she hasn't missed her turn. Because of the decision she made when she disobeyed her sister. Because of how delighted her mother will be to find out that she's gone to the interview and gotten the job. And besides, she's sure it won't be long before she meets the love of her life, too. It'll probably be the interviewer or the manager of the section where she'll work. But above all, she's happy to be one of many. A woman among women.

Jamelia doesn't know that her mother's been standing in front of the supermarket and watching her. Doña Fortu can hardly hold back her tears. She's wrapped up in a black coat, clearly out of season, which obliges her to be quite hot. In her eagerness to remain inconspicuous, she draws the attention of everyone she passes. Made up, perfumed, and excited, Doña Fortu can't stop looking at the automatic doors Jamelia went through. For a while it looked like the girl was never going to do it. Despite the distance separating them, the mother takes a bit of credit for having given her daughter a slight push right before she entered.

"Come on, babe," her ex-husband, Jamelia and Tiffany's father, says to her. "I don't have much time."

"Did you see her? She went in."

"Yes, she went in."

"Her first interview, and she went to it all by herself."

"Come on, let's go. Today we can walk in together—the guy on duty doesn't know us."

Couples aren't allowed in the rooming house where he lives. Occasionally, depending on the time of day, the staff looks the other way. The two of them enjoy a few hours in his room, just for the pleasure of each other's company. They make love now and then. But what they do most of all in their encounters is talk. About when they met, about when the girls were little, about what they'll do when everything's forgotten—even though Doña Fortu never knows what that "everything" refers to. He's as loving to her as he was when they were courting, but sometimes he asks her for money. The man constantly has projects, deals, ideas in his head. Although he claims to be broke, he's always very well dressed; then again, it's true that she irons his shirts on the sly. Tiffany will never let them live together again, and Doña Fortu has often considered asking him some questions about that, but she fears the truth as much as the prospect of angering him. She's afraid she could lose what she's got merely by uttering Tiffany Brisette's name.

When they enter his room, Doña Fortu stretches out on the bed and watches as he undoes his belt.

"Did you remember to alter my new pants?"

"Yes, they're in that bag."

"You can't stay long today."

"That's all right. I'd really like to be home for when Jamelia gets back."

14

"PERCY, WE'RE GOING TO GET ALONG JUST FINE, YOU and me."

The little boy's being stubborn. He's determined to leave the apartment, he's whining and whimpering, and a full-fledged crying fit can't be far away. As for Epi, he has very little patience and even fewer resources for entertaining a child. As the hours have passed, Epi's gradually lost the certainty he cherished early in the morning, when he thought he'd found a logical way to order his world. At that moment, which now seems so long ago, he figured Tanveer's death would put all the pieces back in their proper places. But now, the murder itself—Thor the Avenger, his sinewy arm outstretched, holding up the *Moro*'s head—his flight from the barrio, and his love for Tiffany all seem less real than any fantasy Epi could have imagined. Panic has been rising in him ever since Tiffany's reaction made the normal progression of events he'd envisioned impossible. Now more than ever is the time when he needs Alex's words, his ability to know what to do and to assess the damage Epi's actions have generated.

"I wanna get out of here . . . Grandma! Grandma!"

If he could only rest for a little while, everything would be different when he woke up, he's sure of that. The elves would have helped the cobbler, and everything would be finished and in order. The cocaine in Epi's bloodstream has kept him alert, but he's starting to notice something like red lights in his brain, switching on one by one. A nervous reflex runs through him from his molars to his chest and back, splitting his breastbone in two, and his injured foot is hurting worse and worse. He thinks about doing another little line, but he knows that's not a good idea. He remembers that whenever he's tried to suppress anxiety with more drugs, things have gone from bad to worse. In any case, he thinks there's some tranquilizer or other in one of his pockets that will help him regain control.

"Mama, Mama, Mama!"

Epi tries to defuse Percy, who appears to be on the point of exploding. He's flailing and screaming inconsolably, like a crazed windmill.

"Come here, kid . . . Look, I'll let you play with my cell phone. Look, come closer, look at the neat things it can do . . ."

Percy squirts out of his hands like a bar of soap. The little boy's a machine full of pins, with a superhuman ability to scream, cry, and move at top speed. Epi follows him from room to room until Percy enters the bedroom and the man throws himself on the mattress and catches him. Epi gets on top of him and grabs the child's wrists like a pair of shackles. Percy bawls and squirms nonstop, not listening to anything or anyone. He's an enraged creature, a hurtful little varmint, like his mother: incapable of controlling himself, incapable of listening to anyone.

"Stop it, Percy, please. Shut up! Listen to me! Fuck!"

But the child pays no heed. Not until Epi releases his right hand and gives him a hard slap across the face. Followed by another, and another, and yet another. At this point the boy becomes quiet enough for Epi to tell him that his mother's about to arrive. That the two adults are going to talk, and that as soon as they're through, Percy can go back home with his mother. And as soon as this miserable day is over, he, Epi, freshly showered and handsome as can be, will come and get them—just like he used to do—and they'll stroll through the fair and the car show, and Percy will be able to have anything he wants.

The child twists from side to side, but now with the single goal of protecting himself. His reddened face bears the marks of Epi's fingers. His hair's messed up. Saliva runs down his cheek and onto the mattress. Epi's not sure if the idea that occurs to him is proper or not, but he executes it before he can change his mind. He takes a tranquilizer out of his pocket and bites the pill in two. One piece stays in his mouth, and he puts the other piece, which is smaller, hardly more than a quarter of the whole, into Percy's. It can't hurt him.

"Come on, don't tell me you don't like candy. Swallow it. Then you can stay here and rest for a while. Come on."

The child stops resisting, but Epi doesn't trust him. So he doesn't get up; instead, he keeps straddling the boy and waits for the Tranquimazín to take effect. In the meantime he takes advantage of the opportunity to get his cell phone out of his back pants pocket. He presses the red button, taps in the password—the day and month of Tiffany's birth—and checks to see whether his message has been correctly sent and received. It has, but Alex hasn't answered yet. So then all he can do is wait.

Percy lies on the mattress whimpering but not moving much. Soon his eyes will begin to close. Epi doesn't anticipate any more problems with the boy. He hopes the marks he's left on the little face will have disappeared by the time Tiffany Brisette shows up.

At this moment, having realized that the only solution is to return to the apartment and collect her son, the girl's angrily walking back there. Two blocks to go. It's just crazy-making, the way things have become so mixed up this morning. When she gets home, she intends to take out all her rage on Jamelia, on her mother, and on Tanveer, if he should deign to put in an appearance. She crosses the street with rapid steps, reaches the entrance to the apartment building, and hesitates. Her thoughts are scattered, but she needs to make a smart decision. It occurs to her to call Tanveer Hussein. Now she's got a good excuse, a weighty reason that will allow her pride to remain unscathed: her son is being held prisoner by a madman who's lost his head because of the cock wielded by Tanveer himself. Surely, Hussein won't turn his back on her, he'll come to her aid, he'll play the hero with the kid, and while he's at it, the big lunkhead will fall back under Tiffany's spell. This whole wretched affair will let them add one more chapter. She wants to get him back so that she can dump him into the pit of oblivion when he least expects it. As far as what may happen to Epi is concerned, she doesn't care. Whatever it is, he has it coming. Maybe now he'll leave her in peace. Standing in the entrance, she dials Hussein's number and hears the beginning of his recorded answer. She hangs up, cursing heartily. Then she immediately dials the number again, but this time she leaves a message.

"I don't know why I'm calling you. All right, I do. It's because you and Epi are friends, and I want to see if you can get it into his skull that no means no, and when I say I've had enough, it's over. The son of a bitch is holding Percy in your apartment. I'm sorry to be doing this, but I'm going to call the police and have them come and take care of him unless you get here soon and give me a hand."

Tiffany ends the call. Until that moment, she hasn't thought the matter was so serious she'd have to call the cops, but the idea gathers strength inside her. She can make a scene, get some protection, and be the star of the barrio for days to come. An object of desire for the men. The most motherly mother of all the mothers. Jamelia will look like a selfish, subnormal idiot. Tanveer will be jealous, just the way she wants him. But no. She can't be thinking those things. Her son's up there, and he's too much to bet. So a little less fantasizing is in order. Do what's easiest. Ring the apartment bell and ask Epi to let the child come downstairs and get this whole thing over with.

She rings the bell, and while waiting for a reply she glances at her cell phone. There's a bunch of missed calls, but no trace of Tanveer. He's sleeping off last night's partying, no doubt. Bea and Rita have both left voice and text messages. She taps the keys rapidly so she can have a look at the texts. "How are you? Coming over to your place. We'll talk." She'd keep on reading, but Epi's voice breaks in on her over the intercom.

"Come on up."

"No, bring Percy down here. And stop all this bullshit. If you piss me off, I'll call the police, and then you'll be good and fucked."

"The thing is he's sleeping."

"Sleeping? What the fuck does that mean, sleeping? Epi, Epi!"

An electrical spasm opens the door. Tiffany steps into the lobby and starts to climb the stairs to the apartment. Really, the girl thinks, you can't ever plan anything. Things happen just because. One thing knocks away another, like in a billiards game. The scene changes with every stroke of the blue cue.

Epi has his own purpose in mind: getting a hearing. He wants to talk to Tiffany and let her know what he's capable of doing for love. He wants her to see as clearly as he does that Tanveer was the obstacle to their happiness, that he was something that stood between them. For her part, Tiffany operates on instinct. She's aware that all this will end badly, but not necessarily for her. She has ways and means of dominating

Epi, she's confident in her power, and if it comes to that, she'll know how to get rid of him. That won't be a problem. Not at all, in spite of the people who've told her there's something inside that boy that has yet to appear, people who say he struggles to control his reactions. Like when he starts looking at you in that certain way and you don't know whether he's thinking about something or he can't think at all. That's what they say, but with her he's always been as docile and easily led as a puppy. So what's there to worry about? Tiffany doesn't know. It's like nobody's willing to play his or her assigned role on this miserable goddamned morning. She's been too permissive, too trusting with all of them. With Jamelia, with Epi, with Tanveer. Permissive or trusting. But nothing's been lost. Nothing she couldn't sort out by slamming her fist down on the table. And she's going to start with that guy in there, who's left the apartment door ajar for her.

Epi's nervous. He's waiting for her at the back of the apartment, with one eye on the window. He smiles, but he immediately corrects himself, without being sure why. He'd like to feel raging anger, or he'd simply like to display an attitude that would compel respect and intimidate the girl. But he can't do it. He's trembling from head to foot, his chest hurts, his breathing is labored. He tries to get hold of himself so that he can find the words he needs. He doesn't want to fail to say what he has to say. Or to lose his cool. But from the very first moment, it's Tiffany who takes charge of the situation: "Where's Percy?"

"In the bedroom, sleeping. He came in, he threw himself on the bed, and . . ."

Tiffany goes into the bedroom and tries to awaken the little boy, but he's in a deep sleep. Too deep. Besides, she immediately spots the red marks on his face and neck. She whirls around, intending to transfix and paralyze Epi with a single look, but he hasn't yet come into the room. She plots her revenge against him. She'll fix it so he's killed, so he's thrown into prison. If necessary, she'll petition Hussein to blow his guts out, and if he won't, she'll do it herself. She's afraid the child has suffered a concussion from striking his head against something, but she feels his scalp without finding any blood or any sign of a blow. Planting her feet firmly on the floor, she picks up her son, cradles him in one arm, and turns to leave. She intends to take him to a hospital and hope they can wake him up. Just as she's about to pass through the bedroom door, Epi appears, his eyes staring out at her from the depths of his face. Cold eyes. Bottomless. Different.

"Put the kid back on the bed. You're going to be here for a while."

"Stop talking nonsense, we're leaving now. Epi, let me pass."

"No."

She tries it, but Epi's body tenses in such a way that the real situation becomes quite clear. Their eyes meet. Tiffany's not going to yield, and neither is he.

"Put the kid back on the bed," he repeats, as if hearing him say the same words again will calm her. "Don't complicate things. Listen to what I have to say to you. Is that asking too much? You listen to me, and then you pick up the kid and go. Nothing's happened to Percy. He had a little tantrum, and . . ."

"And what about this?" She shows him the marks on the child's face and neck.

"That's nothing. You know, sometimes my nerves get the best of me, and that's all it was. I didn't hit him, I just grabbed him hard and—"

"You're a coward."

"Come on, Tiffany . . ."

"Don't touch me!" she screams, yanking herself away from Epi's arms as he tries to help her place the child on the mattress. Epi stops obediently, leaves the bedroom, goes to the front room, and sits on the floor. This display of calmness surprises Tiffany. Of course, he's taken his precautions. The door's locked with a key and bolted. Although he's seated on the floor, she knows he's prepared to spring to his feet and snatch her. Getting out of here won't be as easy as it was the first time, but if she escaped once, she can do it again. The second he loses concentration, she'll send a text message or call someone up, and then—

"Give me your cell phone." Epi seems to have read her mind. "I don't want anyone bothering us."

"I don't have it with me."

"Don't hand me that shit."

Epi gets up from the floor to intimidate Tiffany with his physical presence, but she becomes even more defiant. He won't do anything to her, she knows he's not going to do anything to her, she knows he'll fold at the first opportunity and turn back into the kitten he's always been.

"Give it to me."

"Take it from me."

The cell phone's in one of her rear pants pockets. He knows she usually carries it there and grabs for it as quickly as he can, but she beats him to it. However, he's determined to get that phone, so he seizes and twists her wrists until she drops it. When it hits the floor, Epi kicks it into the part of the room where he plans to sit down and explain to Tiffany what happened a few hours ago and how it's changed both their lives.

"You broke it, you're gonna pay me for it, jerk-off."

"Fine, I'll pay you." He picks up the cell phone and checks it. Like a little eye, the phone's screen saver—the shield of the Barcelona Football Club—continues to blink. "It's still working. I'm turning it off. Sit down."

"I don't want to."

"Then don't sit down. Except for leaving before we talk, you can do whatever you want. But no screaming, either."

"So let's hear it, fast, because I have to take Percy to the hospital."

Epi would love to be able to explain himself in a way that would allow Tiffany to see things as he sees them. But how to find the right words? That never happens to him. He remembers arguments that began with something the girl had or hadn't said, with some oversight, some long delay or discovered lie, something clear and evident, and by dint of talking and talking, saying and unsaying, the world turned upside down, and he wound up being the one who asked forgiveness. But today it's going to be different. He won't let her dictate the game. To begin with, he'll come out with what he did and why.

He's not going to ask her for anything. What's done is done. It's no use going over it ad nauseam.

"Tiffany . . ." Epi's kneeling in front of her. He already feels less sure than he did a few moments ago. She notices. "Tiffany, I love you."

"And?"

"And you and me, we used to be happy, before . . ."

"Everything comes to an end."

"No . . ."

"Fine, then no. If you say no, it must be no."

This is the version of Tiffany he hates the most. The know-it-all, the one who's enormously adept at answering quickly and easily, the one who makes fun of him and doesn't give him the consideration he deserves. Can it be so hard for her to take him seriously and not treat him like an imbecile? Is everything he does or says so predictable, so childish? Being here with him is obviously a nuisance for her. But then . . . ? Are the hopes the girl's been tossing to him like treats false hopes after all? Epi tries to understand. All their mutual memories, the dreams they shared—did they count for nothing? The affectionate words she addressed to him over the course of the past several months, when her relationship with Tanveer seemed, for the umpteenth time, to be coming to an end—were those words false? No, no, they were truthful, she spoke the truth. It had to be the truth. He wasn't such a fool as not to have noticed if it was all a load of crap. The sight of her son is what set her off. That had to be it. He shouldn't have hit the kid. But everything would have been simpler if Tiffany had remained in the apartment, if she hadn't run away for no reason, only because he'd made her wait too long.

"Don't treat me this way. I'd do—"

"I'll treat you any way I want to, all right?"

"Let me begin at the beginning. You and I were good together, and then Tanveer came along . . ."

"Tanveer had nothing to do with it. I've told you a thousand times."

"But he came along, and then it was over between us. If you knew how much I suffered when that was happening, the thoughts I had, the things I saw, the things I suspected—"

"How can you say that, if I knew? As if I don't know! Of course I know. I know because of all the times you followed us, because of all your pathetic dead-of-night phone calls, because you've been telling your sad tale to anybody willing to listen—"

"But you said, you said many times, that—"

"Yeah, I say lots of things, it's true, but if you think kidnapping children at nine o'clock in the morning is the way to make me fall at your feet, you better think again, asshole. You're a little shit. Real guys don't act like this . . ."

By this point, she's shouting. A total blowup is imminent. Epi can't find the right words. Why won't she let him talk? Where does all this attitude come from, this insistence on treating him like dirt? Epi moves closer to Tiffany, and she stands her ground, glaring at him. He notices the nicotine on her breath, the perfume he can never forget.

"Real guys do things differently, Epi, you know? Real guys know how to keep a woman. Real guys—"

"Guys like Tanveer, right?"

"Like Tanveer. Exactly."

"Guys who screw whores and then beat the shit out of them."

"That's not true, and besides, what difference does it make to you? Maybe I go around screwing whoever I feel like, too. Whoever comes along. Except for you, of course."

Tiffany knows she's making a mistake. This isn't the smartest way of solving the problem, but she can't help herself. She's overcome by anger and the desire to demonstrate her power, the same power she plans to exercise over Jamelia and over Hussein himself if he doesn't show up to help her this very instant. It's too late to shift into reverse. And when she sees Epi's eyes grow cold and hard again and fix on hers, she thinks that maybe, just this once, she should have controlled her temper, she should have curbed that sharp little tongue of hers.

15

IF YOU SPEND MUCH TIME IN THE WOODS, YOU LEARN to recognize and distinguish the silence that always presages the worst. It's the same in the barrio. When the streets are nervous or drowsy, you can sense it in the shops and among the people. It's the driving force, the reminder that under the asphalt and inside the cement honeycombs, beneath the underground parking garages and behind every door, each concealing a thousand and one stories, the living essence of earth, fire, and water remains. Like a black angel of memory, almost every tale, every occurrence finds an echo inside the walls of the barrio. Old stories, myths, sayings, commandments, angry threats, advertising tips.

Something's going to happen. It's not just another of his premonitions. Alex detects it in the argumentative conversations he hears here and there, in the groups of teenagers crossing the barrio from one end to the other, in the faces of the tradesmen who've already checked the papers in the top drawer behind the counter to see if they're up to date on their plate glass insurance.

The barrio's been fed up for some time. The young people are bored. Whites, yellows, and blacks. On this point they're in agreement, while the older folks don't forget that, in one way or another, they were swindled, too. Tolerance, cultural diversity, and intermarriage are pieces of slogans suited to newspaper editorials no one in the barrio reads, songs no one listens to, or speeches spewed out by politicians for whom many in the audience can't even vote. And the people live, love, hate, and bear up as best they can. Some wear headscarves, others play their radios too loud, and the rest nostalgically remember the city when she was a broad-hipped matron, venerable and distinguished, who knew how to keep her sweepings hidden under rugs and in jail cells.

The boundaries of the barrio are invisible but impossible to cross. Art galleries, fancy restaurants, scooter rinks, painters' studios, and circus workshops have taken up positions around its perimeter like circled wagons. The said enterprises were launched by the others, the clever ones, and are being continued by their increasingly less clever children. They live on the other side of the invisible walls and come to the barrio for a few hours to look around, drink, and pretend to belong there. But as dawn approaches, they return incognito, like thieves, to their homes, their air conditioners, their plasma televisions, and their vacations in Ireland, where they go to brush up on their English. They leave these streets, which function like cages, containers, or cocktails. During the past several years, the neighborhood's been shaken and stirred and pressurized more and more, in the confidence that the plumbing supporting this melting pot of people will hold out. In the hope that fine words will prevail, that the compensations for being an invalid, for being unemployed, for having or not having children, for taking your daughter to school and not removing her clitoris, for going to Mass or to the mosque, may excuse everything. And it's true that everything is forgiven. Everything except boredom. Or the desire to escape, the fascination of turning, for a moment, into the star of the movie.

"Did you know the guy who got killed?"

Two ladies are sitting in the bus and talking. It's only half full, and Alex takes a window seat behind them. One of the women is a Maghrebi, and the other has an Andalusian accent; they're both in their forties, and they're going to or returning from housecleaning jobs. Between her legs, the first woman has set a plastic tote bag with an assortment of floor polish, bleach, and other cleaning products, while the Spanish woman is clutching—quite firmly—the purse in her lap.

"I'd seen him around. A piece of work. I knew his mother better. She was from the same place as one of my cousins. But whatever the man did, he didn't deserve to die like that."

"I don't think so either."

"It's these gangs. Apparently somebody had a grudge against him."

"Moroccans?"

"I don't know. I don't think so. Maybe from down there on the other side of the ocean."

"South Americans? Wouldn't surprise me."

Alex would love to intervene in this conversation. He could make use of these ladies, qualified spokeswomen for the barrio, to spread a theory that would suit his interests. Then again, the best theory may be confusion. If nobody knows anything for certain, the only option remaining to the police will be the simplest one: the first guy who takes it into his head to drink too much or hit his girlfriend tonight is going to seriously complicate his life.

Only a few stops left. By now the ladies are talking about other things. Alex feels the temptation to stay on the bus, to skip going to the police station, to let the cards lie on the table however chance may deal them. But he pushes the button to request a stop, and when the moment comes, he gets off the bus and heads for the brand-new building. His stomach warns him that he'd better put something in it before dinner. Alex hopes the *mosso* he talked to on the telephone is still there. It hasn't even been twenty minutes since he called. His only prayer is that Epi hasn't called in the meanwhile.

The officer on duty behind the counter hardly pays attention to him. He remembers something about a mislaid cell phone, but the matter was handled by a fellow officer who's gone off duty. Someone will come out immediately. Please wait in that room. Alex realizes he's too nervous not to look nervous. He has to try to calm down. And so he takes a seat. He picks up a copy of a free newspaper from two days ago, but he can't concentrate. He gets up, crosses the room with long strides, and goes out the door, passing the counter in the entrance, where the *mosso* opts to carry on with what he's doing. Alex walks to the other end of the lobby, and when he reaches the wall, he turns and retraces his steps.

He notices a gilded plaque that a gentleman more honorable than the rest unveiled to inaugurate the station two years previously. What must it feel like to be an extremely honorable gentleman? Coming here as the guest of honor, being waited for, pampered, even offered a pair of impeccably gleaming scissors and a little flag with four slanted stripes. An immaculate man, well-dressed, well-advised, with no problems related to money, health, or sex. Alex doesn't understand how it can be that there aren't people dedicated to killing for the sake of simple distributive justice: you're dying because you have what I don't. However, upon forming his thought into words, he corrects himself. Indeed, there *are* people with bombs in their underwear, but their motives are pretty ridiculous. They talk about God, about the Next Life, about Good and Evil, about harems filled with beautiful women waiting for them after their immolation. His feeling on this subject is equivalent to the way he used to feel about the biblical films his mother would make them watch during Holy Week in days gone by: that entire part of the planet depresses him. Desert, broiling sun, lizards, dusty robes, jars of water poured onto feet covered with pustules, sulfur rains, tattooed prostitutes, apocalyptic prophets, people raised from the dead behind great stones, rooms like caves, caves like pits filled with the dead, the dead and the living stinking alike. On television, those persons, the losers, the murderers in the name of God, are always the same. And the dead are all carried in coffins on the shoulders of a screaming, fanatical crowd. As they've done for the last hundred centuries or so, they keep grinding their teeth, pulling out their hair, pounding their chests. The women, wrapped up like big black sausages, dutifully bearing soldiers to save the asses of the bigwigs and the sadists with their graying beards and horrible tongues, squeal like pigs and hurl themselves to the ground in a spectacle so painful it cuts them off from any compassion, at least in Alex's judgment. Those people are "scum," as his father would say. *You're a miserable racist,* Alex says to himself. The thought makes him lift his eyes and look out through the tall, smoked windows of the police station at the sky, where Captain America's starry shield will appear, returning from the black-and-white pages at full speed to stand at his side. *No, no I'm not; I'm just telling the truth.*

"Alejandro Dalmau?"

"Yes, that's me."

"Will you please come this way?"

The policeman starts walking, certain that Alex will follow him. The station consists of a multilevel labyrinth, purposefully designed to make escapes difficult. Alex quickens his pace to keep up with his escort. The doors of all the offices are open, and inside he sees police officers, men and women, typing on computer keyboards, carrying papers and folders, waiting impatiently for faxes, or gathered around water coolers. He sure wouldn't mind downing two or three of those brimming plastic cupfuls of cool water himself right now. Maybe he can ask the officer who hands over his cell phone for some water. Every time he sees a *mosso*, whether working in one of the offices or standing in the hall, Alex's eyes are drawn as by a magnet to the pistol in its holster. It's a childhood fascination that has never left him, the attraction of those deadly tools, slung within reach of their owners' hands, cocked and ready to kill. But he knows he'd best avert his eyes and not think about that. Cops don't like it when you obsessively and blatantly stare at their pistols.

"Wait here a minute."

Alex enters a small white room. There's a table with only two chairs on opposite sides, and on the table a computer, several sheets of recycled paper, and a cheap ballpoint pen lying on top of the paper stack. He sits in the chair and tries to personify serenity. He pats his pocket and feels his medication, his little pills. He reminds himself, repeatedly, that they've taken his statement and let him go once already. That he's in this station only because of a moment of forgetfulness. That fate's not playing any tricks on him. That in a few minutes, he'll be back out on the street. But he doesn't manage to convince himself.

"I'm sorry. Nobody likes to wait."

"No problem."

A police officer, not the one who accompanied him here, has entered the room. He has outsized hands, with practically deformed fingers that must make it hard for him to type. However, the rest of his body is completely the opposite; he has long limbs, a narrow torso, and a ruddy complexion. He's not very tall and seems to be an amalgamation of surplus parts left over from different models. He looks at Alex with black, penetrating eyes and speaks to him in a persuasive voice, the voice of a man who gives orders. He sits not on the other chair but on the table. Alex finds himself at eye level with the officer's crotch, his thighs, the black Sharp cell phone inside a plastic bag, and, a little farther back, his empty holster, which Alex notices at once. He glances around, as if the pistol's been forgotten somewhere.

"I'm the police inspector, and this is your cell phone. Is that right?"

"Yes, yes, you know it's right."

"Good, then let's talk about cell phones and phone calls."

At this point, a subordinate interrupts the conversation, which has hardly begun. The older Dalmau brother already knows things aren't going well. Maybe his incessant calls to Epi's cell have caught their eye. On the other hand, it seems only logical that he'd try to get in touch with his brother after being questioned about him no more than a few hours ago. No, but wait, the cops had his phone. There's another possibility, and that one's much worse. He notices that his hands are wet with sweat, that his back and shoulders are soaked under his shirt. But be that as it may, he must remain calm. He'll try to resolve the matter as best he can, but his plans are starting to vary a little.

"We talked to you earlier, and I know what you told us. You don't know anything. You didn't see anything or hear anything. That doesn't surprise me. If I told you how I get along with my brother . . ."

Alex knows that if he lets the officer talk, he'll end up cooperating, one way or another. He'll give away too much, or he'll seek to ingratiate himself, or he'll try not to disappoint this *mosso*, who's taken the place of those others and feeds, like them, on the same ingratitude, the thanklessness of the herds they have to look after. Alex knows he has to cut him off. He needs to make him angry.

"Look, I'm not new at this, okay? I know my rights. Before, you questioned me without a lawyer present, and—"

"Don't get dramatic, Alejandro . . . say, kid, what a name! What did your father do?"

"He was a schoolteacher. How about yours?"

"A cabdriver. Have you been sufficiently impertinent now? Look, if you knew your rights as well as you say you do, you'd know that you were here before as a witness, and therefore no shysters were necessary. Now you've come to pick up your cell phone, which was left here because of your carelessness and only because of your carelessness. You do want it back, don't you?"

Alex makes a move to take the offered phone, certain the policeman will withdraw his hand at the last moment. But he doesn't. Alex cradles the Sharp in his palm. The phone's turned on. He says, "Can I go now?"

"I'd rather you didn't."

"Look, you all asked me about what happened in Salva's bar, and I told you what I saw. Maybe it's true my brother was out running around with Tanveer all night long, but at that moment, he wasn't there, you understand? And as far as I'm concerned, that's all. You asked me about the van and my brother's sprees with Tanveer, and I swear to you on my mother I have no fucking idea about any of that."

"I believe you, Dalmau, I believe you. And you know why I believe you? Because if you knew what we were finding just by pulling on this one thread, you'd be so scared you'd shit your pants."

Alex tries to search the police officer's eyes to see if he's bluffing. What could have been going on in the van? Were they dealing drugs, pimping whores, selling rich kids nights on the wild side? The cop keeps talking.

"As for Hussein's death, what do you want me to tell you? In all sincerity, fuck him. There wasn't the smallest possibility he'd ever do anything good his whole life long. But his demise has led us to other things. I don't know if your brother knocked him off, or if it was this guy Muza you told us about, or if there's something else, but it excites me to think there may be something else, because it gets boring always seeing the same stupid shit in the barrio. I want to know where your brother's van is. All I want to do is talk to him. That's all I want, damn it."

"But I—"

"And I want to do all that before the barrio gets nervous on me and decides to start the holidays early."

"I'll tell you what I told you before. It's all I know." He makes a decision to explain part of the truth. "I've been looking for Epi all day. If you checked the cell phone, you know I've been spending all my time dialing his number and getting nothing."

"Could be he's afraid."

"Could be. But look, I stand by what I said about this morning. I was there and he wasn't. I can tell my brother from a Pakistani. But if he's done something other than that, something with the van or anything else, go ahead and tear him a new one. If a guy's man enough to charge, he's man enough to pay."

"Did your father teach you that?"

"No, I heard it from a cabdriver."

The policeman's eyes harden for a moment, but then he squints and immediately bursts out laughing. "You're a real kick in the pants, Alejandro Dalmau." The latter feels tempted to lower the tension, to do a little joking around himself, to slide between the cop's legs like an aroused cat, waiting for his master to stroke him. But he resists. Nothing has happened yet. The card that troubles him the most remains face down.

"Look, I believe just about everything you told me. I'm not an asshole. But let me be clear. Your brother's gone into hiding, and that's not helping his case, if you see what I mean."

"I'm sure he's sleeping off last night's binge at some friend's place."

"Does your brother have any plans to leave town?"

"No, not that I know of. Where would he go?"

"Granada, for example."

16

ON THE VAN'S STEREO, BAMBINO'S IN TERRIBLE PAIN. Epi turns up the volume. He's either bored or impatient, he doesn't know for sure. Checking for the hundredth time, he touches the Adidas sports bag—MOSCOW 1980—with his foot. The bag contains, among other things, the stolen hammer with which Epi plans to brain that animal Tanveer Hussein, who's bellowing like a young bull in the back of the van, almost in unison with the Gran Bambino's cohort of clapping and shouting *jaleadores*.

Epi lights another cigarette. He feels the snot running out of his nose, a sensation he hates. For some time now, cocaine's been causing what seems to be an allergic reaction in his nasal cavity, but how can he go to a doctor and tell him that? And so he puts everything in one nostril and uses the other nostril for breathing. Smothering him would be so easy. A matter of covering his mouth and half his nose. He wishes it would be that simple to take out Tanveer. But it won't be. He remembers when his mother would fall asleep and look like she was already dead. Her wide-open mouth. The barely audible whistle of her breathing. The nostril holes like candlesnuffers, which had scared him ever since he was a little boy, seemed in her death agony to be caverns directly connected with hell itself.

He's had enough of Bambino for tonight, so he tries the radio. Tanveer's finished with the first part of his circus; for the next few minutes he'll be calm. The monster needs a little time to recover. There's a possibility that the girl he's with may get away relatively unscathed. But not without a good scare, and with her taximeter at zero. Epi finds a classical station, but the music's a bit too prissy for his current mood; farther along the dial, a female voice elicits responses from lonely listeners with sappy poetry and sentences you have to turn over in your head a thousand times before you can think you've understood them. He keeps scanning the dial and comes upon a song in English. The well-informed Epi translates the song: "Tonight's the Night." *A warning, Epi, almost a premonition.*

This isn't the first time he's fantasized about getting rid of Tanveer. Mentally, that sports bag and the hammer inside it have lain at his feet on many other nights. But this time's the last. He wants to feel the relief that comes when there's no longer a decision to be made because you've just carried it out, when you're standing in front of a single door. He lowers his window a little to let out the smoke from his cigarette and immediately raises it again because the next act of the farce has begun. Tanveer insists on entering her rear, but the whore doesn't want to do that, or he can't; in any case, he gets mad, and surely he's going to start slapping her around. Epi puts the van in gear, planning to drive to a more discreet spot. When he hears the motor humming in front of him, when he feels in control of the situation, he calms down. The smoke from his cigarette gets in his eyes. He curses, wipes his nose with his shirtsleeve, and heads uptown. He knows this song, too. Good station. The disc jockey hardly talks at all. The whole program must be recorded. Professor Malick once told him that everything on the radio's been recorded for at least the last twenty years. Apparently, at the end of the 1980s, there were some superhuman recording sessions in which the following years of music were put on tape; from time to time, breaks for news are interspersed to keep up the pretense.

The song's a swindle. At first, the singer—who the hell is it? It sounds like—no, it's not him—says he's crying because he's lost his girl. Then he wishes the guy who took her away from him good luck. He advises him to be there for her, to concentrate on every detail, even the minor ones, and not to let the girl get sad or want for anything. He seems to be suggesting that his rival give her what he himself didn't or couldn't, with the result that she left him. Then comes an exhortation: if he, the rival, can't love her, then he's urged to send her home, where the singer's waiting for her. Epi doesn't know why. So he can give her a piece of his mind? So he can torment himself, so his blood can boil the way Epi's does when he thinks of Tanveer screwing Tiffany wherever and however he feels like? Or maybe so she'll come back to him and everything will be as it was in the beginning, better than it was in the beginning, because now they both know they can't be apart? The night sends coded messages over the airwaves and either can't or won't decipher them to Epi's liking. Therefore he changes stations again and again until finally he gives up and returns to Bambino's CD, turned really loud.

However, he can't get that other song out of his head. At least the protagonist of the song knows where he went wrong, unlike Epi himself, who lost Tiffany and still doesn't know why. No one has taken the trouble to explain it to him. He never neglected her, he always tried to make sure she was happy and content when they were together. He loved her deeply, right from the first moment he saw her. And she was fine with that, you could tell, until Tanveer Hussein appeared. If it weren't for the *Moro*, they'd surely still be together. They could be living under the same roof. He'd have found a better job than making deliveries. Something, anything. They would've left the barrio. Maybe he would've enlisted in the army so he could get big and strong and she could see him in his uniform or his khaki undershirts and melt like butter. But it was never a good idea to leave Tiffany alone for very long. The Peruvian girl was his if he inundated her, if he filled every minute of her time, twenty-four hours a day. When she was alone, she tended to get muddled, confused, and she always wound up running in the direction opposite to his.

Epi lies when he tells himself that had his rival deserved Tiffany, he, Epi, would have accepted losing her. He's lying to himself, but he knows it. No, he would never have accepted that. When Tiffany comes to understand who Hussein is, she won't love him, she'll rip out however much or little of him she carries inside. Epi stops at a traffic light. The whore screams, and he turns up the volume. Louder, Bambino, louder. The songs have soured his mood, bringing him closer to the final decision. Why not do it now? He doubts very much that the blonde the *Moro*'s banging will want to testify against the man who rescued her. Epi turns around to see what's going on behind him and calculate his chances of success. His idea has been to kill him after their night on the town, during the twenty- or thirty-minute nap Hussein usually takes on the carpeted floor of the van, but why not move everything up?

Tanveer's on all fours, on top of the woman. His arms are braced like columns, his hands pressing on her shoulder blades. Epi figures she's put her backside in the best possible position for suffering the least amount of pain. After some thrashing, Tanveer seems to be pinning her with one hand and squeezing his prick with the other to wring out the last spasm of the night. Epi could take the hammer out of the sports bag at his feet now. He could come to a stop, pull up the handbrake, and turn around toward the interior of the van. And once he's back there, he can break open Tanveer Hussein's skull. He won't give him so much as a chance to reply or even the pleasure of knowing why he's being killed. It sounds easy.

He's going to do it. But when he sticks his fingers inside the bag and wraps them around the handle, something in his rearview mirror attracts his attention. A Guàrdia Urbana squad car with its cobalt blue lights flashing is bearing down on them. Epi immediately yanks his hand out of the sports bag and warns his passengers: "Hey, you two, be quiet back there now. Nice and quiet."

The car passes alongside them. One of the officers gives Epi a challenging look, but the car continues on its way. There must be some bad accident up ahead; otherwise, they would probably have hassled him. Would certainly have hassled him. Epi breathes a sigh of relief, but he knows his moment has passed: Tanveer's beside him, asking questions. "What's going on?"

"An Urbana car with its lights flashing. See them? There they go."

They both hear the noise the prostitute makes when she jumps out of the van and starts running. Two in one night. It's practically comical. The Moroccan must have forgotten to lock the rear door—or maybe that was just his way of giving the bravest ones a chance. Tanveer, who's not wearing pants, orders Epi to get out and follow the whore. Epi mentally rebels, but he obeys. He runs after her and chases her down immediately. The woman's desperate and half-naked. She looks at him with horror. Epi doesn't know if her panicked face inclines him to compassion or to the most unbridled fury. "Please, please," the woman implores him, crouching down and covering her head with her hands, as if expecting another rain of blows. *Please what*, Epi asks himself. *What the hell can be done in a situation like this?* She turns away, doesn't want to go back to the van with him. Nonetheless, Epi grabs her by the collar of her blouse and hauls her along the roadway. The avenue is deserted, but he has to be careful, because there will always be somebody curious enough to wonder if such a violent scene deserves a call to the cops. There's no time to lose. "Nothing's going to happen to you. Really. You get in the van, and I'll drive you back to where you were. Or home, if you want." But the young woman—rightly—doesn't trust him. No, no, and no.

A fit of rage is a wicked goblin that takes possession of you. And it disappears as suddenly as it seizes. It gives no explanations and leaves behind no handbook of apologies for later use. It—whatever it may be—simply happens. Violence has no ears. It gives no warning that it's imminent. It neither runs nor jumps; it only explodes. Letting yourself go, releasing all the brakes, proves to be stimulating. Not stopping to consider whether it's proper to plant your fist in a woman's face, to kick her where she's not covering herself, to pull her by the hair until she gives in and starts walking. Like gasoline or glue, blood has a deep, intense smell, it completely fills all the openings in your head, it reminds you that somewhere there exists an order you alone dictate. How can you help liking that?

Epi shoves the young woman, a mulatto, into the van. A blond mulatto, what a rarity. Tanveer's sitting calmly in the passenger seat, looking merry. He must have seen Epi in the rearview mirror, and although he tells him nothing, he must feel almost proud of him. He doesn't speak to the woman, either. He looks as though he's forgiven her for running away, or as though his patience is at an end. Epi sits in the driver's seat.

However, when he puts the vehicle in gear, the rear door of the van opens wide again. Epi gets out to close and lock it. At this point, the whore makes another attempt to escape. Tanveer grabs her with his one free hand, because he's busy knocking the ash off a hashish cigarette with the other. In fact, he holds her back almost negligently. The woman goes over the top of Epi's seat and kicks herself free of Hussein's grasp; in her desperation, she strikes the ignition key and breaks it in two. She jumps out of the van and starts running down the street.

This time, Epi's not going to pursue her. Let her beat it. She's won her freedom by acting like a wild horse. Tanveer doesn't even move. He's through with the woman; he won't do the same job twice. Epi looks at both sides of the street to make sure nobody's seen anything. He gets in the van and immediately realizes he's not going to be able to start it. He looks furiously at Tanveer, but the *Moro*'s sunk in a lethargy due to too much alcohol and too many pills, too many ejaculations and too many lines, too many blows struck left and right in the course of this long night.

"Why didn't you stop her?"

"It doesn't matter."

"She fucked us good, Tanveer. She broke the ignition key. We can't start the engine, man. If she gives us up, they'll come and find us parked here and we'll be fucked."

"She won't do anything."

"Get out of the van."

"What?"

"Get out."

Tanveer seems to wake up. He didn't like Epi's tone. Epi just smacked a slut around, sure, but that's all the credit for heroism Tanveer's going to allow him tonight. If he has to slug Epi himself a few times, there's no doubt he'll do it.

"Get out and push," Epi insists. "The road starts going downhill in about a hundred meters. I'll see if I can get this thing to start."

The *Moro* obeys. It's the first time Epi's ever ordered him to do something and he's done it. The beast manages to climb up into the back of the van when it begins to pick up speed. Epi can't make the van start, but dead engine and all, they glide down the slopes that descend to the city, go through miraculously green traffic lights, circle roundabouts like bright deserts of gray asphalt. At Epi's side, Tanveer laughs like a man possessed. In the end, Epi laughs, too. He no longer remembers striking that woman in the street, that bundle of hair and teeth and fingernails. He no longer remembers the songs on the radio station that was his accomplice for a while. He no longer remembers who he is or where he's going. He looks at his companion, and their raucous laughter resounds against the night. As the streets he turns down become increasingly more level, Epi decides to park the van as best he can and come back for it tomorrow. He no longer remembers that tomorrow he'll most likely have better things to think about.

17

IT'S JUST A MATTER OF TIME. MAYBE ONLY MINUTES. The police may already have realized that "Granada" can refer to something besides a city. A street, for instance, on the border between this barrio and the one with the Casas Baratas, the cheap government housing. It's even possible they were on to that from the beginning and limited themselves to dropping the hook and paying out the line. In the midst of the disaster with the cell phone, at least a text message from Epi, however laconic—"See you Granada"—got through, and it's offered his older brother some hope.

Nevertheless, what he'd most like to do would be to go home. Stretch out on the bed, close his eyes, and let sleep knock him out long enough for everything to take place without him. According to its nature and destiny. But he knows that won't happen. He knows there's no way of getting around the fact that there's something he and he alone can do. He can go and pull Epi out of that safe house and tell him the Tanveer matter is being taken care of. And maybe he can get Epi to start explaining what the fuck's the story with that carpeted van of his, what went on in there when he and Hussein pulled one of their all-nighters. Epi can pin as much of the rap as possible on the *Moro,* save his own ass, and then disappear. Let him never return to the barrio. Let him go to Australia and send postcards with kangaroos and Santa Claus every Christmas.

In the meantime, Alex, as always, will stay here. Stuck in place, dug in like a centaur's hooves. He never could nor ever will fly very far away. There was always something, some better or worse excuse. His abandoned mother, his sick mother, and now his dead mother. But today he's exhorting himself to get out of the barrio, out of the city, at some point in the not-too-distant future. He'll have to do it alone, because there's no rescue operation under way for him. He's known that for a while. He'll go to Ibiza or to Nepal with a load of drugs, and there he'll buy girls, learn to levitate, find peace.

Deep down inside, he envies his brother. He envies the passion he feels, the passion that drove him crazy. All the prodigality of tragedy, of disaster. In the beginning, he figured his brother's crush would last a week. The time it would take to realize that some things are possible and others not. But what happened was that Epi persevered and got the girl.

He crosses intersections when the lights turn amber and looks behind him to see if he's being followed. Apparently not. But he'll make a little detour, just by way of further precaution.

He remembers one of those quarrels with Epi. It was always so easy to be unfair to him. Alex offered the social worker's argument: their apartment wasn't a hotel, and too many people living there could endanger their mother's pension.

"It's strange. When Tiffany appeared, you advised me not to get involved with her because she would be my ruin, and now you're telling me I should set up house with her."

"Don't be an idiot. I'm only telling you you're going to have to make your own way, and don't come whimpering to me with your tail between your legs when what has to happen happens."

"Bullshit. What the fuck is that supposed to mean?"

"I'm telling you what I'm telling you."

"Don't worry. By the end of the month, we're out of here. As soon as she settles her parents' divorce."

But that date arrived and nothing happened. Actually, Alex liked having the girl close by. He even went out with her sometimes, and he had to say, when she was in a good mood, she was very enjoyable company. Epi would rather her go out with his brother than get bored at home or attend parties with her girlfriends. Alex was the eunuch guarding the queen's chastity. The harmless creature. But he didn't mind. He liked entering places with her at his side, both of them caught in the same violet light, with the other couples cooing around them. The guys would look at him and wonder what the hell he had to do to keep that female satisfied. She'd laugh and drink, drink and laugh some more. She didn't do drugs very much. And when she did, it was always by invitation, always someone else's drugs. She rarely spoke specifically about anything; on the occasions when she mentioned Epi, she was affectionate but not passionate. Alex harbored theoretical hopes—never acted upon—of having sex with her someday. The fact of the matter was that lithium had lowered his libido considerably, and his limiting himself to fantasizing about her was due more to pharmaceutical science or laziness than to any self-control. On the other hand, all his masturbation sessions during that period were devoted to her.

By the time he realized Tiffany was using him in order to meet up with Tanveer, it was already too late. How could he have failed to see that sooner? And in any case, what could he have done? Tattle on her to his brother and make an enemy of him? What would be the point? And did Alex perhaps feel an unmentionable desire to be right, to see Epi fail with Tiffany so that he wouldn't be so unbearably happy while his clever brother, his farsighted brother, was lonely and fucked up? Probably so. But when he saw Tiffany's eyes change under her tattooed eyelids at the sight of the *Moro*, Alex understood that all was lost. He had to decide whose side he was on. Would he be loyal to his brother, or would he become a confidant, a double agent, in the service of the morbid sentiment that pushed him, without hope, toward Tiffany? For some months, that was the role he chose to play. He was the beard, the advisor, the last layer protecting the girl's most intimate secrets. But he grew tired of trying to uncouple Epi from Tiffany during the day and weary of acting as a go-between for Tanveer and the girl at night, and that was when he decided to switch sides and stand by Epi. When he said so to Tiffany, she didn't bat an eyelid. As far as she was concerned, Alex had become dispensable.

Returning to reality, Alex concludes that Epi must have gotten in touch with her; it's only logical. Maybe they're together at this very moment. How will Tiffany react? He doubts her reaction will be what Epi wants. And suppose she wasn't the reason Epi murdered Tanveer? Alex's mind dissolves. He keeps up his routine of looking from one side to the other to see if he's being followed. And yes, he is. Someone's following him, and Alex even knows his name: Allawi.

"What's up? Don't you ever work?"

"Fuck, slow down. I've been following you since you left the police station."

"How did you know I . . ."

"Walking so fast and looking over your shoulder all the time like that—you're doing all you can to make the cops suspicious. Besides, what can I tell you? I was behind you a long time, and you never saw me. You can forget about spotting the police."

Alex wants his ideas clear and well arranged, like a perfect Tetris screen, and Allawi's disturbing his concentration. When he's with Allawi, Alex always feels inclined to consider him a good person, but at the same time, he knows Allawi's whole life is business, whatever form a deal may take. And Alex isn't sure that helping him find a brother who's just committed a murder would be something Allawi could put his whole heart into. With great determination, Alex walks faster, but seeing that his friend is nevertheless continuing to follow him, Alex stops and blurts out, "What do you want, man?"

"Where are you going?"

"I'm just going."

"You're going to find Epi, right? Let me come with you."

"I'm not looking for him. Why should I be?"

"Because of the whores."

Alex's face gives him away, and he knows it. They've stopped in the middle of the sidewalk. Nobody passes them. Before Epi's brother can formulate the question, Allawi anticipates him: "You don't know what I'm talking about, right? Okay. The cops have found the van. They say it was abandoned on some street in the upper barrio. A whore lodged a complaint about Epi and Tanveer. Or so I've heard. I've also heard the cops found Tanveer inside the van, whacked by one of the girl's pimps. You know how that goes. Talking's free."

"Allawi, look, I don't know anything. Really." Alex has a practically definitive feeling that he can confide in the barber. Besides, he needs to get his ideas out in the open, out of just his own head, and Allawi has always seemed to be a very clear-sighted guy. But at the same time, Alex isn't about to show all his cards. "Let's say I'm going to find Epi and get to the bottom of all the nonsense that's being talked around here. All right? But what the fuck are *you* doing? Why do you want to come with me?"

"Man, I'm a barber. I'm sick of having to hear about everything secondhand. I want to see things for myself. I want privileged information."

"You're a fucking gossip."

"I don't know what you mean, but sure I am, that's what I am, a cossip. And I'm also your friend, man, I say it to you from the bottom of my heart," Allawi declares sententiously, placing his hand on the left side of his chest.

"It's gossip. Gossip, not *cossip.*"

18

THERE'S NOTHING SO DISTURBING AS A PAIR OF TIMOROUS eyes. Eyes that try to be bright, to convey intimacy, but present only the most complete blackness, like two pools of pitch, like two deep, black holes, the kind of eyes you suspect are capable of turning evil for no apparent reason: a tiny misunderstanding, for example, or a secret sorrow whose existence nobody can recall.

Tiffany sees such a pair of eyes in Epi's face and thinks about a lamb. She's never seen a lamb, but she's sure they bite if you let your attention wander. Like the wolf in "Little Red Riding Hood," disguised as a lamb, no, as a grandmother, in fact, a lamblike grandmother, a kindly, inoffensive old lady. She didn't believe Epi when he first said he'd killed Tanveer. She didn't believe his stories about the whores, either. But it's evident from Epi's behavior that something has happened. Maybe Hussein is indeed dead, and Epi wants to take credit for the heroic feat of killing him. Or maybe he's just trying to impress her. Or maybe love has simply driven him crazy. And why not? It's possible he really did kill Tanveer. People do strange things sometimes.

At first she got the giggles. She was on the point of asking him point-blank how somebody like him could have taken out Tanveer. Now she's glad she didn't. If there's one thing her intuition keeps telling her, it's that those timorous eyes have to remain calm until she manages to get out of this apartment, either by persuasion or trickery.

"Let's see, Epi, let's sit down right here. I don't understand what you're telling me. You have any cigarettes?"

He passes her the almost empty pack. Tiffany looks at his hand and sees what look like traces of blood under the fingernails. As he lights her cigarette, she takes hold of his hand to prevent him from withdrawing it at once. Their eyes meet. There's no need to speak. Her eyes seem to understand. His appear to be waiting for forgiveness, for a reward, for both at the same time.

"Is it true? You really killed him?"

"Yes."

They remain silent, sitting on the floor and facing each other. Tiffany wants to know. She wants Percy to wake up. She wants Epi to let her leave, just like that.

"But why? Did you two fight about something?"

"He said bad things about you. He didn't respect you," Epi lies, childishly striving to justify his deed by inventing more reasons for it.

"But that's not a reason to kill somebody."

"Are you sorry he's dead?"

"But he's not dead, Epi."

"Yes, he is. He's dead. And you shouldn't care, because he's nothing to you, you weren't having any more to do with him, didn't you say that, Tiffany? You told me you two had broken up. You said the worst thing you'd ever done in your life was to be with him, you were sorry for all the stuff that went on with him. You remember that, Tiffany, don't you? That's what you told me just the other day. Last week, when we met in the Barmacia. You said he insisted, but you told him that was it, it was all over, right, Tiffany? Did you say that or didn't you?"

"If I said it, that's because it was true."

"So he won't bother you anymore."

"Don't talk nonsense, man. Tanveer's not—"

"Yes he is, yes he is."

"I know he's not, Epi, don't be tiresome. He survived. He's fucked up bad, but not enough to die."

Without knowing exactly why, Tiffany thinks it's a good idea to do a little improvising and tear down the lie Epi's telling her. She's convinced something's happened to Tanveer—probably a good beating—but she's even more certain that Epi had nothing to do with it. She considers the possibility that they were together at the time. But then something unexpected occurs: Epi starts asking the questions.

"How do you know he's alive?"

"That's what I heard."

Epi rises, goes to one knee on the floor in front of Tiffany, and grabs her by the arms. "Who told you that? My brother? Did you talk to Alex?"

"No, no . . . Stop squeezing my arms like that. You're hurting me."

Epi pays no attention to this appeal. He says, "Who did you talk to? What did Alex tell you? Did you tell him you were coming here?"

"No, no, I haven't spoken to him. A girlfriend called and told me Tanveer was alive. In a hospital, but alive."

"What hospital?"

"How should I know!"

Tiffany sees the fear in Epi's eyes. If he's afraid, it must be that he's really involved in whatever happened to Tanveer. Epi gets up and walks to the window. He's looking for something in his pants pockets. He's out of cigarettes, and he needs a smoke right this minute. Tiffany doesn't have any—she just bummed his last one off him. When he puts his hand in his pocket, he feels the knife. He finds the touch oddly soothing. Because if Tanveer's still alive, Epi will have to finish the job before the *Moro* leaves the hospital.

"I have to—"

"You don't have to do anything. Just behave yourself and that's it."

"I *am* behaving myself. It's fucking awesome how much I'm behaving myself."

"I should go, Epi. Will you help me with Percy?" she asks, giving it a try. Her tone is deliberately sweet. Maybe everything will turn out to be easier than she expects. It's possible that Epi will help her, and then this whole mess will be over.

"You don't understand a thing, do you, Tiffany?"

"What do I have to understand that I don't understand?"

Anger overcomes Epi. He moves closer to her, very close to her face. Epi's a stranger. Something's pushed him to the edge of the abyss, and he can't stop himself. No use cringing and waiting for the fall. What surprises Tiffany the most is his determination. Apparently, he's resolved to take action. Now Tiffany regrets the half-truths and half-lies she's used to prolong the relationship with him. She could never bring herself to break it off completely. Epi was as docile and loyal as a dog. He accepted everything. If you gave him a kick, he'd come back in a while for another one. He didn't know or didn't want to know what was going on. It was also true that nothing in her relationship with Tanveer remained the same for more than two consecutive weekends. No sooner did they declare mutual hatred, break up, come to blows, than—in no time at all, a few hours, a few weeks, a month—they were back together, knowing, both of them, that if there was anyone who was made for someone else, it was the two of them, for each other. During those limbo-like intervals, Tiffany would feel better for knowing that Epi was nearby. Always at her disposal. Ready to love her, pamper her, or take her out somewhere.

"Come on, tell me, what do I have to understand, Epi?"

"Nothing. Forget it."

"No, come on, tell me."

"What can I say? I didn't want you to go wild with joy when you heard he was dead, but I did want you to see things the way I see them."

"Look, you lock me up in here and tell me you've killed someone. Fine, even fucking great, congratulations. Then there's my son, on the mattress where you threw him, covered with scratches . . ."

"I never laid a hand on him."

"Well, then, you tell me what in the hell has to happen to a kid to knock him out cold at eleven in the morning. I have to take him to a hospital and get him looked at . . . And what do you want me to say about all this? What's this movie you're making, Epi?"

"It's not a movie."

"Do you know what you're doing?"

"I know what I'm doing."

"Sure you do."

"You know what I think? I think you're reacting like this because you still love him. Now I see it, I see it clearly. You've been lying to me the whole time."

"What the fuck does that mean? Lying about what?"

"You still love him. You were still with him. But he was bad. He fucked whores. He beat them. Before he came, you and I were happy—"

"Happy? You may have been happy, but me, I was bored to death."

"That's not what you said then."

"How should I know what I said then?"

She goes into the bedroom. Despite all the racket, Percy's still sleeping. He gives no sign of waking up anytime soon.

Throughout the argument, one certainty has kept returning, like a spark, and it gives meaning to the rest of the ideas straying around inside her brain: she's sure the boy is suffering from a concussion produced by a blow to the head. She's checked him for serious wounds without finding anything, but she knows she can't perform an exhaustive examination. Her entire body breaks out in a cold sweat. She flies into a rage. Epi's aware of the change and tries to calm her down. The kid didn't hit his head anywhere, Epi knows that, but maybe children can't take tranquilizers, not even in small doses. No chance he'll die, Epi thinks in an effort to reassure himself. There's still plenty of time to pump his stomach.

Inside the bedroom, Tiffany tries to wake Percy up. The boy's breathing, but he doesn't open his eyes. She calls him by his name, shakes him, seizes his eyelids and opens them. But the child insists on remaining asleep.

"Don't worry, sweetheart. The kid's all right. He had a little temperature, that's all. I put him in the bed and he fell sound asleep."

It could be true. Jamelia went to pick Percy up at his school because he was a little sick. Now, to his mother's great relief, the child opens his eyes. He sees Tiffany without recognizing her and shifts around crossly, determined to keep on sleeping. Tiffany exhales and relaxes a little.

"In any case, I'm taking him."

"Tiffany, let's talk first, and then you can both go."

"Many thanks, lord and master." Tiffany passes in front of Epi and picks up her purse. She slings the strap across her chest crosswise, as always, and heads back to the bedroom for Percy. "Thank you for letting us leave."

"It looks like you don't want to understand anything today. I've got the key. I want to talk, and I want you to listen to me."

Tiffany tries to enter the bedroom, but Epi stops her. "It's easy," he says. "I ask questions and you answer them."

What's in those eyes now? A cornered animal. The classmate everyone beats up, backed up against the schoolyard fence, begging for mercy. The criminal incautiously left behind by the superhero, who thinks him disabled, even as he prepares his next cunning stroke. You shouldn't leave prisoners in your rear. She should never have trusted him. Everything that's happening has enraged her so much, she can't even use subterfuges. The fact that he believes he has some power over her is so annoying she could beat him to death. Not to mention his attempt to swindle her with all that stuff about Tanveer. Who knows if it's true?

"Tell me where Tanveer is. In what hospital?"

"I told you I don't know."

"I saw him dead, Tiffany. Knife wounds are motherfuckers."

There's very little distance between their faces, barely an inch or so. His mouth and nose are so close to her that neither of them can see the other's eyes.

"Obviously, they didn't hit any vital organ. Just belly fat."

Epi's satisfaction is huge. He's caught her. And she's the one who always likes these games. He tries his best not to let the joy of uncovering Tiffany's stupid lie light up his face. He inhales her perfume and reaches down to the hem of her skirt.

Epi thrusts his hand under the fabric. The girl presses her legs together forcefully. She's furious because she senses that he's caught her, that he knows she's lying. Without ending his effort to delve into her panties, Epi stretches out his neck and speaks into her ear: "There weren't any knives, kid. I grabbed a hammer and buried it in his head. He looked at me, and he didn't get it. He didn't expect me to act like a man. He didn't think I'd do that for you."

He shoves her against the wall. He wants her to feel his erect member pressing against her. Raising the hand that's not busy in her panties, he shows her two of his fingers. "This is his blood. It's filled with whatever shit he caught from the whores he fucked last night. He didn't think anybody would love you enough to stand up to him."

Epi sticks the fingers stained with Tanveer's blood into Tiffany's mouth. After brief resistance, she opens her lips. So what if she sucks those fingers? So what if she makes him think she wants to fuck him? So what if she gets carried away by the feeling that there's nothing to be done but to wait for the storm to sweep everything away, to reduce conscience, plans, preconceived ideas, and good intentions to fragments? There he is, stupidly pulling down her underpants, a man capable of risking twenty years in prison to fuck her, to hear her say she loves him, she's never had anyone like him. How she hates him. How she hates his stupidity. And how she hates her own vanity, too. How profoundly she hates yielding to such a demonstration of strength, how she hates being a goddess whose worshippers offend her and offer her sacrifice at the same time.

"Tell me you don't love him. Tell me you never loved him. Because he's gone and I'm here, because I always fucked you better than he did."

By now, Epi's inside her. Tiffany decides to relax and hope Percy doesn't take it into his head to wake up anytime soon. Epi's member slips out of her, but immediately he thrusts it in again. Their legs tense and tauten. Tiffany doesn't know whether she ought to jump up on him and wrap her legs around him. She hesitates. Finally, she does it. She closes her eyes and tries not to think, tries to concentrate on a single idea: a few hours ago, those same hands killed Tanveer. They put a stamp with her name on his forehead so that he'd never forget her. And she still doesn't know if it's true or not. If such a loss pains her or not. But she tells herself that she's sick, because normal women don't get excited when a man kills for their sake. Or do they?

19

ALEX AND ALLAWI ARE STEPPING OUT BRISKLY. THEY'VE taken an anarchic, devious route. For the police, following Alex would be the easiest way of locating his brother, so they've most probably assigned someone to tail him. He has to get to the apartment on Granada Street as soon as possible. It's the only thing he can do. As he walks, he tries to think with the same focused clarity expressed by his long strides, but the presence of his companion makes it impossible for Alex to concentrate on his predicament. He knows that sometimes, as he walks down the street, he talks aloud. It helps him see what he's going to do next. Maybe a deep urge to avoid such knowledge is the reason why he's having such a hard time focusing on the setting and situation he's in. Unlike his brother, Alex orders the world by verbalizing it. His lips move, but he makes an effort to keep his words inaudible.

"You're talking to yourself, my friend."

"I know. I'm fucked up."

In Alex's mind, the idea that he's going to confide in Allawi sooner or later is gaining strength, even though he's not very convinced such a step is advisable.

"At least tell me where we're going. If I know where we're turning, I won't have to keep walking behind you."

Alex stops and moves aside so another pedestrian can pass them. He doesn't look like a cop, but Alex figures that's what "incognito" means. He leans against the wall of a building, takes out the little bottle of water he bought on the way, and swigs from it. After so much off-schedule medication, his stomach is burning. At regular intervals, like a tide, sour liquid erupts into his mouth. It doesn't look like anyone's following them. No cars are passing, either.

"Allawi, listen up, because I'm only going to explain this to you once. The cops in the station interrogated me. They asked me lots of questions about the delivery van Epi drives. I don't know what that's all about, but they're really interested in—"

"I told you what people are saying."

"Look, I don't care a rat's ass what people are saying."

"All right . . ."

"So Tanveer gets iced. By the cops, some say. Others say it was pimps. And I say it was a Paki, because it so happens I saw the whole thing. But anyway. Whatever. I don't care. And to top everything, my asshole of a brother disappears, and now the cops are after him. Just what we need, considering all the shit that's gone down. He looks like a textbook suspect, you see what I mean? I don't know what went on in that van, whether they were dealing contraband or fucking dogs, but whatever they did, let them pay for it. I know my brother, and I know he's very easily influenced, but I'm sure they don't have a reason to accuse him of anything really serious. Anyway, my point was, the cops want to talk to Epi about the van, and Epi goes missing. Tanveer gets killed, and Epi goes missing. He's making it too easy for them to put him in an orange jumpsuit and give one another medals, you see what I mean?"

"I do."

"So, well, I know where Epi is. I want to go there, whack him one across his foolish face, grab him by the balls, and haul him to the *mossos* so he can sing like Camarón. But first he has to sing the song to me. Because knowing Epi, if he takes a liking to them, he's liable to tell them he alone was responsible for the Atocha bombing."

"No doubt," Allawi answers, laughing as he speaks. You can tell he's got a hundred questions buzzing around inside his head, and a hundred jokes, too, but this is probably not the moment for joking. He tells Alex, "Don't worry. I won't say anything."

"Please don't, Allawi, please don't. You know even if you tell the truth, people are going to start making things up and talking nonsense, and I'll get crucified."

"All right, all right. I won't say anything. But if you want a piece of advice . . ."

During this exchange, they've started walking again. Talking to someone about all that has calmed Alex a bit. He's seen things outside his head. Maybe now he can analyze them better.

". . . I'll give you some. The cops have already talked to you. Even they aren't too dumb to figure you'll lead them to Epi. But they don't know anything about me. I could go instead of you, and—"

"You don't have to be a hero for me, pal. I just want to go and talk to my brother."

"I'm saying I'll go instead of you, alone, and tell him what you want me to tell him or bring him wherever you are."

"Well, we'll see."

The elder Dalmau brother acknowledges to himself that this idea of Allawi's isn't crazy at all. It pushes him a little into the background, but it's probably a much safer and more effective plan. He'll keep the possibility in mind for later. They're barely ten minutes' walk from the apartment where Alex hopes Epi's still waiting for him.

"That was a knockout gorgeous chick. And a fucking disaster for those two guys."

"Who are you talking about?"

"Tiffany."

"I don't think any of this has anything to do with her," Alex lies.

"Maybe not, but—"

"But what?" Now it's Alex who wants to know. He stops again in the middle of the sidewalk. He's almost certain Allawi's been playing him from the start.

"Calm down, compadre."

"No. Calm down? No. Don't fuck with me, man. Don't even tease me. I've had it up to here with mysteries. What did you mean by bringing up Tiffany?"

"Nothing in particular. Look, I know she had nothing to do with the *Moro*'s demise, I know he was killed by a Paki or some such, but from what you told me, it could also be . . ."

"What?"

"Well, it could also be that it was Epi who knocked him off. He was the girl's boyfriend before the *Moro* appeared, right? A case of jealousy, my friend. Alcohol, coke, one word too many, and five minutes of madness. It could happen to any of us."

"But, but . . ."

"Admit it, that could be what happened. The real truth."

"It could be, but it isn't. I was there, and I know what I saw."

"But you're his brother, and he's in hiding."

Allawi starts to walk again. After a few steps, he turns around and asks Alex to hurry up. What's he doing, standing there and not moving?

"I don't understand how anyone can believe it was Epi who wasted Tanveer," Alex says, trying to convince himself. "Can't you see he doesn't have the balls to do something like that?"

"No, but maybe the girl's the one with the balls. That chick's good, but she's bad. I wouldn't fuck her, and coming from me, that's saying a lot, I assure you."

Now they're walking side by side, but since Allawi's actually the one taking the initiative, Alex gives up their destination: "We're going to Granada Street."

"That's what I thought. Say, isn't that Tiffany's retarded sister?"

Jamelia's walking along, softly singing a tune she heard when she passed in front of a bar a short time ago. It wasn't even five minutes after she got back home that they called her. And asked her if she could start next Monday! She said yes she could, yes of course. And when her mother came home and heard the news, she went wild with joy and persuaded Jamelia to call them back and tell them that if they wanted, she could return to the store immediately, they wouldn't have to pay her a single euro, and they could explain everything to her, and that way she could start working like a demon first thing Monday morning. Jamelia had never seen Mama so happy. They cried together when the girl hung up after the first, unsuccessful call and continued crying after the second, successful one. Before that, it was as though her mother hadn't fully believed her. She was more worried about Percy and about where Tiffany would take the child; she had visions of emergency rooms or God knew what else. But after the call to the supermarket, Jamelia's mother was all hers. For the first time in a long time, she sensed that her mother was proud of her, and no feeling could compare to that.

Jamelia can't hear her name being called. She's walking fast, wrapped in her own happiness. She wants to get to the supermarket quickly. She imagines what she'll do with her first week's paycheck. Maybe she'll buy one of those tiny television sets so Mama can watch soap operas in the kitchen. Or a pretty dress for Tiffany. One of those extreme ones with a zipper she likes so much. The two of them will go together to pick out the dress, because her little sister's taste in clothes is anything but predictable . . . Jamelia no longer remembers the slap Tiffany gave her early this morning or thinks about what a rude tyrant that girl can be. And for Percy? Jamelia will take him out for an afternoon snack, whatever he wants, mountains of cream and caramel, and afterward they'll go to one of those toy stores, where she'll buy him the toy he likes best. And for herself? Nothing at the moment. But soon she'll have to buy new clothes and get her hair cut differently. The young man who conducted the interview was so handsome, and he treated her so courteously. He seemed very smart, the way he used all those words she barely understood. Her mind expanded, and she could almost see the two of them—him and her—working in the supermarket and waiting for each other at the exit so they could go home together. She imagined herself some time later, expecting a child, because the interviewer was explaining that there would be no problem if she got pregnant, and Jamelia smiled at him. The only problem was the uniform. It was something special, all right, but . . .

"Jamelia! Jamelia!"

Allawi and Alex try to follow her, but before long, they give up. The girl doesn't pause in her excited, headlong dash to the supermarket. Alex isn't sorry. It was hard enough to talk to her this morning, and he can do without a second edition.

"She's carrying a message for her sister," Allawi says, expressing the thought forming in Alex's mind. "When she saw us, she decided she doesn't want to see us."

"You're a real Sherlock Holmes."

"A who?"

"Forget it. A detective. Like Harry Potter."

"Right, Harry Pothead."

They both laugh. Alex still doesn't know what to do. He hopes Allawi has a plan and leaves him no alternative, because they're almost at their destination, and Alex hasn't been able to concentrate, not even a little. All he's got in his head is a catalog of intentions.

20

TIFFANY'S ON THE MATTRESS, LYING ON HER STOMACH with her head turned to one side. Percy's not two feet from her. She stretches out one arm and places her hand on the small face. His breath tickles her palm. Using two fingers, she gives the little nose an affectionate pinch. The boy protests. Good sign. On her other side, Epi begins to breathe even more deeply. She'll wait a bit longer. After doing it with him, she decided she'd try to persuade him to let her leave. She'd make him feel like the unquestioned master of the situation, the hero who murdered the monster and set her free; she'd persuade him that being suspicious of her makes no sense. She'd leave with the child, and then tonight she and Epi could meet and have a nice, calm chat about what's happened and—especially—about what's going to happen.

But after lying down on the mattress, Epi couldn't help falling asleep. The fatigue of pleasure, combined with the number of hours he'd been awake, laid him low; the last lines of coke he'd done had long since evaporated from his bloodstream. Faced with this new situation—that is, with Epi passed out on the bed—Tiffany has radically changed her plan: she's going to leave right now.

Should she be in such a hurry? She should, she knows she should, but suddenly her haste subsides. She savors the moment, which she recognizes as something special, as the precursor of even greater moments to come. Her open mouth presses against the dirty fabric of the bare mattress. She could shut her jaws, but she doesn't even want to do that now. She likes the feel of her tongue against the coarse material, as rough as a cat's tongue. She's not going to run, she's not going to close her mouth. She might even fall asleep. A few minutes would be enough, a few more minutes of lying here, curled up against her little boy. When you most need it, time shows you that it doesn't exist.

But the girl's indolence vanishes as soon as she spots the keys. They're sticking out of a pocket in Epi's pants, and since this article of clothing remains attached to its owner at only one ankle, it would be a simple matter for her to snatch them. She stretches out her arm and thrusts her fingers into the pocket. She doesn't even look at Epi, because she's proud, because she can't be bothered, because she considers that particular precaution beneath her, as she has considered all others. She extracts the keys from the pocket and lets them fall on the bed, gazing at them with the incomplete vision that results from the position of her head on the mattress. The fabric is wet with her saliva.

The midday sun makes the room stiflingly hot. Except for an occasional, unusually loud vehicle, no sound of any kind can be heard. Tanveer's friends chose this apartment precisely because it's so quiet. The neighbors are deaf, old, or dead, and cars go down Granada Street only if their drivers are lost. The windows have no curtains. Tiffany looks around for the violet ones she bought for this room some time ago. They may still be in the wardrobe, along with the mountain climbing equipment left by that nutcase friend of Tanveer's. The stolen hangers must be in there, too, and the bags of unwashed clothes, filthy and paint-stained and smelling of turpentine.

But did he really kill him? she wonders. Something happened. She was sure of that. Epi wouldn't have put on this whole performance if Tanveer were still around. But if he's dead, she ought to feel something she doesn't. If it turns out to be true, people are going to look her in the eyes to find out what she's got inside. And Tiffany's afraid they'll see nothing. For now, at least, she has no tears. No grief. Nor does she know if that will come later. But she ought to feel *something*. Something more than vanity, shouldn't she?

Tiffany knows intuitively that her feelings for Tanveer Hussein are deeper than she'll ever acknowledge. She remembers how she used to feel in the presence of that big son of a bitch with his bad-dog eyes. She felt helpless as a child. Simultaneously protected and exposed. Not knowing where he was would worry her, his lies would alert her, his defeats made her conceited. But when she had him, when she took him inside her, she knew that everything made sense; whether she could interpret it or not didn't matter. But why did that happen only with him, and why in that way?

She can't get used to the idea that she won't see him anymore. For them, "never again" always meant "in a few days." There were so many breakups, so many times when she wished him out of her life forever, when she wished he'd get killed or go back to his own country, if indeed he had any country other than these streets. She's had the feeling it was all over so often she can't take in the idea that it is, that it's come to a sudden, unexpected end. What's left for her now?

Epi's still breathing deeply—snoring, in fact—with his mouth open. What's she waiting for? *Pick up the keys and get out of here,* an inner voice commands her. Her hand closes over the key ring. She gives Epi a look of farewell. His last hours of freedom. His last fuck. His first and last act of heroism. He killed the dragon and came looking for the girl. But he was a foolish Saint George and didn't ask first. He saw things the way he wanted to see them. He never suspected that without the beast, there's no princess.

Why couldn't she fall in love with someone like Epi? What if she made a real effort? Someone who'd ruin his life for her sake. Someone who'd kill, who'd blow everything to hell just to have her to himself. To have her love. To make a private world for the two of them. Is anyone going to love her more than Epi does?

Tiffany's hand closes over the keys. She slithers across the mattress and over her son. No problem with Epi—he keeps on sleeping. She slips both arms under Percy and summons all her strength. She has to choose her moment so she won't make the slightest mistake. She raises the child with her hands and forearms and slowly straightens up. She turns toward the door but has the bad luck to catch her foot in some bedclothes on the floor. She trips and goes flying in the direction of the wardrobe, crashing into it and striking her head hard against the wood. The blow is painful and the noise quite loud. Tiffany stands paralyzed, waiting for Epi to come at her and ask her where she's going in such a hurry. But the moments pass, and there's no reaction from Epi. Tiffany hears only what sounds like a groan issuing from Percy's lips and the creaking of the still-vibrating wardrobe, which she eventually manages to stop with her head.

She leaves the room, heading for the apartment door. As she stands before it, she's aware for the first time that she's frightened. Her hands perspire as she tries to insert the key in the lock without making any more noise. With the child in her arms, the operation turns out to be difficult. Her heart accelerates wildly. She raises Percy higher on her chest, puts his arms around her neck, and presses the little face against her own, thus freeing one of her hands.

When she inserts the key, the doorbell shatters the silence.

Allawi's downstairs, leaning decisively on the intercom button. The sound freezes Tiffany in her tracks; her head feels like it's inside a big metal bell. The ringing continues insistently, stopping briefly only to start again. At last Tiffany reacts, turning the key once to the left and then again, just as her father taught her. "The right tightens, the left loosens," he'd say. Then she hears Epi in the bedroom, falling several times in his attempt to get up. The doorbell keeps on ringing. Somebody knows they're there, and whoever it is isn't about to give up. Maybe it's that idiot Jamelia, Tiffany thinks. Maybe it's the cops. Maybe it's Tanveer Hussein, come to rescue her from this retard.

The lock turns, and the young woman yanks the door open with all her strength, ready to charge down the stairs, dash into the street, and run and run until her heart bursts. Until she gets home, or better yet, until she runs right out of this city, past buildings, over oceans, and back to her country, where her father was good to her and carried her on his shoulders and the sky was bright and blue, back to her grandparents and her Uncle Valle—all of them now in heaven, poor things—who loved her so much and smudged her little nose and taught her to dance and sing songs she barely remembers now. She wants to do the whole thing all over again and do it better.

But reality interrupts the course of her fantasy when a sharp jolt informs her that she's forgotten to remove the chain fastening the door to the jamb. She tries to free the chain with the door ajar, because she's convinced that if she recloses the door now, she'll never be able to open it again. But there's no way. Percy feels heavier and heavier. She closes the door and with the same hand that's holding the keys manages to remove the chain. The key ring falls to the floor, but that doesn't matter. She pulls on the doorknob. Her body's almost outside the apartment when Epi grabs her by the hair and furiously jerks her back in. If Percy were awake, she could let him run down the stairs and at least he'd be saved. If she could do that, then she knows she could deal with Epi, one on one. Or at least she'd have a chance. But having to lug the kid around makes everything harder for her.

Epi's hand, the same hand that split the *Moro*'s head open, releases her hair, yanks her arm to spin her around, seizes her throat, and slams her against the wall. She falls on her butt with the child in her arms. He still doesn't wake up. The doorbell's ringing again, but then suddenly it's as though they don't hear it. Epi's in a rage. His eyes are red with sleep, a rude awakening, and disappointment.

"What the hell are you doing, Tiffany? Did you fuck me so I'd pass out and you could leave? You're a filthy whore! You think I'm a fool! You think I'm some kind of puppet you can do anything you want with!"

"Let me go, Epi, let me go! I have to take the baby to the hospital! And I have to get out of here before I go crazy!"

Allawi keeps ringing the doorbell. Alex has assured him that Epi must be there, that there's no other possibility. He's probably catching up on his sleepless night, and getting out of bed is hard for him. The younger Dalmau brother picks up the intercom phone.

"Epi, Epi! Is that you, Epi?"

"Who is this? Alex?"

"It's Allawi, Epi. I'm here with your brother. Let us in."

"No, tell Alex to come up alone. I'm not talking to you."

Almost immediately after the end of the intercom conversation, Allawi hears someone screaming out of one of the windows in this very building. He can't recognize the voice, but he can tell by the expression on Alex's face that the screams have something to do with them. He runs to the middle of the street and spots Tiffany, waving her arms and shouting unintelligible words. Immediately, someone pulls her back and hauls down the shutter with a single, conclusive jerk.

A Citroën stops a few yards away from the two men. The driver gets out and wants to know what's the address of this building. Allawi doesn't answer. Alex, reacting swiftly, goes back to the intercom. The Citroën's driver is making a call on his cell phone. Allawi walks over to him.

"What are you doing?"

"What do you think I'm doing? I'm calling the police."

"Don't call anybody. We're the police. If you want, I'll show you my badge." As Allawi speaks, he hears a buzzing sound, and out of the corner of his eye he sees Alex enter the building and start up the stairs. Allawi has to hurry if he doesn't want to stay outside. He hopes he's dissuaded the man enough to keep him from complicating things even more.

21

REALITY INSPIRED FICTION. THEN THE LATTER INSPIRED the former, and ever since, everything is copies of copies that don't even remember they ever had an original. That's what Pep, badge number 1465 in the *Mossos d'Esquadra*, is thinking about. His vehicle has been assigned to this particular part of the city, and his mind wanders as he drives the streets, accompanied by Rubén, a devoted son of the force excessively given to prolonged silences and predictable opinions on any subject. So why is he, Pep, reflecting on who copies whom and what copies what? It's an idea that's been recurring to him a lot lately. Looking at city streets with a cop's eyes is like being in a movie you've seen a thousand times. In fact, he knows that the majority of cops—even though few would admit it—are cops because of television and film. And when you see prostitutes displaying their wares, at an appropriate distance from schools and small businesses, you ask yourself if whores dress, speak, and move like whores because that's all part of their job or because they've seen whores portrayed like that on TV programs. And it's the same with everything else. *Moros* are slippery, police commanders have nasty tempers and wear sweat-soaked shirts, the rich snort drugs off glass tables, lawyers take fright at the slightest provocation, and all squatters have eyebrow rings, a German friend, and a big, gentle, collarless dog. Would all this be the same if there were no previously viewed images? Too many shift changes, Pep thinks. He's still not used to alternating shifts. Starting with today, he's got six days of alternating afternoon and night duty. Then one week of mornings. Then it starts over again. It's crazy-making. And it entails a lot of general chaos. So many late-shift Coca-Colas that keep you awake after you get home, so much coffee that your mouth feels like you've been chewing rope and your heart's going a thousand miles an hour, so much nibbling and renibbling of junk food, all those nights turned into days—it ends up killing you. You're dead with sleep, but you suffer from insomnia. You're constipated, and then a few hours later your bowels turn to water.

"Everything's quiet, but it feels like the calm—"

Before the storm, Pep thinks, mentally finishing Rubén's sentence. Like many of Rubén's idiosyncrasies, this one gives Pep no help in penetrating the mystery of the real in the artificial and the false in reality.

"—before the storm."

"Yes."

"I don't trust it. The captain was a nervous wreck, what with burning Dumpsters and rumors and . . . The thing is, all these . . ."

Pep's not sure who or what "these" are. It could be that Rubén's referring to all the people in the barrio who don't root for Barça, for example. But Pep's done more than one shift with him, so he knows the most advisable tactic is to close subjects as they come up over the course of the hours, to seal them off, one by one, like so many blind tunnels. In the end, Rubén gets bored and shuts up for a few glorious minutes.

"The boss is always nervous. And he'll get worse if he finds out his orders haven't been followed."

"It's not our fault, Rubén."

"I know, I know, but we'll sure be the ones who get chewed out."

They're driving around the barrio. It does indeed seem quiet, but Pep couldn't say whether or not there's anything abnormal in so much tranquillity. They've already had one corpse this morning. He hopes and believes that nothing more will happen, at least not this afternoon. If the city goes up in flames, let it happen on the night shift.

"Look, if they mess with me, I'm going to tell them the truth: we never got the orders, not us. We were in the locker room."

"Pep, you know the regulation says that if you receive an order during a shift change . . ."

He knows. But in this particular case, he considers the regulation unfair. If worse comes to worst, he intends to defend his position all the way to the last resort. The captain's orders were to follow the clean Dalmau, the one who was still in the station, and to find the suspect Dalmau, known as Epi. Javier and Magda received the order, but they were going off duty, so they diligently designated it as a matter of urgency for the next pair, that is, for Pep and Rubén. When these two appeared, dressed in impeccable uniforms, armed with pistols properly holstered, but ten minutes late, the brother of the suspect in the van case had been gone long enough to disappear from view. Now Pep and Rubén are trying to avert their fate. They went to the Dalmau family apartment, where they found no one home, and so ever since, like a shark more desperate than lethal, the *mossos'* squad car has been going around in circles, and they've been trying their luck at calculating the barrio's infinite probabilities.

"What do you say we go to Mari's for a while? I'm sick of driving around," Rubén proposes.

"All right."

"Besides, there's always some bad guys in there. We might get a lead."

Pep hates to go looking for informers, as if they were in some 1970s detective movie. But Rubén is Rubén. Pep gives him a sidelong glance. It's always hard to believe that such handsome containers can hold so little substance. Dark-haired, muscular, not very tall but fine-looking, with firm, serene features, he would be a hit in any of the night spots that Pep frequents, at least until he opened his mouth. Rubén, of course, doesn't know that Pep's a homosexual. Maybe he imagines it, but they've never talked about that. Rubén's so preoccupied at the moment with the invasion of Spain by blacks, *Moros*, and the goddamned South Americans that he has little time to worry about fags.

"The thing with the *Moro*—it doesn't seem so bad to me."

"Or to anybody else."

"Will they investigate?"

"Routinely. They say it was a Paki. In other words, good luck finding him."

"Trash killing trash. I have no interest in wasting the taxpayers' money," Rubén answers, imitating the tone and accent of a former president of the country.

"The only crimes we're interested in are the ones connected with the van."

"Do you know what they did to those poor sluts?"

"More or less, but I don't want details."

They enter the barroom and greet Mari. Then they lean on the bar and wait for her to come over and take their order.

"So now you get here. We needed you half an hour ago."

"Shoulda whistled," Rubén says stupidly.

"Right, look, why don't you go play with yourself?"

"What happened, Mari?"

The woman's eyes mist up. She wants to speak, but she seems not to know where to begin.

"What's wrong, Mari? Is it because of the trouble this—"

"It's everything, it's everything. It's what happened this morning, last night, a little while ago . . . I've been shut up in this crummy bar for fifteen years, and I don't see any way out. All I do is work and work. Doing what? Waiting on crooks, drunks, and thugs who don't even know how to ask politely for a glass of water. Anyway, it's nothing, nothing's wrong. I'm getting old. I guess I'm just really tired. What can I get you?"

"Two Coca-Colas . . . please," Pep says with a smile Mari's grateful for.

Just then, Salva comes back from the storeroom. When he sees Mari talking to the two cops, his expression changes. He hurries over to the bar as fast as he can and favors them with his yellow ex-smoker's smile.

"What are you having, boys?"

"I'm waiting on them, Salvador."

"What's with all this attitude, woman? You're mad about Helio? I already told him not to come in here again. I told him it was over, he'd have to do his little payrolls in some other bar. I said there wasn't much in this barrio, but one thing we've got a lot of is bars."

"You didn't say anything to him."

"That's not true."

"What happened with Helio?" Pep inquires.

"The usual. He gets all overheated while he's paying his people and starts making obnoxious jokes, and sure, everything has a limit. Some men need the money so bad they'll take any insult. Others get their balls in an uproar."

"He'll wind up like the *Moro*," says Salva's wife, interrupting him. "I'll get you two some tapas. Salva, you pour two Coca-Colas."

"We ate just a little while ago," Pep protests, without success.

Salva opens the cooler under the bar and takes out two cans. Without asking, he serves the soft drinks with ice and lemon, a practice that never fails to annoy Pep.

"Poor girl. The thing with Tanveer really affected her. Not because of him, but because of all the violence going on everywhere you look. Nobody likes cleaning blood off the floor of their house. By the time she came down, I had already straightened things up a little, but it was still pretty bad."

"Tell me about it. I'm a cop, remember? Fuck! You've never seen *CSI*?"

"You know what I mean."

They all remain silent for a little while, and then Mari comes in from the kitchen with a plate of marinated anchovies.

"On the house," the woman says.

"What's this? An appetizer? A meal? A snack?"

"Marinated anchovies."

Mari goes back to the kitchen. When they're alone again with Salva, Pep decides to try his luck: "I'm looking for one of the Dalmaus."

"For Epi?"

"Whichever. But actually, at the moment we'd like to find the older one."

"Alex left here a little while ago. I think he was going to the police station."

"Yeah, he was there before, but the captain wants to talk to him again," Pep lies.

Salva tenses up. It can't be a good sign that they want more information from him. That idiot Alex—he must have contradicted himself, he must have stuck his foot right in it. Wouldn't it be better, Salva thinks, to tell the whole truth, to describe what really happened? Because when all's said and done, it never does anyone any good to cover up for anyone else. He can tell the cops Alex threatened him if he didn't keep his mouth shut. And it would be better to do it now than to get himself caught later.

"Do you know where I might be able to locate him? We tried where he lives, but no one was home."

"No, I don't know. Listen, I'd like to talk to you in private—"

"It's for you, Salva." Mari hands him the cordless telephone, making it crystal clear that she's not about to handle the umpteenth call from the gas company.

"Just a minute," Salva says, tapping the receiver with one hand and heading for the storeroom. "I have to take this, it's important, but then we'll talk, all right?"

Rubén, back at Pep's side, knocks back some of his drink and vigorously sticks a toothpick into one of the anchovies. With a touch of mystery, he announces his intention to try to get something out of Professor Malick. Then he swallows the anchovy. Pep smiles. For no apparent reason, he's feeling pretty good. And all of a sudden, he's got the distance he needs if he's going to have a little fun with his partner. He asks, "What do you want that psycho to tell us?"

"What we want to know."

"Tell me something, Rubén. If the guy wasn't black, if he

didn't look like some kind of *freak*, would you question him? The logical people to talk to are Mari and Salva . . ."

"I don't understand."

"I'm saying you're going over to talk to him because he looks like an informer in a movie."

"Why do you say that? Because he's colored?"

"Christ almighty, Rubén! That guy's not colored. He's black, he's an African, period."

"I don't care about your shitty mood, Pep. You're not going to ruin my day."

No, no, that's not true; he's not feeling bad-tempered at all. In fact, he'd even be willing to spend the rest of the day in here. He knows he's got the soul of a shopkeeper. He'd spend the time observing Rubén progress from gaffe to blunder, listening to Mari, or watching the sports news on television. Nothing in the barrio appears to justify the paranoia about riots that's fermenting down at the police station. The local people seem the same as always: active, bored, minding their own business. If they set a few trash containers on fire, they'll do it to cause a ruckus and get attention, not to avenge the death of someone who didn't matter to anybody. It looks as though even Rubén has relaxed. He's gone from pumping the Professor for leads to letting his black informer read his cards. Although Pep would very much like some coffee, he thinks it's a better idea to get back to work and try to find the older Dalmau brother. He leaves a five-euro bill on the bar and makes a sign to Rubén, who asks for another minute. As he does so, Salva returns from the depths of the storeroom, prepared to spill the beans before it's too late. And at the same time, Pep's cell phone rings: there's an emergency ten minutes from where they are.

"Rubén, let's go. It's a seven-eight."

"All right. We were finished. Thanks, Prof."

"Don't mention it."

"Land and freedom," Pep jokes.

"*Si la bossa sona*," Professor Malick answers in Catalan. If your purse jingles, if you've got money.

When they're going through the door, Salva catches up with Pep and asks to speak to him a moment.

"Later, Salva. We're in a hurry now."

But later will be too late, Salva thinks, suddenly dispirited. If it weren't for the inertia developed from years of listening to customers, serving them, and collecting from them later for what they're ordering now, Salva wouldn't have the heart to remain upright.

"Officer, remember I wanted to talk to you."

"I'll remember, Salva." As he speaks, Pep gets into the police vehicle; so does Rubén. They decide to switch on the emergency lights and make a dash for the place where a woman in an upstairs window is calling for help.

"Don't be so mysterious. What did Kunta Kinte tell you? Where should we start looking?"

"He didn't say anything about that."

"Fuck, what were you talking about?"

"Me."

"Well, don't give whatever he told you a second thought. Colored—uh, black men are like that."

Rubén doesn't get the irony. Pep thinks he should maybe let up a little. Give the guy a break. The seven-eight will probably offer enough distraction.

22

THE RAGE HE WAS IN WHEN HE SHOOK TIFFANY HASN'T yet abandoned him. The girl's arm bone cracked so loudly Epi's afraid he's dislocated something. She's lying at the foot of the wall, on the other side of the entrance hall. The child, too, is on the floor, stretched out next to the door, lethargic, heedless of all the commotion.

After pulling Tiffany inside and throwing her against the wall, Epi went toward her. She tried to outstare him but couldn't. Epi began to shout at her with all the bitterness he could find inside him. He didn't want to repress or modulate his rage. It didn't matter that its object was Tiffany. It didn't matter who it was. The injustice of the whole thing, in his opinion, exempted him from so much as thinking about restraining himself. Not even when the girl lowered her head and hid her face behind her hair did Epi stop yelling at her or spitting out insults and reproaches.

Adrenaline flooded his mouth. She said nothing. What could she say? After all he'd done for her. The wasted time, the love poured out even in her absence, in the shadows, making the best of a bad deal, looking the other way, always excusing her. And what about him? Like a worthless piece of shit, he'd put up with her rudeness, her contempt, her half-truths, her deceit. He would have bought the whole world for her if he could. He'd defied the opposition of his family, his friends, and everyone else for her sake. And what had he received in exchange? Nothing. Less than nothing.

And now that he'd sacrificed himself for their common future, what did she do? She ran off, she betrayed him, she showed him what a fool he'd been to believe her lies. She couldn't get away with denying so much untruthfulness, all those words and details, those gestures and silences, those mendacious goddamn signals she'd been sending him ever since they broke up, ever since Tanveer took her away from him. No, she couldn't, she couldn't. She had to own up to them. Defend them. Take responsibility for them. At bottom, Epi was only crying out for a just god to descend to earth at once and pass judgment on the outrage committed against him. But failing that, in the absence of such a god, he insisted on a reply that would offer at least the appearance of hope. He wanted a clear definition of the margins and limits of the game, of the masquerade. A lie would have sufficed, but Tiffany couldn't or wouldn't speak it. She remained silent, she who always had a quick comeback, who always knew the answer. Epi shook her so hard that her head was like an empty cardboard box, ready to come loose from her body. The frightened girl began to cry; Epi found the sensation that he had her entirely at his mercy immense, powerful, and intoxicating.

So the perpetually invisible man now has the power to make things move at his whim. He's changed the order of events and the lives of the people around him. This would be a good lesson for all of them. Apparently, he's not as predictable and docile as everyone thinks.

The sense of his power is a lot like being high, combined with the vertigo he feels while he contemplates Tiffany's face, her eyes, her tears, her snotty nose, the blood in one of her nostrils. Nevertheless, Epi would like to know that he can stop; when you're on the Ferris wheel and the rush comes, you need to be holding on to the handrail. But he's not sure he can do it, not sure he can restrain himself in time.

He approaches Tiffany with caution and looks at her closely. He's going to tell her it's passed now, it's over. He gently lifts the girl's chin, and she recites a kind of litany: "Coward, bastard, faggot—"

Epi's hand shoots out again and explodes in a hard slap across her face. When the hand comes back, he can feel it burning. The blow makes a pure and lovely sound that nonetheless almost frightens him. The contact of his hand with that yielding surface, a woman's face. It's absurd; it's as though he wants to do her harm only so that he can then take care of her. It's the endless game the two of them play.

Voices outside the door. Epi turns to answer them. At that moment, Tiffany springs onto his back. He feels her fingernails gouging his face, her teeth tearing at his arm, her weight. For an instant, this too seems enjoyable and exciting, but the pain from the girl's bite makes him instinctively defend himself. With all his strength, he snatches her off of him and dashes her to the floor. And then he starts kicking her: in the legs, in the butt, in the back. When she protects herself with her hands, Epi viciously slaps and punches her, remembering fights in the barrio and the pitiless treatment that was a vanquished enemy's lot. Only when he realizes that she's motionless, sobbing, finally overcome, does he stop.

"You son of a bitch . . ."

Why does she keep insulting him? What is it she hasn't understood? Who started all this? Did he have any other conceivable option? When will Tiffany come to her senses and grasp that all this is for her own good? Is it so hard to see things as they are? Now he wants to caress her. He wants her to say she forgives him. To admit that it was all partly her fault. That he's the one who must forgive her, and not the reverse.

"Epi, for the love of God, open the door."

He recognizes his brother's voice. How different everything would be if Alex had hurried up and arrived sooner, Epi thinks. But now he's no longer sure he wants more characters in this scene. He knows Alex well enough to be certain he'll scold him; he'll tell him he's done everything wrong. He'll tell him to apologize to someone, to put the blame on somebody else, to shut his eyes so tight that when he opens them, everything will have disappeared. But Epi has no intention of opening the door. Nobody can take away his leading role in this film. And no one but him will decide how to end it.

"I'm not letting you in, so just leave me alone."

"Epi, you've spent the whole fucking day sending me messages, telling me to come here, and now—"

"You just said it: the whole fucking day. Now it's too late."

"Don't talk nonsense. Who's with you?"

"Nobody."

Alex turns around and sees Allawi coming up the stairs toward him. With an unequivocal gesture, he cautions the Algerian to keep quiet.

"Is Tiffany in there?"

"No one's in here."

"Fuck, man, haven't you had enough?"

"No! Get out of here! Do you have any cigarettes?"

"No. Yes . . ." Allawi's holding out a pack of Winstons. "How can I give them to you?"

"I'm going to open the door. It's on a chain, so don't try any tricks."

The door opens immediately. Alex can see only his brother's hand. He presses the cigarette pack against Epi's palm but doesn't let go until their hands touch. Alex wants this gesture to convey positive feelings and deep affection, like a sort of electrical charge. Epi closes the door, takes out a cigarette, and lights up. It tastes good.

"Don't let me in if you don't want to, but at least listen to me. Will you listen to me?"

"Talk," Epi replies from inside, wreathing the word in smoke.

"Look, the thing in the bar's under control. Most of the complications came because nobody knew where you were. Salva and I saw a Paki take him out, you understand? The Paki came out of the bathroom and went for him, who knows why, and then he took off running. Salva and I couldn't see him well enough to say any more about what he looked like. Okay? That's what we told the cops. That's what happened. Are you still there?"

Yes, he's still here. It's good news, no doubt, and yet it leaves him with a bitter taste. Although it's absurd to feel disappointed about skating on a thousand years in prison, disappointment is what Epi feels. It seems as though nothing he does has any importance at all; nothing he accomplishes is ever assessed at its just value. Not even killing a man. He has the sudden sensation that he's in the wrong plot. In a story someone else is writing, not him. According to Alex, nobody wants him for Tanveer's murder. If that's so, then what's the sense of staging this episode, shut up in this apartment? What's the sense of this fight with Tiffany? His inability to think clearly returns.

"I don't believe you."

"Well, it's the truth."

Behind Epi, Tiffany has stopped panting. It's obvious that she's listening intently and carefully. And because she is, Epi wants everything made clear. He wants to take back the initiative. *He*'s the hero. *He*'s the lover whom love has driven crazy. It's *his* life he's wrecking.

"But it was me, Alex. You know it was."

"I know, I know, but shut up. I'm not alone. The barber's with me."

"How you doin', man," Allawi interjects. "Listen to your brother. You still have time to get out of this all right."

"I don't care," Epi says, thinking about Tiffany, who's standing behind him. "I don't care about anything. I'm in all the way. If I could take that motherfucker out, I can just as easily end it all. I've got nothing to lose."

"Calm down, Epi, calm down."

"But it was me, it was me who—"

"Christ on a crutch, it was you, it was you, you are the guilty bastard! But enough with that! You want them to put your ass in the slammer for twenty years, or what?"

Silence falls on both sides of the door. Alex and Allawi are glued to it, hoping Epi will react. But he says nothing. There's no sound at all.

"Are you with him, Tiffany?" Alex risks asking.

"Yes, and Percy, too," the young woman shouts.

Allawi sighs and curses. Alex is afraid a neighbor will arrive and show too much interest in why they're talking through an apartment door. He knows that's going to happen sooner or later.

"Holy shit, Epi! What in the hell are you doing? You're fucking up, that's what!" Furious but not surprised, Alex spits out the words. Faced with one good solution and one bad solution, Epi always manages to find a third that's even worse.

Downstairs, the building's main door opens. Allawi leans over the railing and looks down into the stairwell. No, it's not the police. It's a neighbor lady, coming home from shopping. She begins to mount the stairs. Two loaves of bread are sticking up out of the little cart she's pulling. The woman climbs slowly, and the bottles inside her cart clink at every step. Before she reaches the third-floor landing, Allawi's there to meet her.

"Excuse me, señora, but do you know a locksmith? They've locked themselves in, and they can't get out . . ."

"No, I don't know anybody. There was one down the street, but he closed."

"That's all right, ours should be here before too long," Alex says, going along with the farce. "They told me five minutes."

"Thanks anyway, señora. Let me help you with your things."

"No thanks, really, no . . ." the neighbor answers distrustfully. Not for nothing is she a defenseless old lady and he a *Moro* terrorist.

Allawi's aware that he shouldn't give her time to think. He knows by heart that look she's giving him. So familiar is it, in fact, that he no longer minds it. Such poor brutes, these Spaniards, either arrogant or frightened. With full bellies, dead libidos, and hearts withered by solitude. The lady tries to stop him from helping her, but Allawi's already on the stairs leading to the fourth floor, and he's got her cart in his hands. He asks her where she's going, and when the neighbor lady, resigned, designates her fourth-floor apartment, Allawi heads on up at a good clip. Alex has to acknowledge that he was probably right to bring the Algerian along. He remembers some episodes in the adventures of Captain America and the Falcon: "Falcon, why do you always give me bad news when we're fighting?"

asks the Captain, standing back to back with his companion as they face the forces of evil.

Vagi tranquilla, senyora. I que tingui bon dia, Alex says, wishing the old woman a good day in Catalan. His words achieve their object. The lady firmly believes that no Catalan would attack and rape his neighbor, not even through a third party. After she climbs the stairs, Allawi comes back down and the conversation through the door resumes.

"Hey, Epi, listen up," Alex says. "Listen to me, and then think a little, all right? Do you promise? Nobody knows it was you who did that son of a bitch Tanveer. The cops have no fucking idea. They're surprised you disappeared, but that's not a crime. Their focus is on the van. What went on in that van? Is it the one you use for work?"

"Nothing went on. The brakes failed when we were coming down into the city. We left the van up on the road," Epi says, successfully spinning out a half-lie. "I used to lend it to Tanveer sometimes, and—"

"Good, good, it makes no difference. Look, nobody knows who killed him, and the cops won't bust their asses to find out, right? Right. But don't you give them any help, damn it. If they find out you're holding the *Moro*'s girlfriend and her kid, they won't need to ask many questions. It'll be like drawing them a fucking map, don't you get it? On the other hand, if you let them leave and Tiffany keeps her mouth shut, it will be as if nothing happened. You'll go to the *mossos* and tell them the van's life story and that'll be that. They've got nothing. Nothing. You understand me?"

". . ."

"How's the kid? I don't hear him."

"He's asleep."

"Did you understand everything I just told you?"

Epi pauses for a few seconds before answering, "Yes . . . yes . . ." Defeat is swooping down on him. Until this moment he seems not to have thought about the consequences of what's been happening ever since he shut himself up in the toilet in Salva's bar. One thing has led to another, and that other to something else.

Good luck and misfortune keep getting mixed up together. Epi remembers his father saying something like that. Alex can no doubt recall it exactly. The gods mark your path, even though you don't know it.

"I understood everything perfectly."

As always, what his brother says makes sense. If Epi lets Tiffany and the child go and she keeps quiet, it will be as if nothing happened. And if he doesn't give himself away, he'll be free, and without Tanveer. Tiffany will be prepared to forgive him once she grasps that what he did he did for her and for their happiness, hers and his. He'll have all the time in the world to explain to her who Tanveer was and what he spent his time doing when he wasn't with her. He just needs to think clearly, to concentrate on taking the right steps.

"Listen, Epi," the girl says, breaking in on his thoughts. "I won't say anything. I swear to you. At least let Percy leave. He's waking up. Percy, sweetie, everything's all right. Come to Mama."

"Shut up!"

The child is indeed awakening. His mother shelters him in her arms.

"At least Percy, Epi . . . please."

"Epi, can you hear me?"

"Shut up, goddamn it! Both of you, just fucking shut up! I'm trying to think. Let me think! If you keep on talking and talking, how can I think?"

23

HOSTAGE TAKERS ALWAYS COME TO A BAD END. ALEX'S ideas on that are clear. You see it in movies again and again, it's on the TV news, anybody you talk to knows it. The promised airplane is a trap, the negotiator's a cardsharp, your head's about to break, and after you free the hostages, you step outside and someone puts a bullet between your eyes. Moreover, kidnappers and hostage takers are obstinate tightrope walkers who range from innately idealistic to innately stupid. Now, it's true that up to this point, Epi wasn't conscious of having kidnapped anybody. In his mind—before his brother spoke—the entire matter was reduced to a door he didn't want to open.

Tiffany's holding the little boy in her arms, stroking his head as he buries his face in the yielding warmth of her body. Epi turns and sees them. He smiles, but the child pays no attention, and Tiffany remains serious, pretending not to notice him. A few minutes ago, she seemed frightened, but now she's merely alert, and sufficiently stressed to try anything.

"It doesn't have to be this way. None of it does."

"Then let us leave."

"After you listen to me."

"I'm listening to you, but don't you see this is no way to behave? At least let Percy go to your brother."

"You okay, kid?"

The boy doesn't answer. He's still woozy. He turns deeper into his mother's embrace, hiding his little head against her as if he wants to disappear or become part of her, part of her blood and her scent.

"Hey, kid, are you all right? Come on, champ! We're still friends, no? You crazy little guy. We played hard, didn't we? Your boy's got a good strong punch, Tiffany, yes he does. Come on, give it to me."

Epi stretches out one arm, offering his clenched fist to the kid for a knuckle bump, the way he's seen the hard-asses in South American gangs do. With the child in her arms, Tiffany takes a step backward. Contempt and fear, in equal measure, show in her eyes.

"What's up? You're not going to bump with me, Percy? You don't want to bump with me? You don't want us to be friends? Is that it? Are we going to stay mad?"

"He's scared, Epi, and—"

"Please be quiet, Miss. This is strictly between men. No women allowed, right, Percy?"

The guy's not well. Never has been. Tiffany now sees this clearly. He's always been like a soda pop, always getting shaken up one way or another, and now he's about to blow the cap right off the bottle. She'll have to be very careful. As she had to be with her father and even with Tanveer. They're always the same: blind, unpredictable bulls. What they liked yesterday can send them into a rage today. Words they once found flattering they'll take as insults the next time.

"Come on, sweetheart, bump knuckles with Epi. He wants to be your friend."

"Shut up! It has to come from him! It has to be him! He has to do it because he wants to, not because you tell him to."

"Can't you see him, Epi? He's half asleep and scared. He doesn't understand anything. This isn't right, Epi. Let him leave and—"

"Set him on his feet. In front of me."

Epi enjoys making no effort to understand. He's been too weak too long to forget that when you show yourself as you really are, others know how to take advantage of it and use it against you. Like when he was desperate and begged Tiffany not to leave him, when she was already totally in thrall to Tanveer's evil arts, and she petted his face the way you'd pet a dog. Epi hasn't forgotten that. He hasn't been able to, not in all this time.

Tiffany sets Percy on the floor. The kid has trouble keeping his balance. His mother props him up from behind. His little eyes start to close. Epi's sure that all the child wants to do is to go to sleep. To get into his bed and crawl between the sheets, just as Epi used to do when he was that age.

"Come on, sweetheart, bump with Epi."

"It has to be him, Tiffany," Epi repeats, more gently this time.

If only she loved him, if only they lived together far from here, far from all the friends and relatives and acquaintances who think they know everything about them. If only they didn't take drugs or drink. If he had a good job and they lived in a big, pretty house and had kids. *If all that would happen, life would be good*, Epi thinks, while Percy looks at the fist held out level with his eyes. If all that would happen. If they just had the chance, he'd sure know how to take advantage of it now.

"Go on, sweetie . . ."

"It has to be him, goddamn it."

Having recovered a little, the kid's standing on his own, without his mother's help. He looks at Epi, sees the fist, raises his own, and taps the man's knuckles. Epi feels emotion clouding his eyes. He'd love to snort a line right this very moment. He wants to feel strong and see clearly. The unlocalized pain affecting his whole body is worsening. He knows he ought to take the kid's reaction as a sign that everything's going to turn out all right. Even more than that: it demonstrates that the decisions he's made and the attitude he assumed were the right ones. If he hadn't remained firm, if he'd wavered, Tiffany wouldn't be obeying him, and Percy wouldn't want to be his friend.

"Way to go, kid. Look, now we're going to do something, all right? Mama and I have to stay here and talk, but you're going to go with Alex. Do you remember my brother Alex? No? Sure you remember him. He's going to take you to buy some candy, right, Alex? And then you can go home to Grandma and sleep a little more."

The boy nods assent and clings to his mother. Tiffany smiles. Epi raises his voice and shouts through the apartment door: "Percy's coming out, all right?"

Alex answers from the landing. "Perfect. Why don't you let his mother out, too, and be done with all this, Epi?"

"Why don't you fuck off!"

Along with everything else, Alex is in a hurry. He doubts whether he can maintain the situation any longer. Moreover, he's starting to feel his resistance weakening. As soon as he can, he's going to put some tranquillity under his tongue yet again on this shitty fucking day. "Well, come on," he says. "Send him out."

"But you have to buy him candy in that store by the movie theater. You promise?"

"Of course. He can relax. I'll buy him whatever he wants."

Allawi and Alex hear noises coming from the other side of the door, which seems about to open. If that happens and the kid comes out, it will be the beginning of the end. A good way—not the best or quickest way—to start injecting a bit of common sense into all this.

"Don't do anything stupid," Epi warns Tiffany. "The kid's leaving. You don't want to complicate things now."

"Don't worry."

"I just want to talk to you."

"All right."

"I'll explain everything. Then you'll see it all clearly. I'll do a good job of explaining, but you have to let me talk. Tanveer was bad. If you had known what I know about him, fuck, you would have killed him yourself. But I did it. When you kill the cause of the problem, you kill the problem. I just want—"

"Okay, Epi, but I don't want the child to hear all this."

"You're right."

"You let him go and we'll talk calmly, right?"

"I am calm. I'm not crazy, only angry. Don't talk to me as if—"

"Okay, I won't talk to you like that."

"Are you going to say I'm right about everything?"

"No, but the thing is—"

"You're going to say I'm right? You're going to do everything I want?"

"Yes, if you want me to, yes, but—"

"Okay, then lemme see 'em."

"Fuck, Epi, don't push it. The kid's here, and—"

"It was a joke, woman."

Epi smiles from ear to ear, and at the sight of that smile, Tiffany gets scared again. She's had it with his stupid, shitty little games. Of course, it occurs to her to seize her chance and slip through the door when he opens it and, with the help of the people outside, get out of this hell she's in, but if she did such a thing, she knows it would be extremely unlikely to end well. She considers other possibilities. She could hit him on the head with something when his back is turned. Maybe with the ashtray. But it's in the bedroom. She could go and get it. No, it would take too long. Or maybe not. Why not try it? Or while Percy's being liberated, she could raise the shutter, hang down from the window ledge, and drop to the street. Two floors, more or less. Not so high you'd kill yourself, unless you landed wrong. But she'd have to run over to the window, and he'd have time to catch her, and . . .

Epi takes Percy by the hand and opens the door. Tiffany knows she must do something, but she can't even move. She tells herself it's because of the child. But there's no denying that fatalism has settled over her like a cloak. She's resigned, certain that nothing she can do is going to work. She looks at them, hand in hand, like father and son. What a strange sight, however often she may have seen it before, in parks or on walks. At birthday parties. At Epi's mother's apartment. But this time is different: they're kidnapper and hostage. A madman and a bewildered child. And Tiffany herself, the mother, the ex-girlfriend, the other hostage. The little boy turns around and says, "Good-bye, Mommy." Tiffany can't reply. Weeping fills her chest and throat, but she doesn't want either the child or Epi to see her cry. Nor does she care to dwell on the thought that this guy's going to brain her the way he did Tanveer, maybe even with the same hammer. Or that she'll never see her son again, his little face, his hands, his eyes, his way of waking up or walking. Or that she'll never know anything more about him. Or that she won't see him grow up and become a man. Or that now it won't make sense to save the best kisses for anybody. Or that she hasn't been a good mother, no she hasn't. Or that she wasted a lot of time. Or that this will be her last image of her little son: walking away, his back to her, hand in hand with his mother's murderer. Opening a door and disappearing. She can't stop the tears; they're already coursing down her cheeks.

24

ALEX EMBRACES THE CHILD AND THEN GIVES HIM A superficial inspection, tousling his hair, looking for marks or scratches. He appears to be all right. It's true he seems very drowsy; maybe he just woke up. Alex asks him how he feels, but Percy doesn't answer. He looks like he's about to burst into tears. His entire face is pouting. He starts to turn toward the door to take refuge with his mother but realizes that's impossible.

"Say, barber, why don't you take him out and buy him some candy?"

"Candy?"

"Yeah, fuck, caramels, nougat, sweets, whatever they've got."

"Okay. Come on, kid. But wouldn't you rather go yourself? Epi might listen to me."

"He's my brother. I'm staying."

"All right." Allawi doesn't seem interested in disputing the point. "We'll go buy some candy, and then I'll take Percy home. His grandmother has to be worried about him. I'll come right back here."

"Sounds good to me. But go on now. The fewer people who see there's a kid involved in this, the better. Buy him some caramels, some nougat . . ."

"Yes, Alex. I got that."

"The store's near the movie theater. Get him some candy and stuff like that."

Allawi scoops up Percy an instant before the pout disintegrates into weeping. The barber tries to soothe the child by whispering in his ear, telling him about the pile of candy he's going to be holding in his hands in just a few minutes. Percy says nothing. They descend the stairs and go out into the street. The sunlight surprises them and activates the energy stored in Allawi's legs. The time spent on that landing upstairs has stiffened his muscles and darkened his mood. Almost with pleasure, he quickens his pace. They're practically at the corner; from there to the candy store is only a five-minute walk at most. Then however long it takes to get the kid home.

The flashing red and blue lights of a police car parked on the corner tell him that things are about to get complicated. There is, he remembers, more than one problem. Two policemen are walking on the sidewalk toward the apartment building Allawi just left. There can be no doubt about where they're going. That guy in the Citroën or maybe one of the neighbors must have called the *mossos*, and they, with their usual diligence, have come to preserve order. Without stopping, Allawi picks Percy up and carries him on one arm. Taking out his cell phone with his other hand, he looks for the number and dials it. While the rings succeed one another, Allawi ponders the question of whether or not he's really interested in returning to that apartment, which is about to become fiendishly crowded. He skips Alex's voice mail and presses the redial button. This time he has more luck.

"What's up?"

"You've got cops in the street downstairs."

"Holy shit!"

"I'll be back soon. Stay calm."

Alex steps over to the stairs and believes he can make out a scarlet-and-blue reflection in the glass of the building's main door. He's not mistaken in believing that the police want to find out which window the girl was calling for help from. But what Alex doesn't know is that they're going to get this information quickly from the Citroën driver, who called the *mossos* and has been waiting for them across the street.

So in spite of all he's been through, Alex believes he has more time than he actually does. He looks attentively at the door and immediately regrets it. He knows that if he detects a face in the wood, some capricious contour reminiscent of a profile, he's not going to be able to stop staring at it, to keep from watching it almost come alive. He pats his pocket. Then he puts the tranquilizer under his tongue and drinks from his little water bottle. He can't lose his cool, not precisely *now*. He closes his eyes. The image of something he's seen in the wood of the apartment door has remained as though stamped in his brain. That edge forms a snout and a chin, and this . . .

"Epi, listen to me. It's important. Epi? Can you hear me?"

But his brother doesn't answer. It's possible that he's standing right next to the door; however, it's also possible that he's at the other end of the apartment, killing his girlfriend. Why not just start running and abandon them to their fate? Alex tells himself, without conviction, that he's done more for Epi than Epi would ever have done for him. But he, Alex, made a promise. To Mama. He swore an oath to her. So let's recapitulate: He's done everything he could. He concedes this point. He's tried to think clearly; he's coordinated his version of the murder with Salva's; and he's gotten the cops off their backs, or so he thought. They may well have followed him, but wouldn't it have been much worse if he hadn't tried to come here and talk some sense into Epi? At least he managed to get the child released from the apartment. He's afraid, he is most definitely afraid. Then why not take off? If the cops come, he's not going to be able to do anything. Except maybe stop them from killing his brother. In the presence of witnesses, those people control themselves; they're not the animals they turn into when they're alone with a suspect. My God, how could all this have happened? What diabolical course of events has brought the two Dalmau boys to this place? Where are the rest of the people in his world? Why is there no one behind him, no mother or father to support him? And no one at his side, a woman, a companion, someone to salve his wounds, to advise him to go back home and leave Epi to a destiny that Epi and Epi alone has forged for himself? All Alex has in life is on the other side of that door: a crazy, homicidal brother, and the girl Alex fantasizes about when he wants to ejaculate rapidly and well.

The cops are in the building. They've opened the door and entered the lobby. With all the gear they're carrying—handcuffs, nightsticks, cell phones, gold insignia, all as though copied from a child's police costume—they make an unmistakable noise.

"Epi, listen to me. Do you hear me? The cops are here. Let Tiffany come out right now, and nothing will happen. She can just say you two were in there together and that's all. Tiffany, can you hear me?"

The sound of Tiffany's voice restores his calm. She replies that she thinks his proposal's a good idea. Alex hears nothing more from the other side of the door. He doesn't hear Tiffany trying to make Epi understand that letting her go is the best solution for everyone. For him, for her, for both of them. They can leave together, she says, or better yet, they can wait for the police to knock, and then she'll open the door, half-dressed, and it will be obvious that the whole thing's a mistake, an embarrassing mess they've wound up in because of some evil-tongued, attention-seeking, officious neighbor. Epi doesn't reply. He's sitting silently on a chair next to the door, staring at the tips of his sneakers. Tiffany goes over to him, and when he notices she's so close he could touch her, he reacts. They gaze into each other's eyes, but Tiffany can't read anything in Epi's.

Once again, they're two deep, black holes. She asks if he heard the plan and then repeats it to him: when the police come, I answer the door and tell them it's a mistake, and then they go away. But although by now Epi's looking at her and listening to what she's saying, he continues to make no reply.

The police officers are climbing the last flights of stairs. Alex straightens up and heads for the landing on the floor above. From there, he can look down into the stairwell and see without being seen. Pep and Rubén walk up to the apartment door and ring the bell once, twice, three times. No one answers. The policemen look at each other. Maybe they've got the wrong door. One of them tells his partner to try the other apartment. With any luck, someone's home, he says. But Alex doubts it. Considering the commotion that's been taking place on the landing, if anybody's in the other third-floor apartment, they'd surely have given signs of life by now.

"Rubén . . . do you hear anything?"

Rubén shakes his head. Alex wonders what they'll do next if they can't find anybody home on this floor. If someone called in a complaint, the cops can't just leave without further investigation. If they're here just because they've been following him, it makes no sense that they wouldn't look for him on every floor. Whatever the case may be, he has to keep quiet until he's had enough time to relax and think clearly. Maybe the best idea would be to go down and talk to them. Persuade them to let him try to reason with his brother. Explain to them that it's a jealous argument, a simple lovers' quarrel that has nothing to do with Tanveer or anything else. But Alex is very nervous. He shuts his eyes, but that makes everything much worse. They're back. At critical moments, they're always so punctual . . . His medication will start to take effect very soon, but in the meanwhile . . . He feels presences surrounding him. They smell like old people, like damp wood, like corpses, saints, and demons.

Suddenly Alex hears a click behind him that dissolves his visions into nothing. He opens his eyes and springs back instinctively from the railing, over which he's been observing the policemen. A neighbor, apparently lost in thought, steps out of his apartment with a bunch of keys in his hand. He locks the door, and when he turns around, the sight of Alex surprises him. He utters an involuntary, astonished, irrepressible shout.

"You scared the hell out of me! What do you want? Who are you looking for?"

Alex tries to reply, but while he's searching for the words, he can tell from the neighbor's face that at least one of the policemen has appeared behind him. The cop speaks to the neighbor in Catalan: "*Passi, senyor, passi. No es preocupi de res, senyor. Passi, si us plaus . . .*"

The neighbor obeys the officer—Rubén—who's taken his pistol out of its holster. When the man passes in front of him, Rubén lowers the weapon, effectively hiding it. Alex faces him and, without knowing exactly why, puts his hands up. At this point, the policeman shows him the pistol, as if the effect has produced the cause and not vice versa. From the next landing down, Pep abruptly calls out: "What's going on up there, Rubén?"

"Bet you can't guess who's here."

"Today's most sought-after brother?"

"Bingo."

"Come on down, both of you."

Alex is convinced they're not looking for him. They don't know a thing. This *mosso* is probably even more scared than he is, and that's why he pulled out his gun when it was completely unnecessary. As if reading Alex's thoughts, Rubén puts the pistol away and tries to ease the tension in the air: "Don't you know we've been looking for you all day?"

"No. I've been to the police station twice today. It's not like I'm hiding out," Alex replies crossly.

When he reaches the third-floor landing, Alex grasps how bad it looks for Epi to be playing possum on the other side of the door. The whole affair has become too complicated, Alex thinks. It has to be brought to a close, quickly, and the consequences controlled insofar as possible.

"Well, what's going on here?"

The proper question. This cop, at least—unlike the other, who's remained behind Alex—has no apparent desire to perform feats of heroism. What he wants to do is to resolve the matter right away, without too much noise.

"My brother's in there."

Pep nods interrogatively toward the door of the apartment where Epi and Tiffany are. Alex confirms the policeman's assumption.

"Is he alone?"

"No, he's with his girlfriend."

"Right."

"His friend was murdered, and he's scared. He doesn't have any prior arrests. It's just that he's confused . . . I was talking to them when you and your partner arrived. They were on the point of coming out. Let me talk to him some more and everything will be fine."

"All right. Tell him to come on out. We'll take him down to the station and ask him some questions, and then we'll see."

Alex silently vows to get Epi out of that apartment, whatever it takes. He makes himself promises, just as he used to do when he was a boy. If he successfully jumped the vaulting horse in gym class or held his breath for a minute underwater in the swimming pool, he would pass the exam, or the girl would be his. If he succeeds. If he manages to get Epi out of there. If this all ends well.

But when he speaks, nobody replies. The silence thickens. The policemen look at each other. With a certain brusqueness, they move Alex out of the way and replace him at the door. They identify themselves as *mossos* and demand entrance. Seconds like eternities pass. There's no sound, and then, suddenly, Alex's foot starts tapping against the railing. Pep urges him to cut it out. Alex withdraws his foot from the metal structure. There's not much more he can do. His temples are thumping against the cotton walls that the tranquilizer has been erecting inside his head. But in the midst of the ambient disaster, he discerns it clearly. Amid the shouts and footsteps of the policemen, the pistols and the radios with their droning, metallic messages, there it is. Its outline stands out on the door. Alex has seen it now, and he won't be able to stop seeing it. It's a Donald Duck silhouette, and it's going to entrance him for a while; all at once, everyone and everything else will seem to shift into the background, and that image will become for him like *Christ walking on water,* as his mother would say, if she were still alive, if she were here, and if she would ever have been given to blasphemy.

25

"TIME EATS UP TIME," EPI'S FATHER USED TO SAY. EPI remembers that now and thinks it's true. Time, it seems to him, has an almost physical presence. It's a runaway animal made of minutes, which in turn are stones, bones, teeth. Every second matters so much it hurts. Every moment is the last.

He thinks Tiffany won't or can't listen to him. She's afraid, and it seems that frightening her more is the only way to make her understand she has nothing to be frightened of. He has no wish to do her harm. In reality, he never has. Now he knows that. The glimpse of her elusive eyes through the tangles of her hair is enough for him.

"Tiffany, you're not listening to anything I'm saying, are you? Until we talk and you know everything, and I mean everything, nobody's leaving here. Nobody. So I don't want any more nonsense, all right? Is that so hard? And if you fuck me around too much, remember one thing: I don't care what I do. If I've come this far, it's because I know I can't turn back. I don't care what I do, you understand me? The easiest thing would be to make a clean sweep. That way, all of you will stop fucking me around."

She understands him, and how. She tells him so without speaking. She whimpers so he'll know she's in defeat. From the very first moment, she's misjudged this situation. She underestimated Epi and the prevailing circumstances—the safe house, the shortage of neighbors, the time of day, Tanveer's death—and failed to see how serious things would become. Now she needs to be cautious, she needs to be smart; Epi's on the alert, and her life's probably in danger. The girl perceives her body in a way she's never perceived it before. An entity with concrete dimensions that she has to protect with the greatest care. It's as if there were a time bomb in the room, and she must make sure Epi doesn't touch anything that will make it go off. She notices her toes. She notices her weak stomach, transparent to the touch of a knife blade. She pictures her defenseless face, exposed to a slash, a blow, her skull caving in like plaster under the force of a madman. She'd love to be able to draw a circle, place herself inside it, and disappear. But the chalk she must use is invisible, her drawing must be perfect, and she must retrace without tremor or hesitation the line of points that she and she alone has to be able to read. With Epi, she needs to use the right words, make the necessary promises, execute the flawless caresses.

"Are you going to listen to me?" Epi asks insistently.

She nods her head. She's going to listen to him. She's going to tell him he's right. She's going to promise him eternal love. This time she's going to do it properly, all of it.

"Where shall I start?" Epi says aloud, as though he wants Tiffany to tell him what he should say. "You know I'm no good at talking."

He's sitting cross-legged on the floor in front of her. The image seems strange to Tiffany; it's like Epi's about to teach her some sleight of hand. Nothing in my left. Nothing in my right. Look, see for yourself. Now a knife will appear, and with it I'll cut your throat. Guess the card: one chance out of a hundred. Tiffany calculates the distance between them. She assesses whether or not she could avoid a sudden fit of rage directed at herself. What are her possibilities of parrying a blow or a knife thrust? None, she thinks. She'd be safer on her feet, but she's afraid Epi will get mad if she stands up. So she embraces her folded legs and presses them forcefully against her body, as if trying to make herself small enough to vanish through one of those open doors in the baseboards that mice in cartoons use to frustrate cats and brooms. Not far from Epi, who's still trying to find the words, she sees something that fills her with anxiety and dread. It's the mountain-climbing rope that was in the wardrobe earlier and is now lying in coils on the other side of the room. When did Epi take it out? With that rope he could tie her up. With that rope he could strangle her.

"Sometimes a person doesn't see things as they are. Tanveer was part sorcerer, you know? That's not a stupid thing to say, it's true. He enchanted people. I can't explain it, but it probably happened to you. And his name wasn't even Tanveer Hussein. His mother told my mother that one day. At home one afternoon. His birth certificate says his name is José María. But it's true that his father was a *Moro* from Morocco."

"I knew that about his name . . ."

Epi rises to his feet and goes from one side of the room to the other. He looks somewhat calmer now that she's listening to him.

"He didn't love you. He never loved you. He saw you and wanted to have you because having you is like having a lucky charm. Do you see what I'm saying? It's hard to explain. When a guy has you beside him, he feels like everything's going to work out fine."

"My mother didn't think so, and neither did yours."

"But I did. To me, you were like a guardian angel. That's it: like an angel that doesn't believe in God or heaven. When you were with me, you—"

"We were good together, weren't we?"

"Yes."

"I always end up destroying what I love the most, Epi. It's always the same story. I'm crazy. They should lock me up. Send me to a funny farm. Or maybe to a psychologist. I could get it all out, all the stuff I carry around inside, the stuff with my father, with Percy."

"We were a couple."

"Yes, fuck, I'm very sorry. Forgive me. I know I treated you bad," Tiffany ventures, praying to the God and heaven she apparently disbelieves in that Epi doesn't grow too suspicious of the new role she's playing in this production.

"We used to make plans. You remember?"

Voices that aren't yet shouts come from the other side of the door. Epi figures Alex and Allawi are getting impatient. He says they're pretending to be the police, but Tiffany's not so sure about that. If she could just tell them to wait a few minutes, if she could let them know that everything seems to be going well now, that Epi only wants to blow off some steam, and then he'll let her leave and they can come in and haul him away to prison to rot for the next many years while she goes around telling everyone about her adventure, describing it on TV, in the newspapers, to friends and neighbors in the barrio.

"Shut the fuck up!" Epi yells at the door. "If you keep bothering me, I swear to God I'll do something crazy and we'll all leave here feet first!"

The voices fall silent. Something changes, all of a sudden, in the girl's spirits. Epi's not acting as unconsciously as he seems to be. He's got some kind of plan. It could include killing her and/or killing himself. Maybe he only wants her to listen to him before he slaughters her. Maybe her life can't be saved. Nevertheless, fear inspires her. "Leave us alone," the girl shouts. "We're talking. Nothing else is happening. Go away from here, and the two of us will come out in a little while. Leave us alone. Go away."

Epi smiles. He likes Tiffany's new attitude, even though he doesn't trust it. He's put everything on the line for her once already. What was it his father used to say that annoyed his mother so much? He can't remember it clearly; it escapes when he tries to keep it on his tongue. He says, "It won't be so easy."

"Why won't it be easy? Why can't it be? You're talking to me. Didn't you want to explain everything? Then explain. I'm listening. This doesn't have to be the end; it can be a beginning. I realize a lot of things now." At this point, Tiffany believes, she has to talk and talk. "I realize I've been blind. I didn't see anything. I didn't see who was good and who was bad. Who loved me and who didn't."

"I loved you so much . . ."

"And I loved you, too, in my way . . ."

"I used to wait for something, anything: a telephone call, a meeting in the street. I'd see you everywhere and I'd close my eyes and I'd keep seeing you."

"I'm sorry, Epi, I'm so sorry."

"And I didn't understand what was happening. I'd see the two of you go off, and I'd—"

"I was blind. I don't know what came over me. You were what I needed. You calm me down. You always did. But I fought against that. You satisfied me in every way. In bed, on the street."

Well, in that case, Tiffany, Epi thinks, *why did what happened happen? Why the endless humiliation?* Now it's starting to come back to him, the quote his father used to recite. Alex even learned it by heart. How did it go? *The power of speech is granted to the woman, who is herself the gift of the gods . . .* What came after that? *In the woman's presence, the hero—any hero—feels confused, drained of energy.* Epi strikes out at the ambient air, like a boxer blinded by fatigue and anger. Something about how *the woman has false words in her mouth and the temperament of a thief.*

"Her words cast spells . . ."

"What are you saying, Epi?"

"Nothing."

"Shit, don't scare me."

"So I satisfied you? I fucked you good?"

"Yes, yes . . ."

"Well, then . . ."

"Well, then, what?"

"My father always used to tell us stories. It was as if everything that happened to us had already been written down; it was part of a story told long ago."

"I really wish I'd known him."

"Why?" Epi asks, squashing what sounded like a pleasant fantasy. *So he could fuck you the way yours did?* he thinks. But where did those other words come from, the ones from the past? It's as if the tension he's under has let loose words that have been shut up inside his head for a long time. Words his father said, words his brother said, like neon lights Epi's always kept switched off, and now the recent short circuit is turning them on. For a moment, they serve to illuminate the scene. *No, I can't believe her. She's lying, I'm sure she's lying.* He looks away from the girl's gaze. He doesn't want to see what he sees. He doesn't want to read her thoughts. All at once he feels the way he used to when he was sick and his mother would bathe his eyes with salty water to get the sleep out of them.

The thing is, Tiffany's not Tiffany anymore. He looks at her tattooed blue eyelids, and they're no longer the distinguishing mark of the pharaohs; now he sees them as the clumsy work of a clown who doesn't know how to make people laugh. Likewise, Tiffany's warm and friendly attitude is a fraud, one more in a long line. Like her words, which she uses to snare his. False words, and this time he's sure he knows what they mean, every one of them. Liars all. He's not even listening to them. The goddess he imagined at his side forever now seems to him ugly, ridiculous, clumsy. He peers into her eyes and sees only eyes. And he thinks about the words that apparently meant different things, depending on whether you looked at them from one side or another. How to explain that mystery? Why didn't "I love you" mean "I love you"? Why did "Leave me" signify "Wait for me"? Why was "Get out of my life" equivalent to "Stay here"?

"Don't waste any more words. You're talking so much, it's making me tired."

Tiffany shuts up. She'll do whatever he asks her to. But suddenly, he wants nothing from her. Oh, maybe he'll bang her one more time to break the spell once and for all, to see her as the bad magic trick she is, full of blood and fluids and shit inside. He no longer wants her to love him, because by a strangely lucid insight, he sees that he can never know whether or not her love is true. He'd have to keep the woman at his side always just to assume that, to guess it, to deduce it from each and every detail of her being. No, he doesn't want anything from her, Epi tells himself as he turns his eyes away. He goes to the window and looks down at the street through the gaps in the shutter. He sees the police car, and it's a relief: at last, all is lost.

He's standing with his back to her. Now, if she should start running for the door, he wouldn't stop her. In fact, he'd really love it if she would disappear, or better yet, if she'd never been there at all. If that poisoned gift had never crossed his threshold. He'd like her to die. He'd like to kill her while she looks at him and begs his forgiveness because everything was her fault. The key that opened up paradise was the same that bolted prison doors and sealed graves and locked dungeons. All he had to do was to think about her father, about Percy's father, about Tanveer, about himself. He'd kill her, and no one would notice. He'd bury her somewhere, and at that precise instant, his life would begin again. The streets of the barrio would be balmy boulevards, not pitfalls or ambushes. Friends, bars, buses, and cars would gleam in the sunshine. There are so many things to do once you've found the road to freedom. But when he turns around, Tiffany's still there in front of him. She's risen to her feet, and she's waiting for him to say something.

"Ask me to let you leave."

"Please let me leave."

"Not in that tone of voice. Purr like you used to do when we made love and you pretended to like it. Use that voice, please."

"Let me go, Epi, please, don't humiliate me. I never pretended to—"

"Ask me to kill you."

"No . . ."

"Masturbate in front of me. Standing up, right now. Do it and I'll see what to do with you. Kill you or open the door."

Tiffany watches Epi put his hand in his pants pocket. He shows her the knife handle, which suffices to remove all her doubts about whether or not he's serious.

26

PEP'S ABOUT READY TO CALL FOR BACKUP, EVEN THOUGH he understands why Rubén doesn't want to. There will be time for that, his partner's gesture seemed to say. They can't kick the door down. It's too stout, and it appears to be double-locked besides. However that may be, the decision is his, not Rubén's, and the consequences will be his as well. Up until now, something that seemed like luck was lending them a hand. They started off by losing the bait, and then, by sheer chance, they found it again on the end of their fishing line. Now their catch is in that apartment. With a girl.

Pep's been trying to make sense of the case, trying to arrive at a mental image of it in which all the elements fit. The guy in the apartment is the one who wasted the *Moro*, and the woman must be mixed up in it somehow. That's what he thinks, even though he finds it difficult to imagine how a woman could be mixed up with the rest of that garbage, with beating up prostitutes and raping them. As a matter of fact, working such cases is always like sticking your hands into a garbage can. And once you've done that, everything—however perfumed and lovely—gets stained and soiled and ends up rotting when exposed to light. Drugs, success, violence, ambition, money. At bottom, all circles of the same desperation, like drowning in a whirlpool.

Nothing can be heard from inside the apartment. At one point, the girl called to them and told them to go away, but she was obviously speaking under duress. Moreover, it's possible she had nothing to do with the murder of Tanveer Hussein. They could be dealing with yet another creep in a long line of creeps eager for a kind of cruel notoriety and intent on making their girlfriends pay for it. Then again, maybe it's a case of score-settling. What if Epi's frightened because his buddy's just been killed and he could be next, as his brother suggested? But in that case, wouldn't it be a much better idea just to disappear? Or maybe he's shut himself up in this apartment simply because he's so terrified.

The presence of more policemen won't bend Epi's will or make him free his hostage. But if this mess ends disastrously, it's a sure thing that Pep will be asked why he didn't notify the police station and ask for backup. He and Rubén have to act fast and prevent the worst from happening.

"Does your brother carry a weapon?"

"No, no."

"Do you know that, or are you making an assumption?"

"I know it. He's a good kid. He's very peaceful. I don't know what could have happened."

"Is this what you call being peaceful?" Rubén interjects. "He's got himself in a fine mess. Does he use drugs?"

"No, no. He smokes. Hashish. But he doesn't use anything that would make him do something like this."

"Rubén, I'm going to make the call."

"Don't call them yet. Wait a few more minutes, and then, if you want to, you can ask for help, but I think the two of us can do it by ourselves."

"Let me talk to him again," Alex adds.

"You can try, but it looks to me like he's not going to listen to anybody."

Rubén steps closer to Pep. A premonition watered with the venom of silence is growing larger and larger inside Rubén's head. He could have taken care of this matter by now. Pep's radio signals a response to his recent request for communication.

"Listen, we've got a five-seven-two here. Can you send someone to open a door for me?"

"Pep, is that you? It's Natalia."

"Hello, Nat, how you doing?"

"Probably better than you two. Is it very urgent?"

"I don't know. I think so."

"I'll send you a squad car and a shrink as soon as I can."

"All right."

"Oh, by the way, Pep, they caught the guy who killed the *Moro*."

"Are you serious?"

"Yes, they're putting him in tomorrow's lineup. He's a Paki with priors. A nasty piece of work."

Pep turns toward Alex. There's no need to tell him anything, because Pep knows perfectly well that Alex has overheard the conversation. And now the elder Dalmau brother is sure they're not going to pin Tanveer's murder on Epi; if he lets the girl leave, the incident will come to nothing. It's true, however, that Alex is standing with his head pressed against the wall and his eyes closed, trying in vain to stop hearing Donald Duck's voice imploring him to look again, to keep on watching him. Alex has to concentrate. He has to know what to do. He has to choose the appropriate words, the surest path to Epi's feelings.

"Epi, Epi, it's me again. Please listen to me . . ."

Meanwhile, Rubén approaches his partner and says something in his ear. Pep immediately acknowledges that he's committed a rookie error, and Rubén goes down the stairs like a shot. His purpose is to take up a position in front of the building and foil any attempt to escape through one of the apartment windows. The distance from window to ground isn't great enough to deter Epi from taking a chance, dropping to the street, and getting away.

In the entrance, Rubén encounters the returning Allawi, who's seen the *mossos'* squad car parked on the sidewalk outside and the curious onlookers gathered around, unsure of where or what to look at. Allawi was afraid he wouldn't be able to get back inside the building, and now, in the very doorway, he runs into a cop.

"You can't come in here."

"I live here," Allawi lies.

"At the moment, you can't come in."

"But . . ."

Rubén asks Allawi not to insist. The *mosso*'s in a great hurry—too great to continue arguing with this supposed neighbor—to get himself under the windows and prevent, if need be, the flight of the suspect. Rubén knows Allawi's going to enter the building as soon as he walks away. And this is just what the barber does, having held the door open with his foot during the entire discussion.

One of the two windows of the apartment where Epi and Tiffany are still has its shutters lowered. The other window has one shutter raised. Rubén believes all four shutters were down when he and Pep arrived. Maybe the suspect's already flown the coop. Rubén looks up and down the street, just in case he might be in time to see someone running, when he realizes he has no cause for worry on that account. Admittedly, there's that raised shutter, but he can tell from the glass panes that the window itself remains closed, and he knows such windows can be closed only from inside. "Brilliant deduction," Rubén says aloud, cheered up by his own sarcasm. Now all he can do is wait for events to unfold. There was a time when he would have much preferred being in the middle of the action, but ever since that incident in La Seu d'Urgell, he's become much more cautious. He almost wished the suspect would exit by the apartment door and Pep would arrest him.

"Maybe we are few in number," Rubén hears himself say, as if he were being recorded by a high-definition video camera as part of a TV series or some film about policemen committed to the defense of law-abiding citizens.

Epi still hasn't answered. Pep inwardly berates himself for being stupid. What's happening to him? Stupid, yes, stupid and slow. Over his radio, Natalia assures him that they're doing all they can. Then she immediately calls him back to tell him that the locksmith on duty is fortunately in the barrio and will be with them very shortly. Allawi has silently placed himself behind Alex, who recognizes him without even needing to turn around. He's turned out to be a good friend, a loyal guy.

"Epi, I know you can hear me. Think the situation over a little. Don't be afraid. Nothing's going to happen to either of you. You'll be protected. The police are worried on your account, but they've assured me that nothing will happen to you or Tiffany. They've arrested the guy who murdered Tanveer. You all have nothing to be afraid of. The police will protect you."

Pep receives a call from Rubén, who tells him that the two subjects are still inside the apartment. He further reports that he sees no movement and hears nothing. He doesn't think anyone's going to escape through the window, not unless they feel like breaking a leg.

"Epi, Tiffany . . . Come on out and that'll be the end of it. Don't make things more complicated. It's all been a misunderstanding."

Pep's radio crackles. He's informed that the locksmith is already at the door of the building. The policeman asks Allawi to go down and let him in, and Allawi complies. The murmuring that becomes audible when he opens the door comes from the rising number of people waiting outside to see what will happen. A small man carrying a toolbox mounts the stairs to the third-floor landing and presents himself to Pep. After praising the coincidence that placed him so close at hand, the locksmith sets to work. Allawi has to step back, and Alex watches with some relief as the guy with the white mustache cautiously but resolutely thrusts a screwdriver into Donald's eye. As the screws in the door hinges are removed, one after another, it dawns on Pep that this affair is straddling the line between a glorious success and a botched job. If the guy's armed, it could be a real bummer. He steps back from the door and calls the station again.

"Any news about backup?"

"A squad car's on the way. They've already left. They'll be however long it takes to get from here to there."

Pep gestures to the locksmith, indicating that he shouldn't go so fast, but the job's almost finished. With great difficulty, he holds the door in place to keep it from falling off its hinges. Alex is going to make one more try, maybe his last.

The silence snaps like a bone. Tiffany screams, calling out for help. Pep thinks about his mother, about his boyfriend, about the dinner he's been invited to this very night. A silly melody runs through his head, adding a soundtrack to his excited state, caused in equal parts by fear and by the necessity to act. Allawi retreats farther when the locksmith backs away from the door, aware that the last hinge is liable to give way any second now. Pep pushes Alex against the railing, takes his pistol out of his holster, and tenses his entire body. Alex stares at the officer's prominent jaw and intense eyes, which are fixed on the door that's about to come down. Jamelia screams her sister's name, and the sound of her voice enters from the street, passes through the front door, and climbs the stairs.

Alex knows he's failed. As has happened so many other times, he's seeing the whole thing from outside. He hasn't been able to get his brother out of that apartment. He's been three steps behind ever since the early morning, in Salva's bar. He could have stopped Epi at that moment, and he didn't do it. He could have been shrewder about figuring out Epi's hiding place. He could have hesitated less, during a shorter period of time. He could have done more for Epi. He could have listened to him more and not humiliated him so much by pointing out everything he did badly or did at the wrong time or simply didn't manage to do. He could have gone after Papa when he went away. He could have stayed with his mother when she became ugly and dirty, when she was dying.

His head fills up with images. Of the two of them going with their father to buy picture cards in the Mercat de Sant Antoni, or that time at school when Epi got his face split open while defending Alex, or that other time when he didn't and remained hidden in the darkened classroom, waiting for the fight to be over. He remembers the promises he made to his mother regarding his little brother, and he remembers her, young and pretty, coming to pick them up at school or drying their hair with a pink towel that smelled like soap. He remembers laughing fit to die at the movies the four of them would see together on Saturday nights. The one about the bumbling police detective, and the one about the mountain lion that escapes and no one can find. When Alex learned to ride a bicycle, Epi and the other kids from the street, who were theoretically holding him upright on the saddle, ran ahead and showed him their hands in an uncontrollable expression of joy. That same day, his parents hung wallpaper on the walls of their home. Alex remembers long rolls of paper on the dining room table, cans of glue, thick brushes that seemed to click their tongues every time they were applied to the back of the wallpaper.

What can he do with all that? Here he's got a guy with a pistol, and in there he's got his brother and Tiffany, alive or dead, he doesn't know, not in either case. He can try to stop the policeman and go in first himself. He can do that. Or at least try. He sees the locksmith give the policeman an unequivocal nod, move away from the door, and go down three or four stairs, obliging Allawi to go down a few more himself.

A good push is all the door needs to make it fall. And at this point, Alex decides to be a man of action and, though many years too late, confront Helio. More clumsily than adroitly, he shoves Pep against the wall and slams into the door, breaking its remaining hinge and precipitating everything, as the valiant Hector—the best of men, according to his father—would have done, had he been there when it all came down.

27

A FEW MINUTES BEFORE ALEX'S SURGE THROUGH THE door, Epi crossed the room in Tiffany's direction. As he did so, she thought without much conviction that he was going to escort her out of the apartment. But she also feared that he was coming toward her with the single objective of killing her, of ending it all. Epi wasn't carrying anything in his hands, so if he wanted to take her life, he was going to have to strangle her. She tried to read something in Epi's face, but in vain. He avoided her eyes. Obviously, he was playing with her. He'd kept her standing there, fulfilling her part of the deal, and now he was making it clear to her that it hadn't sufficed, that the performance had bored him.

Epi was drunk with the power bestowed on him by his conviction that he'd become unpredictable and intimidating. It can't be said that he was following a preconceived plan, because he'd always been very bad at that sort of thing. It had simply, suddenly happened. Like a flash, as though inspired, he knew what to do next. Everything, except for that, remained in darkness. Persons, objects, words. It was like one of the games on his computer. You found the object that allowed you to open the door, ascend to a higher level, trigger mass destruction all around you.

A few seconds earlier, he'd understood how the huge ruckus he'd caused ought to end. He couldn't bring the most important day of his life to a close by simply offering a few apologies. Or by opening the door and letting Alex and everyone else fix the mess in their way. No, this day had to end with something that would galvanize its memory forever and project an image many, many years into the future. He was going to renounce life, having children, making money. And in return, the world should miss him. Afterward, if it wanted to, the universe could begin again, reset the pieces, adapt to the new order of things, but from now on, nothing would be the same in the lives of those who knew him.

It was so bizarre for such an object—a practically new climbing rope—to be there, in that apartment, that it absolutely had to mean something.

As Epi walks back and forth, Tiffany watches in terror. *He's got some idea in his head, that's for sure,* she thinks. When he passes close to her, he keeps his eyes averted. The girl gets up to go and hide in the bedroom. Epi doesn't stop her. She figures that if she disappears from his immediate field of vision, maybe he'll forget about her. But barely a few seconds later, he enters the bedroom behind her. He's holding that climbing rope in his hands. Tiffany looks into his eyes again. This time they meet hers. They're not black holes. They don't say anything bad. To her surprise, Epi throws her one end of the rope. It lands on the bed beside her.

"Come and help me."

"Why? What are you going to do?"

"Tie the rope around the feet of the wardrobe. Come on, hurry up."

Tiffany senses that Epi's plan is to let himself down from one of the windows. The relief of knowing she's not going to be a murder victim activates her. She picks up the end of the rope and tries to help him, but not very competently. Nevertheless, the two of them pass the rope around the wardrobe's four wooden feet, and Epi ties a triple knot.

"Are we going to escape, Epi? Is that what we're going to do?"

He doesn't answer. He could, but today he's discovered, among other things, that thoughts and desires, as well as dreams, are stillborn as soon as they're formed in words. He prefers to keep Tiffany's attention fixed on each and every one of his movements, like a rare and precious possession to take along to the next world. He leaves the bedroom, intent on performing his new chores. He moves quickly and efficiently. His first thought is to open the window, but when he sees the cop keeping watch in the street, he decides to invert the order of his actions. Back in the bedroom, he knots the end of the rope around his neck, the closest thing to a tie he'll ever wear in his life. He looks at Tiffany, and although he no longer knows what it is that he feels for her, he figures he ought to tell her good-bye.

"You can leave after I jump."

In a certain way, Epi expects something from Tiffany. Some words, some final gift. Something he can take with him. And the girl's tempted to cooperate. What he said has surprised her. Her first impulse is to dissuade him, but something stops her. The wish that he'd kill himself is immediately stronger than any desire she may have to find another solution for this impasse. Let him jump and break his neck; nothing but good can come of it. Tiffany's silence irritates Epi more and more with each passing second. There she is, standing in a corner, her face soiled with tears and sweat, dust and panic, far, very far from the panther that paraded her elegant silhouette through the streets and bars of the barrio, and far from the naked body Epi used to imagine as a big jar filled with warm oil, with perfume, with future children, with never-ending, never-cloying pleasure. Now she's ridiculous, with the elastic clothes she wears to please men badly wrinkled and covered with stains. *When we're afraid*, Epi thinks, *we all look pretty much the same.*

"You're still afraid, aren't you?"

She doesn't say anything. She limits herself to gazing at him steadily and sternly. She's getting used to the idea that she's facing a man condemned to death. Tiffany visualizes the moment when he'll jump through the window and the rope will tauten, when he'll drop down the front of the building and his neck will break like a rotten branch. He'll get a hard-on, too. *At least, that's what the urban legend says*, the girl thinks. The whole barrio will see, raised in homage to the woman for whose sake he killed another and then himself, his erect dick, like a proud banner of unrequited love. The war will have ended. He'll have lost it, and his carcass will provide her with food and drink and make her stronger than she's ever been until now.

"If you'd only been true to me, just a little true . . ."

"You don't understand."

"I sure don't, Tiffany. I'm going without understanding a thing. That may be why I'm killing myself. Because I don't want to know if you loved me or not. Or if you were fooling me the entire time. I'm going so I won't know the truth."

Epi doesn't notice his tears, which well up and course down his cheeks. Tiffany looks at him and finds his crying contagious without knowing the reason why. It's not compassion. It's not sorrow. Her tears aren't for Tanveer, and not for Epi, either. Maybe they're for herself.

Maybe they're for nothing. Weeping for the sake of weeping. Falling in with the mood of the company. Tears like big drops of paint. Like tears in animated cartoons. Epi interprets them as signs of love. And because of them, if the girl asks him not to jump, he won't. He's already demonstrated that he's a man, that he's capable of anything. But she remains silent.

"I'll be the last thing you think of tonight before you fall asleep . . . Do you remember telling me that?"

"Yes."

"I suppose you'll have other guys after I'm gone . . ."

"No, no . . ."

"Yes, yes, don't lie, not now . . . It doesn't matter anymore, but when you're with them, ask them what they'd be capable of doing for you . . . How much does a person have to love someone to do all this? To kill for you, to kill himself for you. Who's going to love you more than me?"

"Nobody, nobody . . . I . . ."

"You . . . what?"

It's true. Nobody will ever love her so much. This certainty suddenly causes her to become again the cruel, all-trumping queen; all at once, she has recovered her power. She'll do the deciding.

"Epi, you're not going to do it, and you know it."

He recognizes the change. Her words are strong again, and they weaken him. He should have kept his mouth shut. He shouldn't have tried to extract a final caress, a last assurance from her. Tiffany doesn't look scared anymore. She's picked up the leash and she's rubbing his nose in his shit. What an idiot. He let her do it to him again.

"You won't do it because you don't want to do it. Because you've never even thought about killing yourself. You just wanted to scare me, didn't you? Scaring a woman and a child. Quite an accomplishment. All right, that's done. Big fucking deal, and you're a real man. Now you can go back home, Epito."

Tiffany's words and their fearlessness surprise them both. Epi knows he must regain the initiative as quickly as possible and—if there's still time—snatch the power back from the woman's hands. What he wouldn't give to have kept the gym bag. He could slip his hand into it and feel the wooden handle. He could pull the hammer out and wave it in front of this little bitch's eyes and turn her back into a frightened child.

He clenches his fist as though he's clutching the hammer. He pretends to feel its weight, its consistency. He goes at the girl with his face contorted, his arm raised, and violence in each of his gestures and sounds. Tiffany screams. She screams with all her strength, simultaneously crouching down and covering her head with her hands. One of the wardrobe doors opens, and Epi sees his reflection in the mirror inside the door. His image is sharp and clear: he doesn't have to die yet. Whatever he may do, he won't die. He'll close his eyes and slice off Medusa's head. He'll put Pandora back in her goddamned box. He'll tear out Tiffany's heart and eat it.

He deals a furious blow to the wardrobe door, which rebounds and strikes him in the back. He feels ridiculous. How did he do it this morning? Fast, that's how. His tensed arm had only to attack that head with force, and his own hurt would disappear. His pain would be over; his wound would stop bleeding. Or so he thought. But maybe the evidence indicates things won't turn out that way. Maybe ghosts stick around more stubbornly than the living themselves. Departed fathers, the stories of Orpheus and Eurydice, of Daniel in the lions' den, of the lepers' cave where Job sat down—all these are much more real than a constantly ill mother who died one day, or friends who grow up and get married and go away, or brothers you can't find a moment's time to tell why you love or loathe them. Perhaps it was only his hatred for Tanveer that sustained him in the hope of a better life, whereas now, in reality, the mortal blow has only brought him to a different, sadder place. He no longer has enough faith in this enormous planet to fill his guts, his breast, his brain and persuade him to go on. Epi lowers his arm and opens his hand, and the imaginary hammer he was holding in that hand disappears when he opens it, like part of some macabre magic trick.

He won't wait any longer. He opens the window. He steps back two paces to get a running start. He tightens the knot around his neck, leaps up on the windowsill, steadies himself, and jumps. A great crash at his back confounds the sound of the capsizing wardrobe with that of the apartment door, which Alex has just knocked down.

In the void, there are no clouds and barely any air to breathe. An instant ago, Epi wanted to die, and now he wants to land on his feet and do himself as little damage as possible. An instant lasts an eternity, but, incomprehensibly and simultaneously, an eternity lasts hardly any time at all. He'll no longer be alive. He'll see nothing more. He won't know any more about anything or anybody. And his brain, terrified by the pain of the impact that's about to occur, remembers nothing of his life. That was a lie, too. He has no especially emotional childhood memories. Tiffany's image doesn't pass before his eyes, not even when she loved him, if she ever did. Nothing like that. Instead, an absurd recollection comes to his mind. Something his memory has preserved whole and intact, right down to the smallest detail. While he falls, Epi remembers a little girl who accidentally got a ballpoint pen stuck into her palate. They had to call an ambulance and take her to the outpatient clinic, where a doctor gave her three stitches. The name of the boy who caused the accident by pushing her down was Roger. The girl was Genoveva. Some of their classmates said they liked each other. Roger denied it. Genoveva remained silent. How absurd that *that* should be his last thought before dying.

Alex bursts into the room and falls facedown on the door. From the floor, he can see his brother jump out the window. He starts to get up and go to it, but the *mosso* presses his shoulders down and clambers over him. Pep has a better take on the scene and heads for the other end of the rope, which is in the bedroom. The elder Dalmau brother tries to get to his feet and follow the policeman. His thoughts hurtle at full speed from one bit of foolishness to another. If he grabs the rope, he'll only burn his hands or help to hang his brother. What if he tries jumping too and catching Epi in his arms in midair and cushioning the impact with his own body? What if . . . ?

He reaches the window, looks down, and sees the other *mosso* moving toward his brother's body, which is hanging from the climbing rope and about to slam into the wall of the building. The policeman's peaked cap has fallen off, and he's stepping rapidly along the sidewalk with his arms outspread, as if someone has thrown him a bundle of clothes. Alex perceives that the two of them, his brother and the policeman, are going to do themselves harm, grave harm, and implicit in Alex's thought is the feeling that his brother's going to get out of this. For sure.

Pep enters the bedroom and spots the girl in a corner. Good news: she's alive. The wardrobe has crashed onto the mattress and shattered like a clumsy wooden giant. The rope's still attached to only one of the wardrobe's feet. Pep throws himself on the wardrobe, and while his body staves in the back of the ruined piece of furniture, he manages to free the rope at the precise moment when Epi is waiting to feel either the impact with the concrete or the mortal jolt that will break his neck. One or the other.

The liberated rope runs like a breath between Alex's legs. It goes through the window, following the same destiny as its master. The rope seems to fall lazily. Rubén's arms and Epi's legs snap almost in unison, with a dull pain. Then Epi and Rubén are lying on the ground, motionless, in agony, whimpering. People draw near to help them. Alex sees it all from a distance. As usual.

28

THE NIGHT SEEMED TO BURST INTO TANVEER'S AND Epi's ears. They were making the racket themselves, descending the steeply graded streets at a gallop, both of them all too aware that their refuge lay farther down, farther down, a little farther down, in their barrio near the sea, which was felt or smelled or imagined but never seen. A dog barked, but the sound was immediately lost in the distance. They were two perfect machines. Everything—arms, legs, head—was working on command, just as it should. *So few people living in these enormous houses,* Tanveer Hussein thought as he passed through one of his city's wealthier neighborhoods on the last night before his death. After some time had passed, he looked back. No one was following them. They were going to get away, but not by much this time. They should go to the nearest police station and report the van as stolen. Then, if things didn't get too agitated, in a few days they could go back and find that whore on the job and bribe her with money to keep her pretty little mouth shut.

"Stop, stop, stop . . ."

He thought it was crazy to keep going at this speed. Besides, it made him laugh to see Epi running his ass off like that, with his hair looking electrocuted and his generally slovenly appearance, hanging on to that gym bag as it bounced here and there, out of control.

"Stop, son of a bitch! I'm gonna piss in my pants!"

Epi halted his headlong plunge a few strides farther on and retraced his steps. His heart was about to jump through his mouth, he was almost unable to speak, but even so, he felt he was in good shape. Much better than the *Moro*. He's going to be able to do it. He's going to be able to take him. For sure.

"Man, I was watching you run and practically pissing myself. What the fuck are you carrying in there?"

"In this?" Epi said, holding up the bag. "Papers for the van and tools for work."

"Let's go pee."

They went up to the wall of a mansion, one of those former summer houses that had been converted into clinics for old folks with rich children. Without saying anything, they pulled down their zippers and began to urinate. The yellowish fluid crackled against the wall. As he'd done on many another occasion, Epi gave Tanveer's equipment a sidelong inspection, checking out what he put in Tiffany's mouth or between her legs. The sight always revolted him, infuriated him, and covered him with absolute sadness, as if someone had dropped a blanket on him from the sky.

"That was some fucking whore, huh?"

"Yes, but . . ."

"But what?"

"But you go too far."

"Why do I go too far, dipshit? Why?" Tanveer asked, taking Epi's face in one hand, which still smelled of urine, and squeezing until Epi's lips took on the shape of a kiss. "You think they don't like it?"

"Let go of me, man!"

Epi shook off Tanveer as best he could. The *Moro* was already on to something else. He came up with a pack of cigarettes and began to smoke one, sitting on the curb not very far from the wall they'd pissed on. Epi remained standing. The cocaine made it hard for him to keep still.

"We should keep moving. If a patrol car spots us alone out here, they're going to stop us."

"What's with that? You don't have the right to smoke on the street in peace in your country?"

"It's your country, too, Tanveer."

"What country, nutball? You all don't even know its name. *Sóc català. Visca el Barça*. Fucking right. I'm from the Country of Allah, and we're going to screw all of you bastards to the wall."

"If they stop us, I've got the papers for the van in here. We should go and fill out a stolen vehicle report."

"*You* should. I haven't been here. Besides, no way I'm getting close to a police station. You go. We'll meet up tomorrow."

"Let's go together. You can wait outside, and then we'll go by Carlos's to see if he's open."

Tanveer smiled but said nothing. When he finished his cigarette, he bounded to his feet, went up to Epi, and put his arm around his shoulder. They began to walk south, toward the barrio. "If Tanveer didn't love you so much," he said, "you'd get yourself fucked up for sure."

They crossed two squares without talking. Epi remembered that there was a police station near a hospital, and the hospital seemed to be the one they were approaching. Tanveer, who was subject to sudden spells of drowsiness nobody appeared to believe in at all, started to feel very sleepy. With all the shit he'd been mixed up in today, he hadn't yet been able to take a little nap. He decided to wait inside a cash machine kiosk already occupied by a homeless person he knew from somewhere, for some reason. The beggar opened the door and greeted him.

In the police station, Epi filled out the form. He indicated that the vehicle had been stolen the previous afternoon, almost twelve hours earlier. The policeman didn't ask him what he'd been doing since then and why he was reporting the theft at that hour.

As he left the police station, Epi had his doubts as to whether he'd find Tanveer in the kiosk. But there he was, and wide awake.

"I didn't expect you to be here."

"I didn't sleep at all. This bastard can really snore. Come on, let's get out of here."

"Where are we going?"

"To Carlos's, no?"

Carlos had renovated an old two-story cafeteria and converted it into a trendily seedy nightclub where the music was mostly Brazilian and the hours of operation very ill defined. On Thursdays there was salsa music, on Tuesdays free daiquiris, and, on the upper floor at all hours, drug trafficking. When Epi and Tanveer arrived, they were welcomed with hugs and two drinks of unknown origin.

"What *is* this shit?" Tanveer asked Epi.

"Looks like a Cuba libre."

"Since when do people buy me Cuba libres?"

"They've mistaken us for two other guys."

"Don't talk nonsense."

"It was a joke."

"Yeah, I know."

"They must have had them already made."

The black singer La La could belt out heartrending boleros with great precision, but he didn't know Bambino or Los Chichos. Professor Malick was delivering his spiel to a couple of young South American yokels, and Clara, the Chilean woman, drunk and crazy, was going around looking for a few good whacks no one would give her. Her ex-husband was a policeman, and she always used that fact as a threat when she was getting ready to let herself go a little. Some posh-looking ladies in their fifties with recently premiered implants came in, accompanied by an older man wearing a ponytail and the look of one who'd arrived late everywhere he'd gone for the last twenty years.

"This bar is full of crazies. I don't know what we're doing here."

Epi didn't answer. He pressed the gym bag containing the hammer between his legs and counted the passing minutes as what they were, a countdown. He drank his Cuba libre in four gulps and asked for a Tanqueray and tonic. No, two. He knew Tanveer, and he was one of those types who always order what the other guy has ordered.

"Thanks, nutball."

They were both sitting on stools far from the bar, looking at the fauna in the room as if they weren't part of it.

"So what about you?" Tanveer asked him.

"What about me?"

"I don't know . . . Do you have a girlfriend, or are you a fag? You're never with anybody."

"I'm doing without women."

"Or women are doing without you."

This was followed by silence. Carlos came by and explained something about an argument with someone they were apparently supposed to know.

"I know what's up with you."

"What's up with me?"

"You still like Tiffany."

"That's not true."

"Yes it is."

"No, that happened and now it's over."

"Don't fuck with me, Satan. Things are never over."

Epi raised his glass to his lips and took a long sip of his cocktail. If that was Tanqueray, he was the pope. His mother once saw the last pope in Rome. She had proof. She kept a photograph hanging on the wall in her apartment. Even though at first glance, it looked as though it was the pope who had come to the Vatican to visit Señora Dalmau. How strange life was. There they were, he and Tanveer, the two of them together, like old friends talking about old loves. Like in those computer games where if you undress all the characters you see that nobody's who they say they are. Look at the people at the bar. Look at yourself. Carrying a one-pound hammer in a sports bag and buying your victim a gin and tonic.

"Why do you like to go with whores?"

"What do you mean, fucker? *I* don't like to go with whores. It's the whores who like me to go with whores. In the Country of Allah, there are no whores. Here the women are all whores."

"Does Tiffany know about it?"

"Are you crazy, or what? But they like it if a man penetrates other pussies. Believe me."

Another silence. La La began a rendition of "La vida loca." Tanveer said, "I like this song. So, do you want to fuck Tiffany again? She's willing."

"What are you saying?"

"Would you like to or not? She told me you would."

"I'm not paying attention to you."

"But it'll have to be a threesome. I do her from behind while she's sucking you off and all that sort of thing."

At that moment, Carlos climbed on the bar and asked the crowd to leave the premises. One of his sisters was arriving from Brazil this morning, and he had to be at the airport by seven-thirty. He barely had time to straighten up the place and change his clothes. Then he asked La La to sing the song about the night saying good-bye. It was a Rubén Blades song whose title no one, not even La La, knew for sure. Epi suggested going to Salva's. He'd be opening in a little while. Outside the night belonged to those who slept, to children and the innocent.

Carlos Zanón is the author of four volumes of poetry and three novels, which have received wide critical acclaim in Spain. *The Barcelona Brothers* is his first novel to be published in English. A literary critic and screenwriter, he has also collaborated as a lyricist for rock bands. He lives in Barcelona.

John Cullen is the translator of many books from Spanish, French, German, and Italian, including Yasmina Khadra's Middle East Trilogy (*The Swallows of Kabul*, *The Attack*, and *The Sirens of Baghdad*), Christa Wolf's *Medea*, Manuel de Lope's *The Wrong Blood* (Other Press) and Eduardo Sacheri's *The Secret in Their Eyes* (Other Press). He lives in upstate New York.